W9-BRP-168

Darkbeast

REBELLION

Also by Morgan Keyes

Darkbeast

Darkbeast

REBELLION

MORGAN KEYES

Margaret K. McElderry Books
NEW YORK   LONDON   TORONTO   SYDNEY   NEW DELHI

MARGARET K. McELDERRY BOOKS

An imprint of Simon & Schuster Children's Publishing Division

1230 Avenue of the Americas, New York, New York 10020

MARGARET K. McELDERRY BOOKS is a trademark of Simon & Schuster, Inc.

For information about special discounts for bulk purchases, please contact
Simon & Schuster Special Sales at 1-866-506-1949 or business@simonandschuster.com.

The Simon & Schuster Speakers Bureau can bring authors to your live event.
For more information or to book an event, contact the Simon & Schuster Speakers Bureau
at 1-866-248-3049 or visit our website at www.simonspeakers.com.

Interior design by Mike Rosamilia

Jacket design by Russell Gordon

The text for this book is set in Adobe Caslon Pro.

Manufactured in the United States of America

0813 FFG

2 4 6 8 10 9 7 5 3 1

Library of Congress Cataloging-in-Publication Data

Keyes, Morgan.

Darkbeast rebellion / Morgan Keyes.—First edition.

p. cm.

Sequel to: Darkbeast.

Summary: When twelve-year-old Keara and her friends are captured
for not sacrificing their darkbeasts—animals they have bonded to with a psychic
connection since birth—Keara meets the crown prince and realizes this fight
is bigger and more political than she had imagined.

ISBN 978-1-4424-4208-5 (hardcover)

ISBN 978-1-4424-4210-8 (eBook)

[1. Fantasy.] I. Title.

PZ7.K52614Dd 2013

[Fic]—dc23

2013000055

To Jake and Eli,
who are getting old enough to understand
what this darkbeast thing is all about

ACKNOWLEDGMENTS

Books like *Darkbeast Rebellion* only happen when many people pitch in over weeks, months, and years.

I greatly appreciate the support I have received from everyone at Simon & Schuster Children's Publishing—Karen Wojtyla and Annie Nybo and all the other hard-working souls who have been responsible for bringing *Darkbeast Rebellion* to you.

The entire Darkbeast series would not exist without Julie Czerneda, the editor who published the short story where Caw first appeared. I am, as always, grateful to my agent, Richard Curtis, who read that story and saw the potential for these novels. Bruce Sundrud continues to be an author's dream of a first reader, and he made this book better with his timely and astute comments.

Throughout my writing career, I have enjoyed an incredible level of support from family—Klaskys, Fallons, Maddreys, and Timminses. Mark Maddrey remains my absolute bedrock when it comes to the often crazy life of being an author.

Of course, no novel is complete without readers, and I love to hear from mine. I hope you will stop by my website: morgankeyes.com.

PART ONE

Self-Pity

Chapter One

I was hungry. And tired. And cold. More hungry and tired and cold than I had ever been before.

When I lived in Silver Hollow, in the cottage I shared with Mother, I thought I understood. I was cold when I spent a night or two with the north wind blowing, when snow drifted up to my knees as I stepped outside our cottage door. I was tired when I spent a full day in the fields gathering herbs, when I helped out in the vineyard harvesting ripe grapes. I was hungry when Mother took too long to stir honey into porridge, to ladle hearty stew into my smooth wooden bowl.

But now, as I trudged down a narrow path in nameless woods in the far reaches of the primacy of Duodecia, I knew I'd been wrong. I had understood nothing. Life with Mother had been a game, a frolic. I had never wanted for anything when I lived with Mother, when I enjoyed the safety and the comfort and the security of my tiny village. Mother had loved me and protected me. She kept me safe from every harm.

"Feeling a bit sorry for ourselves, Keara?" Caw's voice cut into my litany of woes. Some part of me must have been aware that my darkbeast was hovering near; I did not startle as he flew out of the swirling snow and sank his talons into the pad on my shoulder.

"Don't start with me." I slurred the words. My lips felt numb as they slid over my teeth. Caw was the reason I'd left the simple perfection of Silver Hollow. By tradition in my village—in all of Duodecia—I should have killed my darkbeast at the full moon following my twelfth birthday.

I hadn't been able to kill Caw though. He was my best friend. He knew everything about me—everything I thought, everything I believed. He had been magically bonded to me when I was an infant, and I truly could not imagine a life without him.

"A deep first snow is a good thing," Caw remonstrated. *"The red-fruit will grow larger next summer."*

"If we're even alive next summer," I said. My sullen voice caught on the last word as my boot slipped on a particularly icy patch in the snow. I gasped as I regained my balance, and then I sniffed loudly, to emphasize my frozen nose.

Caw shifted his weight as if he'd never considered falling. He cocked his head at a sly angle. *"I know your problem. Your pack is too heavy. You'd have a much easier time walking if you shed a little weight. Say, maybe an apple cake?"*

I glared at him and picked up my pace. I didn't want him to fall off my shoulder—not exactly—but I took a little pleasure in the way he needed to tighten his talons. "The apple cakes are long gone. We finished them two nights ago. Just before we left the main road." My stomach growled at the memory of the sweet treat.

"Then I'll have to settle for seedcake," Caw said matter-of-factly.

Fool. We'd finished the seedcake well before the apple. Even so, my mouth flooded at the memory of the honeyed sweetmeat. I swung my arms as I lengthened my stride, shrugging elaborately.

Caw merely flapped his wings, keeping his perch by digging still deeper with his claws. *"You are vicious when you're cranky. I take your hunger. Forget it. It is mine."*

If only things were that simple. If only I could offer up my hunger as I had my darkest emotions, my most evil deeds, throughout all my childhood. Caw was responsible for taking those, for absorbing them, for freeing me to live a life of goodness and light, like every child of Duodecia.

Except his taking didn't always work with me. Despite my darkbeast's best effort, I was usually left with my dark impulses intact, with the same old urges to think bad thoughts and do dark deeds. Even now my belly twisted, yielding an enormous gurgle that might have been heard all the way back in Lutecia.

Caw looked so startled that I had to laugh. The sound echoed through the woods, and for the first time since dawn, for the first time since we'd set out on this narrow path through this uncharted forest, my human companions turned to look at me. "Sorry," I said to Goran and Taggart. And then, by way of explanation for the two Travelers, I nodded toward my darkbeast and said, "Caw."

Goran and Taggart had to be used to my sometimes-strange behavior by then. After all, we had journeyed together since the summer, since I left my home village of Silver Hollow for the excitement of crossing Duodecia with the Travelers. I had originally been drawn to the actors for the magic of their revels, the plays that they performed along the Great Road. I had stayed when I discovered true friendship, from humans and darkbeasts alike.

Now, Taggart merely shrugged in the face of my inappropriate laughter, turning back to the trail he was forging. His breathing was ragged in the cold night air. Snow had crusted in his beard, making it seem as if he wore a blanket woven out of clouds. By the glint of moonlight the night before, I'd seen him tuck his ornate iron neckpiece beneath his tunic. His darkbeast, Flick, lived on that iron ornament.

Flick was a lizard. Even though the magic of Bestius, god of all the darkbeasts, would keep Flick from hibernating through the winter, the tiny creature could not help but grow sluggish with the cold.

Goran's toad, Wart, wasn't much better off. He kept her in his pocket, doing his best to warm her with his own chilled fingers. I wasn't sure who hated the snowfall most—man, boy, lizard, or toad. Or me. Caw wasn't in the running—his spirits never seemed to dim.

Caw was utterly oblivious to the danger we faced on the road. All three of us humans had passed the age of twelve—Goran and me just a few months earlier, Taggart many decades before. Each of us had sworn to execute our darkbeasts in the dark ritual mandated by Bestius and all the Twelve. And yet each of us had chosen to spare our closest companions, to brave the wrath of all the gods and their all-too-human Inquisitors.

The six of us—humans and unlawful darkbeasts—believed in the ancient stories, believed in the secret tales. Taggart had woven the stories for us every night since we had fled the safety and security of the Primate's capital, Lutecia.

The old man had spoken with the magic of the Travelers, his voice strong as he chanted about free darkbeasts, about humans called Darkers who dared to defy the ancient order of the Twelve. Taggart had spent a lifetime performing before crowds, and he had honed his ability to weave images, to share a vision. He had made me believe in—made me long for—a society where our darkbeasts would be free to live out their lives in peace.

Now Taggart turned toward me, his heavy eyebrows knit into an angry line. "Keep up, Keara. We won't come back for you if you slip into a ditch." His voice sounded raw, scraped across the back of his throat.

I started to retort—there weren't any ditches on this narrow passage through the woods—but the soles of my leather shoes chose that moment to lose their purchase on the icy road. My knee slammed hard against the frozen earth, and my teeth snapped shut so hard that my ears rang. Caw squawked and flew off my shoulder, one jet-black wing buffeting my cheek as he swept past.

Without a word, Goran turned back to help me. His fingers were rough as he clutched my biceps, as he tugged me back to my feet. His teeth chattered as he stared into my eyes, silently asking if I was able to continue. I nodded once, squaring my shoulders. He stayed beside me as I took a tentative step.

I could put my weight on my right knee, but it hurt. A lot. Immediately I thought of the herbs that Mother used for bone bruises. The best was snowlap, but we'd be hard-pressed to find any of that. The deep-rooted plant grew high in the mountains of central Duodecia, far from this stretch of northern woods.

I grimaced and took another half dozen steps, Goran's hand on my arm the entire time. There. The pain was easing. Or maybe my leg was simply freezing, now that I had dipped my knee into the slushy snow. With any luck, we'd find a stream when we stopped for the evening, find a willow tree. Fresh bark would not work as well as dried, but a willow tea would help ease the pain in my knee.

Assuming that we ever *did* stop for the night. "Tell me again why we're doing this?" I muttered, pitching my voice low enough that only Goran could hear. Truth be told, I was still a little afraid of Taggart, despite the fact that he had spared his own darkbeast. Despite the fact that we had been on the road together for nearly a month.

"You know as well as I do. Taggart says we're close to the Darkers now. They'll never come close to the main road, to the Inquisitors."

"If there even *are* any Darkers," I complained. I didn't keep my voice low enough, though, because Taggart turned round to face me.

"Doubting again, are you?" His grey eyes flashed in the moon-light. As he filled his lungs, I could hear him wheeze. The rattle sounded like dried leaves of sheepleaf. "Have I misled you yet?"

Taggart had saved us from the Inquisitors in Lutecia, guiding us out of the city and into the marshes. He had given up a lifetime of secrecy, of balancing his hidden darkbeast against the Traveler troupe that he loved, all so that he could help Goran and me. He had led the way when the Autumn Meet was over, showing us how to melt into the crowds of merchants heading south, journeying toward home. He had made sure that all of us had food, even the darkbeasts.

It was only after we turned west that things became difficult. Taggart insisted that he had good sources, that there was excellent reason to believe that Darkers were hiding in the nearby woods. Nevertheless, it was hard to believe him as our packs grew lighter. And it was almost impossible to have faith now that our supplies had run completely dry.

For the past two days Taggart had chivied us on with promises instead of facts. I took little satisfaction that he had tired even more than Goran and I had. Now the old man's eyes glowed strangely. His lips had grown chapped, and I suspected that he was running a fever.

"No, Taggart," I said, finally responding to his peevish question.

As if in response, the old man veered from the path we were following, choosing an even narrower way through the woods. At least the snow was shallower there. More of it had caught on the broad pine branches that loomed above us. I wanted to ask Taggart how he got his information, how he knew that Darkers were hidden close by. I could only imagine, though, how the old man would react to *that* challenge to his authority.

Caw landed back on my shoulder. *"There should be pinecones beneath the snow,"* he said. *"Pinecones mean pine nuts. You could roast them by tonight's fire. Mix them with a bit of lard and flour, a touch of honey, and fry it all up for a snack."*

"That would be a grand idea," I said, rolling my eyes. "If we had lard and flour. Or honey. Or oil for frying."

"Then you agree! Let's dig for pinecones now!"

Caw's optimism made me smile—as he had surely meant me to do—and I stumbled farther down the path. I tried to ignore the clutch of pine needles, the looming presence of snowbound trees, the occasional shift of branches as Taggart or Goran brushed free a dollop of snow that landed on my head.

Lard and flour would be lovely. Honey, too. I closed my eyes and imagined the finest treat I'd ever had—toffee bread from the village of Rivermeet. I could remember the hot steam rising from the baked loaf, the rich, buttery aroma as I tore mine into bite-size pieces.

We were leagues from Rivermeet, though. Leagues and months away from that simple time in my past, from that easy passage along the Great Road.

Taggart coughed, a deep rumbling that was anchored in his chest rather than his throat. My mind leaped back to Mother's herbs, immediately searching for a cure. Marrin berries would do the trick—roasted over a slow fire. Taggart could chew them, one by one, until the phlegm broke loose in his lungs.

There were no marrin berries in the winter woods, though.

And none stored in our packs. Taggart coughed again, as if a dam had been breached and he could no longer hold back the sticky sound of grippe.

Worry sparked within me at the sound. If we had been back in Silver Hollow, Taggart could have gone to sleep in the Men's Hall. He could have been surrounded by eager youths, by young men who would tend to his needs until he was well again.

But here there was no Men's Hall. No Men's Hall, no Women's Hall. No supportive community like the one I had always known in the village of my childhood. We were alone, destined to live or die beneath the winter trees.

The Frost Moon glared, icy and unforgiving as its light filtered through the tree branches. *Frost.* That sounded so benign. Nothing at all like the frozen, slippery mess I fought through. Who had named the Moons, anyway? Who had decided the endless cycle—Frost to Wolf to Snow, and on through the rest of the year?

I would have given the Moons different names. I would have tied them to darkbeasts I had known. Caw could take the place of the Frost Moon, standing in for unpredictable weather, for unexpected change. Wart could be the Egg Moon, heavy and waiting in the middle of spring. Flick could stand in for the Flower Moon, for the busy industry of midsummer.

What other darkbeasts could I name? None that were alive—

all the other shadow creatures I had ever known had been slain by their owners in a timely rite. All the other darkbeasts were gone, dead, cold.

Gone.

Dead.

Cold.

So very, very cold. I stumbled forward, suddenly freed from a pine tree's clinging fingers. For one terrible moment I thought I was going to fall again, was going to jam my knee another time.

Goran's fingers closed around my arm. He held me upright, gripped me tightly until I caught my breath. "Must rest," I whispered, surprised to find that my lips were chapped, raw, and swollen from the wind.

"No," he said.

I shook my head. "Jus' a second." The words slurred, frozen as they left my mouth.

"We can't stop, Keara." Goran looked exasperated. Exhausted. And something else. Something I could not read. Something I should understand. Something . . . And then it came to me. Goran was afraid.

I took another step and slipped on the ice that had frozen in Taggart's footsteps. I sat down hard in the snow. I was too weary to cry out. I started to shiver, great racking waves that shook me from my chin to my toes.

"Keara," Goran pleaded. "Stand up. I know you can. Come on."

I shook my head. The motion freed my jaw enough that my teeth began to chatter.

Goran knelt beside me, gritting his own teeth in frustration. I watched through slitted eyes as he fumbled in his pocket. I could see his fingers close around something, and I watched indecision swirl across his face.

What? What was he holding?

Goran caught his breath and drew his hand from his pocket. Despite my fatigue, despite the bitter cold that shook my body, despite the clatter of my teeth in my aching jaws, I craned my neck to see what he held.

It was a bracelet. A fine black bracelet, spun out of delicate fibers. Careful, ornate knots marked the circumference at regular intervals.

"Wha' is it?" I asked. My curiosity was piqued, even if I found it even harder to form words.

"It belonged to my mother," Goran said. I understood the importance of that simple statement. Goran *never* spoke about his mother. His mother. Taggart's daughter. "She gave it to me when she . . . left."

Left? Where had she gone? I peered closer at the treasure. I had a dozen questions I wanted to ask.

Goran seemed to understand the most important one. "It's

from her darkbeast, a ferret. She spun the fur after she killed Streak. Tied the knots to make it stay on her wrist. To remember the lessons she took to her darkbeast."

I'd seen such things before. My mother had stuffed her rat darkbeast and kept him by our hearth. My sister had turned her snake into a belt. But this bracelet was finer than those tributes. It was beautiful. Precious.

"It's yours," Goran said. "But you have to get up, Keara." He dangled it in front of me.

I shook my head. He asked too much.

"Keara. I'll give it to you. But you must walk."

I heard the tears in his voice. The desperation. The terror.

And I looked at the darkbeast bracelet again. He had never shown it to me before. It must be precious to him, perhaps the most valuable thing he owned. I caught my tongue between my teeth. I flexed my toes within my soaked boots. I caught my breath. And I stood.

Goran nodded, taking a few steps down the path. Jerkily, I followed. One step. Two. Three.

Goran slipped the bracelet around my blue-veined wrist, covering the tax tattoo that showed I was a loyal citizen of Duodecia. He tightened the knots carefully, cinching the jewelry so that I could not lose it in the snow.

And we continued down the forest trail.

I could not say how long we stumbled. I could not say how many times I fell. I could not say how many hours we trudged through the snow. But finally, when I thought I would never take another step—precious darkbeast bracelet or no precious dark-beast bracelet—I caught myself against the edge of a gigantic black stone.

Dazed, I looked around. We stood in the middle of a clearing. I had grown up in the woods near Silver Hollow; I knew my way around a forest. I immediately realized that something was different about this space.

The line of trees behind me had been groomed. Nothing obvious, nothing that any casual traveler would notice. But the more I stared, the more I could see that the clearing had been shaped into a definite square.

The black stone only drove home what my mind had already started to accept. It wasn't perfectly smooth beneath its cap of snow. There were indentations on the two sides visible to me, and I could see a groove in the top, along one long edge.

The clearing was shaped to resemble a godhouse, a building sacred to Bestius. I tilted my head back to gaze at the lowering sky, almost as if I were a toddler trying to catch snowflakes on my tongue. The clouds loomed over the forest, closing in the space, making the clearing feel even more like the holy home of the god of darkbeasts.

A shiver quaked down my spine.

I had not been in Bestius's godhouse since the Thunder Moon. I had not been in the presence of the god of darkbeasts since I had been instructed to take Caw from his iron cage, ordered to wring his neck and take my place among the adults of Silver Hollow.

My raven chose that moment to alight on my shoulder, startling me so badly that a wordless cry burst from my lips. *"Hush,"* he said. *"All will be well. They might even have a few treats to share."*

"Th-they?" I stammered, fighting the urge to turn my back on the black stone and Taggart and Goran, to push my way back into the safety of the forest.

Before Caw could answer, though, before I could flee, the meaning of his words became clear. Two dozen shadows detached themselves from the trees. Two dozen dark figures glided toward the altar in the center of the clearing. Two dozen people surrounded Taggart and Goran and me.

I opened my mouth to scream, but no sound came out.

Chapter Two

Fortunately, Goran was not as tongue-tied as I. "What do you think you're doing?" he shouted at the hooded figures. Angry as he was, he kept his left hand deep in his pocket. I was certain his fingers were curled around Wart, keeping his darkbeast warm. Gaining some comfort from the toad's lumpy skin.

Caw's talons tightened around my shoulder—not enough to draw blood through the padding, but enough to command my attention. He cocked his head toward the stone, toward the altar. I understood what he was saying. I should move forward, get the rock at my back. I should take a stand beside Goran and Taggart.

Except Taggart was not standing beside the altar.

Instead the old man had stepped back toward the edge of the

trees, closer to our attackers, closer to the slippery, frozen path we had created reaching this cursed place. As I gaped, the old man reached inside his cloak, his fingers diving deep beneath his tunic. I was shocked to see him pull out Flick, to display his living darkbeast to everyone. "Well met, good friends," he croaked.

"Well met, indeed."

The voice belonged to a woman. She stepped forward from the shadows, simultaneously raising her hands to push back the hood of her felted wool cloak. Her fingernails flashed and her hair glinted in the light of the Frost Moon. The icy blond strands sparkled, nearly as bright as the snow.

She stared hard at Taggart for several heartbeats. Still silent, she glanced at Goran, and then her gaze settled on me. In the moonlight it looked as if her eyes were clear, as if her irises held no color at all. Her pupils were very wide, and I somehow felt as if I might fall through them into another world, a place as dark as the altar at my back, a place where there was no Frost Moon, no snow. Only endless, velvet night.

"Keara," she said, and her voice thrummed with power. Those strange eyes narrowed, and she shifted her gaze just the slightest, to take in the raven on my shoulder. "Caw," she said, the word dropping down to a whisper.

I longed to reach for my darkbeast, to find comfort by stroking his feathers. I dared not move, though. Not with the woman staring at me. Not with her knowing our names, knowing so much more than I. I concentrated on the bracelet Goran had given me, trying to draw comfort from its knotted strands, even as I feared to say or do anything.

It was Goran who broke the spell. "My lady," he said, collapsing into the deepest bow the Travelers used on stage. "You have us at an advantage. You ken more than we do."

I recognized the rhythmic line from one of the revels, one of the Travelers' plays that Goran had memorized from the first day he could talk. A quick glance at Taggart confirmed my suspicion; his cracked lips twitched into a painful smile. Even exhausted, even freezing and ill, he was proud of his grandson. Proud, and apparently relieved that we all were safe.

In for a sapling, in for the woods. I'd cast my lot with Taggart and Goran when we fled the Primate's city. I'd be a fool not to trust them now, the first time we were seriously challenged on the road. On the road, or *off* it, to be more precise.

The woman looked gravely at Goran, never suggesting that she was even faintly amused by his Traveler airs. "I am Saeran," she said. "I am the leader of these folk."

Goran seemed to gain courage from her gracious reply. "These folk, then? Who are they?"

Saeran's brow was smooth in the moonlight. She seemed utterly unaware of the bitter cold, completely oblivious to the snow that spread beneath her narrow boots. "We are the ones you seek. We are the Darkers."

Darkers. At last. Just as Taggart had promised—wary people who kept their secrets in the wilds of Duodecia. They held on to their darkbeasts, child and adult alike. They defied the Primate and Inquisitors. They banded together, traitors and heretics all, to fight the injustice of the Twelve.

As if to prove her words, Saeran shifted her weight, extending her left arm in front of her body. A ray of whiskers appeared from her sleeve, followed by a frantically twitching, jet-black nose. The darkbeast edged into the moonlight, its tiny claws gripping Saeran's arm. A rat. Only when the creature had emerged fully from the woman's sleeve did it curl its long, naked tail around its body, hunching its shoulders as if it felt the midnight chill. Or as if it were afraid.

"This is Twitch," Saeran said.

I heard a lifetime of conflict in that pronouncement. Saeran said her darkbeast's name with honor and respect. But there was something harder underneath her tone—something that sounded like teeth gritting together in a nightmare.

Caw heard it too. He shifted his weight on my shoulder with the ease of long practice. I could feel his chest move close to my ear. I imagined I could hear his heart beating, fast and wild beneath the stars. *"What?"* I asked. *"What is wrong here?"*

"Perhaps nothing." Caw tilted his head to one side, as if he were trying to peer into the rat's mind.

"Can you talk to him? Can you hear Twitch?"

"Yes. No."

"What does that mean?"

Caw made a chittering sound at the back of his throat. It wasn't the noise he made when he was afraid, though. Rather, it told me that he was curious, that he was nearly lost in thought. *"I can hear the rat think,"* he said at last. *"And I can feel its bond to the woman. But that bond is . . . different from yours and mine."*

"Different? How?"

"I cannot say, precisely. I can sense mudroyal—the taste is strong in the ties between them."

My tongue curled in reflex. Mudroyal was one of the most bitter herbs Mother had stocked in our cottage. *"And ladysilk? Is it there too?"*

Mudroyal and ladysilk were the herbs used by Bestius's priests in the bonding ceremony that linked a newborn child to a dark-beast. The herbs somehow enhanced the god's magic, cementing the ties between human and animal.

"Aye," Caw said, bobbing his head. *"There's ladysilk, too. That much is like any other bonding."*

I might have asked Caw more questions. I might have struggled to learn more about what worried him, what felt different. But by then Saeran was speaking again. "You must be tired," she proclaimed. "Fear makes the road stretch long."

I wanted to argue that I wasn't afraid. But I had only lived with the Travelers for a few months before the disaster in Lutecia, and I had not yet mastered the confident tone that came so easily to those who spent a lifetime performing on a stage. I could not make my lie believable, not to one with a gaze as shrewd as Saeran's. I stayed silent and let Taggart answer for all of us.

"We would be grateful," he wheezed, "if you would conduct us to your darkhold."

Darkhold. The word was new to me. But Saeran did not hesitate. She merely raised those long-fingered hands, gesturing imperiously to a trio of her shadowed companions. The robed followers glided forward, their only sound the crunch of snow beneath their boots. Without pausing, the Darkers produced lengths of jet-black silk from under their cloaks.

I started to protest as the man closest to me reached out to bind my eyes. Taggart shook his head, though. The movement was tight, precise, as if he were shoving away an annoying gnat in the heat of a summer afternoon. I recognized the gesture for what it was, of course. A command, as sure and certain as if he had barked in his deepest voice.

I caught my tongue between my teeth and let the Darker

blindfold me. My temper was not eased by the flutter of Caw's wings as he took to the air. I wanted to cry out, to beg my dark-beast to stay close. I felt sorry for myself, suddenly alone.

But that was foolish. Caw wasn't going anywhere. Caw was my constant companion. When I calmed down enough to draw another breath, I could reach for him with my mind. He was close enough for me to think a panicked, wordless question, for him to answer with silent reassurance.

As soon as my eyes were bound, the clearing seemed to shrink. The air grew more icy with every breath I struggled to pull past my dry lips. My heart pounded in my ears, and I longed to reach for Goran's hand, for the touch of a known ally.

But Goran was too far away. Instead of the Traveler boy, I felt robed figures close by. One person took my right arm; another took my left. Their fingers felt like iron wires through my cloak.

Saeran said, "Now!" and I braced myself for some attack. Instead I heard stone grating on stone, a laborious groan from the direction of the black altar in the center of the clearing. The Darkers' fingers tightened above my elbows, and I was forced forward—half walking, half carried.

My feet slipped on the snow, but I was not allowed to fall. Rather, I was pulled toward steps, stairs that marched steeply down. I tried to find each riser gingerly, but the Darkers on either side moved me faster than I could control. One rough palm settled over my forehead, and I sensed that we passed beneath a stone arch, a lintel that could have smashed my head.

I told myself to count the stairs. I told myself to remember the turns we took through hallways. I told myself to measure the narrow doorways that forced my escorts to move closer to my sides. I told myself to memorize the route in case I ever needed to flee along it, on my own, when I could see again.

But I was tired. And hungry. And cold. And we walked for a very long time, twisting through too many corridors, ducking under too many low arches. Through it all, at least, I could sense Caw following the party, always keeping me in sight.

At last our journey ended. My guides loosened their grips, but I could still feel them standing close to me, closer than I would have tolerated aboveground. I could hear them breathing. The man to my right stank of rancid grease, as if he wore a filthy beard.

"Now!" Saeran commanded again.

The midnight silk was pulled from my eyes. I blinked to find myself in a cavernous room that was easily the height of three men. Torches flickered at regular intervals on the wall, barely penetrating the gloom to the stony roof. Goran stood to my right. Taggart was to my left. Caw flapped noisily to my side and settled on my shoulder.

But my attention was not held by Goran or Taggart or Caw.

I had expected them to be there. I had known what they would look like.

I had not expected to see all the *other* people in the cave. I had not expected to see a group of perfectly normal men, women, and children. They all wore identical clothes—black trousers, black tunics, black cloaks all held at the shoulder with matching silver brooches.

Aside from their clothing, they looked like any other people we might have encountered on the road. I half imagined they might be waiting for us to perform, to share our Travelers' tricks. I caught welcoming smiles on the faces of many adults. A handful of children eyed us with suspicion, but no one seemed angry, or even truly frightened.

But even as I studied the group, I realized that these people were not common villagers. These people were not ordinary Duodecians, living out their lives under the benevolent eye of the Primate.

No. These people were different.

Every single one of them—men as old as Taggart, women the age of my mother, children the age of Goran and myself—every *single* one of them had a darkbeast close at hand.

Mice.

Snakes.

Starlings.

Each animal more midnight-black than the one before. Each animal clinging to a wrist, an arm, a shoulder. Each animal gazing intently at us.

I heard the moment that Goran recognized the oddity. His breath caught in his throat, and I suspected that his fingers tightened around Wart. Taggart made no sound, but I felt him become very, very still.

"Welcome to the darkhold!" Saeran announced.

Her voice seemed to release the crowd. One woman laughed. A girl shrieked as a boy poked at her side. In ragtag harmony, though, every voice was lifted in singsong greeting, repeating Saeran's words. "Welcome to the darkhold!"

As if in reply, Caw shifted closer to my cheek. "*Well*," he chortled, in a voice that only I could hear. "*They look as if they haven't missed many meals. Will you ask them for treats? Or shall I?*"

Chapter Three

In the end, no one needed to ask the Darkers for treats. Saeran clapped her hands and issued some sharp orders, and the entire community scuttled about. Scrubbed wooden tables were dragged into the center of the room, along with matching benches. A great wheel of cheese was rolled forward, and baskets of bread appeared as if by magic. Carved bowls were produced, each containing tiny apples and pears. One of the largest men trundled in a cart from a side corridor; I could smell the apple cider in its keg even before he started filling cups.

Saeran held up a hand to command everyone's attention. As Taggart, Goran, and I gaped like ill-schooled villagers, the Darkers recited a brief prayer, offering up thanks to all the Twelve for the food they were about to enjoy. Soon enough, though, I was surrounded by Darkers, each person collecting enough food to satisfy an entire marching army. Despite my empty belly, I hung back from the feast.

"Quickly now," Caw urged. *"Don't let that bread go to waste! There are raisins in those rolls! Hurry!"*

"Hush," I said, answering my darkbeast aloud, confident that no one would hear me in the clatter of the crowd. I lowered my voice, though, to whisper, "We can't be sure the food is safe."

Caw's exasperation exploded as a wordless cry. Then he said, *"Look at them!* They're *all eating! Ah, currants . . . Don't pass by the currants. I'm ravenous!"*

"What else would I expect my raven *darkbeast to be?"* I snapped. My own mouth flooded as I caught a whiff of the braided bread Caw coveted, but I had our safety to worry about. *"They might have poisoned the food, Caw. Poisoned it and quaffed an antidote before they dragged us here."*

"Aye. They might. That would explain their going to the trouble of taking in three frozen travelers in a snowstorm. Poison would explain why they have exposed the secret of their existence, including this hidden stronghold. Poison would be the perfect *reason to offer up a Frost Moon feast the likes of which we haven't seen since Silver Hollow."* His sarcasm was cut short as another laden basket passed before me. *"There! Do you smell that? Truffles, baked into the very bread!"*

"Caw," I moaned, thinking that my darkbeast was more head-strong than I had ever been. Was this the way I had sounded to Mother when she told me to listen to her, to obey her rules, to do as she instructed?

"Well," Caw said, fluffing his ruff and settling closer on my shoulder. *"At least Wart is getting some food."*

I followed my darkbeast's gaze and found Goran already seated on one of the benches. He had a trencher in front of him, and he was helping himself to a thick slice of creamy cheese. From the way Wart was bobbing her broad black head and blinking her eyes, I knew the toad had just swallowed something.

I glanced around the chamber, desperate to find Taggart. He was easy enough to pick out in the crowd—his tattered beige cloak leaped out from the unrelieved black of the Darkers. The former leader of the Travelers was seated on a bench, surrounded by adult men and women.

His iron neckpiece was on full display, and I watched as Flick darted down Taggart's sleeve, skipping across the old man's plate and scuttling back to gulp some newly seized treasure. Taggart was eating too—slowly, however, as if he did not have the energy to chew. As his jaws worked, his eyes stared straight ahead, and I wondered if he even heard the animated conversation around him.

I sidled up to Goran and whispered his name as harshly as I dared.

"What, Keara? Here. Try this apple bun. They're amazing!" He thrust a fist-size treat toward me. My fingers closed around it automatically.

"Stop it!" I hissed. "We can't eat this!"

"Aren't you hungry?" He stared at me in shock.

"I'm starving!" The Darker children were staring at us now, and I lowered my voice. "Goran, we don't know if we can trust these people! Their food may not be safe!"

He laughed.

Goran laughed as if I were standing in the center of a stage, decked out in the crisscross costume of the Primate's jester. He laughed as if he were a wise grown-up, and I were nothing more than a very silly little girl. He laughed and he said, "Keara, don't be ridiculous. If these people wanted to harm us, they would hardly need *poison*. They could simply pull a knife and carve away, and no one in all of Duodecia would be wiser."

"They might not want to dirty their knives, though. Not if they needed to cut away slices of cheese after."

"*Caw!*" I glared at my darkbeast, recognizing his sarcasm immediately.

Reluctantly I had to admit that Goran was right. Saeran could have merely ignored us in the forest clearing, left the three of us to collapse from hunger and cold and exhaustion. She could have drawn a blade and shed our blood on the black stone altar, a mockery of offering to Bestius. She could have lured us underground, and then stabbed us, or tied us up, or locked us in a cage.

Managing not to gloat, Goran passed me a trencher and reached toward a huge basket of bread. I noticed that he took care to select a bun that was studded with extra currants. He added a hunk of cheese and a matched pair of apples. When he passed the bounty to me, he let his fingers linger for just an instant, brushing against the bracelet he had given me. "Eat, Keara," he said, in the softest voice a Traveler could summon. "Trust me. All will be well."

I stared at the food.

I could continue to make my arguments. I could continue to ignore the yeasty aroma from the roll, the spice of the fruit. I could continue to deny that my belly was crying out for nourishment, that my mind was already drowning in the imagined flavor of the feast. I could feel sorry for myself all the rest of my days.

But what good would any of that do?

I looked across the room and saw Taggart slam his tankard down on the table. A bit of cider sloshed over the top, and he started to cough, long and hard, even though the sound was lost across the cavern. When he recovered, he reached for a crimson-skinned winter pear, studying the fruit intently, as if it could heal the sickness in his lungs. He began to eat with steady dedication.

At my side Goran shrugged before he tore a massive bite off his own hunk of bread.

Caw shifted on my shoulder.

Fine. I would eat with the Darkers. I would share their food and drink. I would sit at their table, offer up a story or two, go through the motions of meeting new people, of settling in.

And I had to admit that the bread was the finest I had ever tasted. The apples were the sweetest. The cider sparkled in my throat as I emptied my tankard and held it out for more.

Caw wasted no time demanding the tastiest bits of the food I loaded onto my platter.

Three days later Caw's belly seemed to have doubled in size.

The Darkers might have lived a rough life, confined to a series of underground caves, but they lost no opportunity to indulge in fine food. I soon learned that the cheese and bread that had broken our fast was an uncharacteristically limited meal, made necessary by our unexpected arrival. The children said there was always meat in summer—coney and venison and a variety of birds caught by Darker hunters who roamed the woods. For now, in winter, we had to content ourselves with rich stews heavy with root vegetables that were stored well beneath the frost line. Whoever had harvested those crops had kept an eye out for herbs, as well. There were copious braids of the usual kitchen bounty—rosemary and sorrel and mint. There were rarer finds as well—honeywort that made food sweet, and spinewood that offered a pleasant bite at the back of the tongue.

While food preparation seemed to be one of the most important tasks for the Darker society, it was not the only one. Teams of workers tended a small flock of sheep, mucking out their cavern and seeing that the animals got all the hay they required. One group of women was devoted to combing out fleeces that had been shorn the previous spring—mountains of wool remained to be washed and carded. Every woman and child who sat still for even a few moments used a drop spindle to create fine yarn for the weavers. Of course there were always garments to be mended as well—every one of them fashioned from the same black cloth, every one stitched with the same black thread. The older women laughed good-naturedly that they could barely see their stitches in the flickering torchlight.

The Darkers also possessed a surprising amount of armor, and all of it had to be kept in good repair. Leather had to be oiled and blades carefully burnished for a variety of disciplines. Boys and girls regularly used real weapons in fighting drills.

The children were tested on other skills as well—Goran and I along with the others. We were expected to know how to count out money and how to give fair measures of grain. We were quizzed about the Twelve and about the history of the primacy. We memorized the names of each Primate who had reigned since

First Primate Kerwen, noting the rulers' wives and every single royal child, even if they did not live to see their first nameday. For those sessions we were all required to leave our darkbeasts in a distant chamber, far enough away that no one could cheat by asking our bonded creatures for answers.

It bothered me to be kept apart from Caw, but the other children did not seem to care. I wondered if their complacence was due to the different darkbeast bond that Caw had sensed, the strangeness he had described. I wondered, and I worried, but there was nothing to be done about it.

Goran was not troubled at all. Of course he had no problem memorizing all the required information. He was accustomed to learning the revels, to mastering the rhythm and rhyme of the Travelers' stock in trade. After one particularly grueling session about First Primate Kerwen's distaff nephews, a half dozen Darker children gathered around my companion, scattering parchment pages and inkwells in their urgency to learn his tricks.

"Tell us how you do that!" one boy said. "How can you memorize those names, hearing them only once?"

"Anyone could," Goran said. For a moment I thought he was being modest, but then I realized his intention was precisely the opposite. He was boasting as he spoke, glibly hinting at the Darkers' own failings.

"Try this, then," a girl said. Wynda, I reminded myself. Her name was Wynda, and she had turned twelve at the previous Hunter's Moon, same as Goran. "Bestius. Screech. Spider. Godhouse." She went on, rattling off several other words. She wrote them all on a scrap of parchment, her fingers flying over the page, and then she challenged Goran. "Go ahead. Say them back."

He took a deep breath. I'd seen this Traveler's trick—he was bracing himself to recite a long passage, to cast out an entire speech at one go. His inhalation served to heighten the tension in the crowd around us—all the Darker children drew closer. Goran exhaled, and then he said, "What order would you like? The way you quoted them to me? Or backward?"

Wynda stared him down. "Forward is fine. If you can."

Goran filled his lungs again. Everyone leaned forward, looking first at him, then at Wynda. They caught their own breaths, charmed by the Traveler spell he was weaving. I heard my heartbeat pounding in my ears, and I struggled to remember the list myself. I could recite the first four words. And I knew the last was Inquisitor. But I wasn't certain of all the words between.

Goran raised his hand, as if he were going to make a proclamation in the name of the Primate himself. Half the children bit down on their lips, eagerly concentrating.

Then Goran exhaled and said, "Are you sure? I can skip every other word on the first pass. Or maybe you'd like them in the order of the alphabet?"

Wynda huffed. "You can't do this at all. You're just hoping to slip the net."

Goran's grin was familiar. "Will you make a wager, then?"

"For what?" Wynda was suddenly shrewder than any merchant in any market in any city throughout the primacy.

"If I recite correctly, you'll take my turn at making soap tomorrow."

Wynda nodded. "And when I win? I'm not on the schedule for soap." Goran shrugged and turned his hands up, inviting Wynda to name her price. She narrowed her eyes and enunciated carefully. "Mucking out the sheep stalls." Goran started to grin his acceptance, but she cut him off. "For three days."

Goran's eyes widened, but he extended his hand, offering a fair clasp to seal the deal. Wynda took his fingers in hers, and I could see she squeezed tightly, grinding his bones together as if she were punishing him for his audacity. Goran only grinned wider.

"For soap, then," he said, and Wynda smiled with absolute confidence. He threw his shoulders back, as if he were standing on the finest festival stage. He filled his lungs, and then he recited: "Bestius. Screech. Spider. Godhouse. Ladysilk. Rat. Darkbeast. Nameday. Altar. Onyx. Mudroyal. Inquisitor."

Wynda looked up from her parchment, her mouth gaping

with shock. The other Darkers laughed loudly, shouting out their compliments to Goran. My friend took a sweeping bow, as if he had just performed a complete revel. He let the momentum from his action carry him forward so that he completed a triple somersault, leaping to his feet so quickly that he seemed only a blur. The tumbling earned him a round of applause—along with a grudging smile from Wynda.

"That's amazing," the Darker girl said. "Are there others who can do that? Other Darkers that you know?"

Goran snorted. "It's a Traveler skill. It has nothing to do with Wart."

Before anyone could challenge Goran with a longer list, a bell tolled from deep within the caverns. It was time for everyone to gather in the central chamber for supper.

"Go ahead," Goran said to his crowd of admirers. "Keara and I will stow away the books."

Eager to be spared even that slight burden, the Darkers left the chamber, filling the corridor with chatter as they recounted Goran's accomplishment. Wynda was subjected to some good-natured teasing about her looming stint making soap.

I shuffled across the room and opened the storage chest against the far wall. "How did you do that?" I asked.

Goran blinked. "Vala never taught you how to memorize?"

I shrugged. Vala Traveler had been my best friend in the company. She had taught me lots of things about life as a performer, about living on the road. But she'd never given me the secret of rattling off a string of vaguely connected words like that.

"It's simple," Goran said. "Just focus on a place familiar to you. I use Taggart's wagon. You know, from . . . before."

From before Vala denounced us to the Primate's Guard. Before we left the Travelers. Before Taggart had been forced to abandon the troupe he had led for decades so that he could protect Goran and me and our darkbeasts.

Goran closed his eyes, and a peaceful smile came over his face. "I connected every word on Wynda's list with an item in Taggart's wagon, going widdershins about the space. The rectangular stairs were like the altar in Bestius's godhouse. The hinges needed to be oiled and they screeched, like the name of Wynda's darkbeast. The baskets just to the right of the door had a pattern that resembled a spider's web."

I must have had an odd expression on my face, because he laughed. "It's easy," he assured me, "especially when you know the place well. To recite the list, I just have to walk through Taggart's wagon in my mind. I imagine touching all those things, setting them to rights."

Even as he explained, I remembered how Wynda had looked at him. It seemed as if the two of them had exchanged some secret conversation, some private words behind their playful wager. I grunted as I stooped to collect an ink bottle from the floor.

Goran grinned at me across the half dozen books he had already gathered. "You're allowed to smile, you know." His light words reminded me of all the times we had laughed together in the past. Months before, Goran and I—along with Vala—had spent the better part of our days playing pranks on each other. We had tumbled like puppies in a pen, happy and content in ways we had not truly understood. In ways that were now lost forever.

I wiped ink from the quills everyone had left behind. "I know."

"What is wrong with you?" Goran sounded exasperated. Or maybe that was only the exertion that he spent pushing the table back to its place against the stone wall.

"Nothing."

"Of course," he said, and his voice thinned into a tone of perfect innocence, a Traveler's trick for portraying a child who was too young even to understand the notion of wrong, much less act in such a way. "You always shred feathers between your fingers when nothing is wrong."

I stared down at the quill pen I had been dismantling, all unaware. "It's just that life here is not what I thought it would be."

"Let me guess," he said. "You have taken a sudden dislike to regular meals."

I gave him a dirty look.

"To being warm, then," he prompted. "To being safe, without fear that an Inquisitor will appear at any moment."

"I am not mad!" I shouted, and the anger behind my words made them sound like a lie. I swallowed hard and forced my voice back to an urgent whisper. "Hasn't Wart told you? The bond between the Darkers and their animals is strange. Different."

"According to whom?"

"According to Caw."

"And is your darkbeast one of Bestius's sworn priests, that he can evaluate dozens of bonds between others?"

"He is bound himself, Goran, and you know it. He knows what mudroyal and ladysilk are supposed to feel like. Are you honestly telling me that things don't seem odd here? The Darkers all think alike, all memorize the same lessons!"

"Travelers memorize the same revels."

"But the Darkers aren't performing on a stage!" I curled my fingers into fists, desperate to put words to the foreboding that had tickled the back of my skull since we arrived. "It's not just the memorization. It's the routine tasks. The mindless repetition."

Goran laughed. "Everything about your life was routine before you took to the Great Road. There was baking day and laundry day and what else? Butter-churning day."

My bottom lip began to quiver, and my tears made me angry.

I slapped away the fingers that Goran extended to take the ruined quill. "Be quiet. You don't know anything about me!"

The flash of my hand against his hardened something in Goran's face. "Fine, Keara. Pretend you're angry with *me*. But we both know the truth."

"What truth is that?"

"You're jealous. You don't like me making new friends."

I laughed at his outrageous words, so shocked that I could not make a verbal retort.

"You forget," he said. "I watched when you came to the Travelers. I watched as I lost my best friend, but I never held that against you. I never blamed you for taking Vala."

My heart clenched around her name. She had been more like a sister to me than Morva and Robina, the blood family I had left behind in Silver Hollow. Vala and I had been inseparable—until she discovered the truth about me, about Caw. Then she became my enemy, sworn to destroy me no matter the cost.

Goran went on. "Vala was my friend long before you joined the troupe. Now it's my turn to make new friends. You get to watch me with the Darkers. You can join in, or not. But if you don't like them, then you can just stay here in the schoolroom. Alone."

I was still gaping in shock when he turned on his heel and left me in the cavern. Unbidden, my fingers went to the darkbeast circlet I wore around my wrist, the gift he had given me in the snowstorm. *Goran!* I wanted to call. *I'm sorry! We can talk!*

But he was already gone. I said nothing, and the torches guttered in a stray air current as I stared at the ruined feathers in my hand.

Chapter Four

K eara," Taggart wheezed. "Everyone is waiting for you to join them in the upper chamber. Put on your cloak now. Don't delay."

I sighed and shifted my weight on the wooden bench in the storeroom. I had hoped no one would think to look for me here, near the stacks of unsewn black cloth. Caw shifted on my shoulder, and I wondered if he had secretly communicated with Flick, if the darkbeasts had conspired against me. "They don't need me," I said aloud to Taggart. "There are plenty of children heading to Barleytown."

Taggart eased himself to sit beside me. His face was flushed, and I felt the heat of his body—not a deadly fever any longer, but still warmer than he should have been. The Darkers had provided nothing stronger than willow bark to treat the old man, and Saeran had been stinting with that. I could still hear the congestion in Taggart's lungs, and I longed for Mother's stock of herbs.

The old Traveler's voice sounded as if it had been rolled over gravel as he said, "Don't tell me you're going to let that girl take your place in the troupe."

That girl. Wynda. Goran's closest companion. I sighed and sank deeper into the pile of cloth. "We're not a troupe," I pouted. "We're nothing more than a ragtag group of rebels."

Wynda reminded me of that often enough, talking about how long the Darker stronghold had stood against the primacy. She regularly challenged me, asking how many Darkers *I* knew, how many times *I* had watched children spare their darkbeasts. Over and over again, I'd needed to confess my ignorance, my solitude before I'd had the good luck to meet Taggart and Goran.

"Ah," Taggart began slowly, as if he were aware of my spiteful thoughts about Wynda. The exclamation of wisdom sent him spiraling into a short coughing fit. When he had recovered, he said, "That's what has you concerned. Our rebellion is not progressing as rapidly as you hoped. We've spent four and a half weeks with the Darkers, and you thought that the Primate, the Inquisitors, and all the Twelve would be overthrown by now, and your darkbeast would be feted in the streets of Lutecia."

I glared at the old man, even as Caw said, *"Me? Feted? Does that mean everyone will throw seedcakes?"*

I did not bother to answer his absurd questions. Instead I started to pick at a knot on my darkbeast bracelet. Goran probably wished he'd never given it to me. He probably wanted to give it to Wynda now. "I'm not an idiot, Taggart."

His bushy eyebrows met above his nose. "You're not an infant, either."

I bristled at the unspoken accusation in his words. He wasn't being fair. He had no idea how difficult the past month had been for me. Ever since we had arrived at the darkhold, Taggart had been treated differently than I had been.

At first he had been too ill to participate in the Darkers' endless discussions, the adults debating long-term plans while we children were drilled on history, over and over and over again. At one point Taggart had even been feverish enough to rave about riding to distant villages, about stirring up peasants, about urging them all not to pay for their annual tax tattoos, not to slay their darkbeasts.

I had longed to get him out of the dark tunnels then, to take him aboveground. Even if it was winter outdoors, even if snow was falling, I thought that the old Traveler would regain his strength more quickly if he could breathe fresh air, if he could see the sky above him. After all, he had spent decades sleeping out of doors, staring up at the stars on all but the coldest of nights.

But we had not been allowed to wander aboveground. We had not been permitted to return to the clearing, to the fresh air, to the cold winter sky where the Twelve blazed out like beacons among the stars.

Instead Taggart had been questioned, over and over. Saeran herself had come to him daily, demanding to know if there were other Darkers on the Great Road, if Taggart had found other resisters who needed her help. Every day she mourned those brave souls who might be suffering at the hands of an Inquisitor, those loyal girls or boys who might be wandering lost in the woods, desperate for rescue.

Aside from Saeran's daily interrogation and ministrations from Goran and me, Taggart was kept separate and apart from the Darkers. He had been confined to a pallet in a distant chamber, lest he make the others ill. And so he had not needed to fit in with the strange company. He had not needed to conform. Now that he was finally recovering, he was welcome in so many ways that I was not.

"Taggart, the Darkers are not what I expected." I had not realized I was going to say the words before they were out of my mouth.

"What you *expected*? And what was that, in the name of all the Twelve?"

"*Yes,*" Caw said. "*Do tell!*" I glared at my darkbeast. He was the reason I'd taken to the road in the first place. He was the reason I was stuck here in the underground caves, the reason I was so unhappy.

"I thought there would be more . . . activity."

"Activity?" Taggart made a curious sound, as if one of his coughing fits was threatening to turn into a guffaw.

"All I've done for weeks is cook and clean. Spin and weave. Sit and memorize. With work like this, I might as well be back in Silver Hollow!"

This time Taggart actually did laugh out loud. He threw back his head, sending Flick scrambling for a secure grip on his iron neckpiece, and he cackled until he wheezed. "Keara!" he exclaimed when he could catch his breath. "Keara, Keara, Keara . . . Most of *life* is routine. Routine is what keeps us fed, keeps us safe. Keeps us ready for those few, heart-stopping moments when we must fight for what we believe."

Caw turned his head to a jaunty angle. *"Fight?"* he said. *"I do not plan on fighting. At least not on an empty stomach!"*

I echoed my darkbeast, in part. "I'm not saying I want to fight, Taggart. I'm just saying there should be more to life than skulking in caves."

"We're in agreement then, Keara. There *is* more to life. Specifically, there is a Wolf Moon market, a chance to trade for winter goods. And I wouldn't blame the Darkers if they've left you behind by now. You've kept them waiting far too long."

And that was when I realized I *had* been ridiculous. I'd been sulking because I was bored, because I wanted life to be exciting. And I was missing out on the very opportunity to make it so. I clambered to my feet and held out my wrist for Caw. Gently, he closed his talons on either side of my bracelet.

"Taggart?" I asked, suddenly afraid of what I would find aboveground. "What if they didn't wait? What if Goran has already headed out of the clearing, through the woods?"

What if he's no longer my friend? What if he demands that I return his bracelet? Those were the questions I could not make myself ask.

Taggart stared at me down his long nose. "Goran will be there for you, girl. You're bound together, after all that happened in Lutecia. Don't you worry about Goran."

I heard him. I understood his words. But I could not bring myself to believe. He spoke about his own grandson. How could he possibly see the truth, understand the real way things were?

Nevertheless, I made my way out to the clearing in the winter woods, consulting with Caw at the most confusing tangles of tunnels. I remembered my hopeless counting of twists and turns when I'd first been brought underground, blindfolded. Thank the Twelve, Caw had been left free to memorize the path. Otherwise I would never have found my way out.

Standing aboveground for the first time in over a month, I

was blinded by the brilliance of sunshine on the snow in the clearing. I blinked hard as my eyes started to water.

Goran hurried to my side. "*There* you are!" he exclaimed. "I thought maybe you'd changed your mind!"

"I lost track of time," I lied. "Caw was supposed to remind me." My raven squawked an indignant protest.

Goran frowned at him. "He'll have to stay here, you know."

"What?" My fingers immediately reached for the sleek familiar feathers, stroking Caw from his crown to his tail in the way I knew he loved.

"Only children ten and younger can bring their darkbeasts out of the caves. We don't want to call attention to ourselves in any way. All it would take is one adult to slip up, to let a single curious person glimpse a darkbeast, and we'd all be found out."

"But I still look young enough!" I protested. "Anyone will believe I'm still eleven!"

Goran shook his head. "Those are the rules," he said. "I've already left Wart behind."

Before I could structure an argument, Wynda came out of the crowd of children. "Ready, Goran?" She glanced at the sun, high above the clearing. We had a long way to travel to reach Barleytown. We planned to gain the Western Road that night so that we could find the best deals at market before noon the following day. "We can't tarry any longer."

Why didn't she ask me if *I* was ready? Why didn't she include *me* in her broad smile?

Instead of arguing, though, I said to Caw, "Go ahead, then. Back underground with you."

He cocked his head, settling one gimlet eye on a brilliant spray of carkle berries. *"If you're going to abandon me, at least let me eat first."*

I sighed. "Fine. Eat. But then it's back to the caves for you."

He took wing without bothering to reply. I wondered if Wart or Flick had ever been as exasperating.

I turned back to find Wynda staring at me. "You're wearing that?"

I glanced down at my black attire, the tunic, leggings, and cloak that I had worn since my first morning with the Darkers. "What else would I wear?" Even as I spoke, though, I realized that everyone else was clad in ordinary clothes—hearty garments made of brown homespun and dyed wool. I caught glimpses of ribbons on some of the girls and women, bright bands in the shades of rubies, emeralds, and sapphires.

Of course. We could not look like Darkers if we were heading out among regular people.

Wynda sighed. "One person in black will have to do."

I started to protest. I would love to wear ordinary clothes like Wynda did. I would love the glint of embroidery at my wrists, of careful stitches all along my garment's hem. I would love a ribbon, a touch of finery, of rich promise. But no one was going to wait for me to find some cache of clothes in the underground tunnels. No one was going to wait for me at all.

Wynda was already turning around, nodding to Saeran and saying, "We're ready. At last." She tucked her pitch-black hair under her crimson hood. I tried to swallow my jealousy as I noted the shade of the garment. Red had always been my favorite color. Even more importantly, the wool was twice as thick as the common cloak I wore. Wynda was taking no chance she'd grow cold as we journeyed through the winter woods.

The Darker girl had made certain that Goran was dressed smartly as well. He wore a rich green cloak the color of pine needles. Lucky Goran, who had friends among the Darkers. I might as well just stay with Taggart and the handful of Darker workers who remained behind, feeding the sheep, guarding the caverns. No one would notice, in any case.

And that was the last chance I had for a self-pitying thought. Instead, my attention was soon snagged by the treacherous journey through the woods. Much snow had fallen since we had arrived at the darkhold, and laden pine boughs blocked the narrow path. I soon grew accustomed to cold slush on my face as branches sprang away, and I pulled up the thin hood on my black cloak in hopes of sparing my neck from a similar bracing bath.

After our narrow path joined up with the main trail through the forest, the Darkers came to full life. We had no intention of sneaking about. Rather we operated under a simple story—we were from a clutch of villages, far to the west. We had kept company on the long road, traveling to this rare winter market to stock up on supplies, to offer some excess cloth and harvested winter berries and fine woven ribbons in exchange for goods we could not have at our isolated homes.

That much, at least, was true. Our entire reason for heading to Barleytown was to restock for the frozen months ahead—herbs and spices and other things that the Darkers could not grow or make among themselves.

I soon discovered that Goran had integrated himself into the company even more than I expected. He had shared Travelers' tricks for passing the time on long roads. On the broader path I watched children as young as five walk along, juggling wooden balls that had been wrapped with brightly colored yarn. A pair of older boys bounced a baton between them, sending the wooden rod flying off their wrists and elbows, their knees, their backs.

I shouldn't have been surprised. I had seen the trick often enough among the Travelers.

The sun was almost in its early winter bed when we reached the Western Road. The Silver River rushed beside us, flowing fast enough to stay free from ice even as its frozen spray coated the largest boulders. Saeran barely noticed; she kept us walking until nightfall, until we were nearly on the outskirts of Barleytown.

Only when the light was completely gone did she gather us close. She ordered the men to build a massive bonfire. Three women were instructed to share out food from the woven hampers they carried. Waxed cloth was stretched over wooden frames; we had tents to take refuge from the cold night air.

Pondera's godhouse would have been more welcoming. But we Darkers shied away from the hospitality of the Twelve. We had too many secrets to spend time with priests. And we did not have the coin to take rooms at a regular inn—not all of us, men and women and children.

I collected a pear-infused biscuit and a generous serving of cheese. Even as I joined up with Goran and the other children, I studied the bread, determining the fairest split so that Caw got no more than his share of the sweet fruit within. My face flushed when I remembered my darkbeast was not beside me. He was foraging on his own, and the treat was all mine.

I should have enjoyed the laughter in our group as we downed our simple fare. I should have taken pleasure in the easy camaraderie. I should have reveled in the surprising warmth of a pair of woolen blankets draped over my shoulders, keeping out the chill of night.

Instead I watched Wynda offer Goran half her cheese, and my own food settled heavy in my belly.

Before I could think about my motivation, I gathered a pair of apples and went to stand beside Goran. "So," I said. "You shared the Travelers' tricks for juggling balls and batons. Did you think the Darkers could not handle rolling?"

Goran took my meaning immediately; his eyes gleamed with a spirit of friendly competition. "I did not want our new friends to surpass your limited knowledge. I would not have embarrassed you that way, Keara-ti."

I brushed aside the easy endearment. "I can roll better than you," I said. "And for longer, too."

For answer, Goran whipped off his cloak and held out his hand for an apple.

The children gathered around us in a circle. I made a deep bow, letting my fingers flare wide as I invited our audience to watch Goran's feat. For his part, he brandished the apple above his head, cocking his wrist at the perfect angle, as if he held the Primate's largest gemstone in his fist.

I started the competition by clapping, slow and steady, cupping my palms to make the sound louder. The other children took up the beat immediately, laughing and jostling for a better position. Goran wasted no time. He placed the apple on the crown of his head, balancing it as he turned a perfect circle in front of the watchers. Then he leaned his left ear toward his shoulder, taking care that the apple stayed balanced as it traced an opposite path, coming to rest against his right ear. It was easy enough to continue the motion, catching the apple against the side of his neck, rolling it around so that it nestled beneath his chin.

The crowd laughed, and I saw that the adults had drawn close. Goran noticed as well, and the knowledge made him bold. He started to straighten, prepared to roll the apple down his chest, most likely to his side. He moved too quickly, though, and the fruit slipped into the slush at his feet.

Ever the showman, Goran acted as if he'd intended to end his performance there. He swooped into another regal bow, gathering up the apple and flourishing it toward the crowd. There were hoots and whistles and more than a few feet stamping the ground to show their approval.

And then Goran gestured to me, inviting me to do my best.

I shrugged off my blankets and chose to play another of the Travelers' types—not the bold performer, but rather the shy maiden. I dropped a delicate curtsy, gathering imaginary skirts out of my way as I ducked my eyes in semblance of modesty. I raised my own apple and balanced it on my head, making a tight circle to build suspense regarding what I was about to do.

The crowd was with me immediately, counting out a rhythm with strong, even clapping. I followed the general pattern that

Goran had set, rolling the apple from my head to my ear, from my ear to my neck. Once I had the fruit tucked under my chin, I sensed the watchers' excitement. Every last one was waiting to see if I could best my friend. Allowing myself to grin, I edged the apple back to my shoulder. The fruit tracked down my arm, to my hand, to my eager, agile fingertips.

On and on I worked the routine. Truth be told, I performed the best I ever had, feeding off the Darkers' enthusiasm. I chose when to finish the game. I chose to kick the apple off the toe of my boot, to send it arcing through the air, to sail easily toward waiting hands in the crowd.

Toward Wynda's hands.

Well, I hadn't planned that. I wouldn't have chosen to grant her that recognition.

But I could afford to be gracious as the Darkers burst into applause. Half a dozen children ran over to the hampers, snagging apples of their own. They clamored for me to show them how to work the magic, how to perform the trick. I laughed for the first time in weeks, for the first time since I had followed Goran and Taggart into the darkhold clearing.

Out of reflex, I reached for Caw's thoughts, to share my joy with my darkbeast.

Nothing, of course. Only dim, dark distance—there was no way to contact Caw across all the space we humans had traveled.

I winced, but I told myself all would be fine. I would see Caw in another two days.

Using my pride to plug the hole in my heart, I set about teaching my Darker friends how to perform like a Traveler. The lessons were made easier when Goran joined in, working by my side as if we would always be together, forever and ever.

Chapter Five

The following morning Goran was still beside me as we made our way down a winding street in Barleytown. He glanced at a scrap of parchment that Saeran had pressed into his hand before we left the group. "Two dozen iron needles," he intoned, as if the words were as important as a revel. Saeran had sketched a map, too. Goran clutched his fingers around the pair of silver coins the Darkers' leader had given him so that he could complete the purchase.

I swallowed down a healthy dose of jealousy. No one had given me a scrap of parchment. No one had drawn me a map. Certainly, no one had given me coins newly minted with the Primate's face.

At least Goran and I were allowed to work together. Wynda had been assigned her own tasks, and all the other children too. We were each charged to gather in front of Venerius's godhouse at the far western edge of the village by no later than sunset. Then we would proceed back to our roadside camp together, with an eye toward regaining the darkhold the following day.

Goran and I turned a corner and found ourselves in the middle of a paved square. A stone-lined well hulked in the center of the space, and a line of women waited with buckets.

A grin broke out on my lips, and I cast a quick glance to my companion. He was smiling as well—we both remembered the days we had spent crying villages along the Great Road, announcing the Travelers and their revels. Even now a part of me waited for Goran to take the lead, to swing into action, to clamber on top of the shed that sheltered the well.

By reflex I started to size up the assembled women. That one was heavy with child; she stood with a friend who cradled an infant. Another woman held forth on something important—she commanded the respect of her fellow townsfolk, and three or four nodded in agreement with whatever she said. Yet another pinned Goran and me with narrowed eyes—she had no friends, and she was wary, watchful. Exactly the sort of woman we would have avoided months before, a lifetime before, when we had regularly cried the revels.

"What do you think?" Goran asked, and I could see him longing to be the center of attention. "We could juggle for them. Entertain them while they wait. Add to Saeran's coins, and make the D—our companions proud."

My heart seized as he almost spoke aloud the secret name of those companions. Still, I was reluctant as I shook my head. "No, Goran-tu," I said, flavoring my words with real regret. "This is neither the time nor the place."

The last thing we needed to do was call attention to ourselves. To the Darkers.

As if to emphasize my words, there was a commotion on the far side of the square. All conversation died as a newcomer arrived. A newcomer clad in snow-white robes. A newcomer whose face was obscured by a tall hood. A newcomer who was still too distant for me to see the fine white thread embroidered across his chest, symbol of the specific god he served. An Inquisitor.

In a rush I remembered everything I had ever been taught about the Inquisitors—how they trained with Marius's priest-soldiers to become dangerous fighters and studied with Pondera's priests to learn the rules of justice. Inquisitors worked with Tempestia's priests to master the signs of weather, until they could foretell the future by a single wisp of cloud and a breath of wind. They studied everything, mastered everything. They held all power and offered it up in perfect dedication to the Twelve.

Without intending to, I clutched at Goran's hand. His fingers squeezed mine, cold and clammy and every bit as desperate as my own. His touch eased back to the pulse point in my wrist, settling one of the darkbeast bracelet's knots against my pounding veins. I was paralyzed, like a mouse praying that a hawk would not notice her from its distant circle in the sky.

As the Inquisitor crossed the square, one woman found the courage to break the silence. "Blessed be Aurelius!" she cried. It was the suspicious woman, the one who stood alone. She was obviously close enough to make out the stitchery on the Inquisitor's snowy robes.

So this man was sworn specifically to the god of wealth. After completing all his studies, he had bound himself to the cause of money and counting, of proper order in all things monetary. The Inquisitor responded to the woman: "Blessed be." He raised one fleshy hand in acknowledgement of her salute.

The other women freed themselves from their spell of silence then, repeating the greeting. Goran cleared his throat beside me, and I heard him join in. I was only a fraction of a heartbeat behind as I, too, greeted the robed figure.

The Inquisitor crossed the square so slowly that I thought he had to be drawing out his passage intentionally. The line of women parted to let him by. At first I thought he was going to pass directly in front of Goran and me, that we would be close enough to touch his robe. Close enough to hear the chains that all Inquisitors wore around their waists, the better to restrain the Lost.

I longed to reach out for Caw's cool thoughts, to consult with my darkbeast about what I should say, how I should move. But Goran and I were alone here, without our lifelong animal companions, without even the support of our fellow Darkers.

No one would know if the Inquisitor clapped us in chains. No one would tell Saeran. Word would never reach Taggart. How long would it be before Caw and Wart registered the true meaning behind our absence?

Goran's fingers slipped from the bracelet and tightened around mine. It seemed as if I could read his thoughts; the words were as clear as Caw's inside my head. *"On the count of three,"* he seemed to say, *"we'll run. We'll try to reach the Western Road, make our way back to the darkhold."*

Or perhaps that was merely my plan.

We didn't have any hope of fleeing, of course. The Inquisitor would raise an alarm long before we could ever escape. Nevertheless, I could not think of a different path, a better option.

I clutched Goran's hand—once. Twice. I relaxed my fingers for a heartbeat, drew breath to shout, *Now!*

And then the Inquisitor turned and walked away. He chose the corner of the square to our left, a path that headed deeper into town. Like a massive ship sailing on a calm sea, the robed man drifted out of sight.

I scarcely heard the women come back to life beside the well. I could not quite make out the stories they told each other, the gossip, the news. I was barely aware of Goran standing beside me, his breath as harsh as Taggart's had been during the worst of the old man's illness.

I dared a glance at Goran's face. The spray of freckles across his nose stood out like grains of millweed pollen. He swallowed hard, rubbing a hand across his upper lip, wiping away a sheen of sweat. I could smell rank fear upon him.

"Well," he said, and it took him two tries to force more words out. "Saeran's iron needles aren't going to walk here to meet us, are they?"

I made myself laugh, even though his words weren't actually funny. But somehow, laughing eased the knot in my belly. Goran joined me, tentatively at first, and then both of us were cackling like mad hens discovering their very own clutch of juicy worms at the corner of a dusty garden.

The women at the well shook their heads at us ill-mannered brats, but no one called after us as we ducked back into the warren of the Barleytown streets.

Goran was better at reading Saeran's map than I was. He'd had more practice with unfamiliar villages during all his years with the Travelers. He counted out the twists and turns, nodding as we passed scribbled landmarks. The shop, when we found it, was deep inside a tangle of storefronts. I nearly missed the wooden sign that was nailed to the wall beside the door—a slender representation of a needle.

An old man sat inside, warming his bottom before a small fire. His eyes gleamed as we stepped over the threshold. I knew he was measuring us, calculating just how much he could charge for his wares. My palms itched; I remembered listening to countless stories of how Mother had gauged interest in her herbs, how she had negotiated for profit from ill-prepared customers who did not know the true value of the goods they sought.

Goran, though, seemed perfectly well prepared. In fact he started his negotiations with a price that was insultingly low. The old man barked a harsh laugh and said he could not part with two dozen needles for anything less than a dozen silver pieces. Back and forth the pair argued until Goran took a break to scrutinize the quality of the wares. After that we prepared to leave the shop, Goran shaking his head and denouncing the old man as a scoundrel, a thief, and worse.

In the end, we got all twelve needles, and a handful of coppers in change. Goran made a show of checking the edges of each coin, determining they had not been shaved to a lighter weight. The old man scowled, but he shook on the deal before counting out the needles into a soft leather pouch. Goran shoved his prize deep into a pocket at his waist.

I followed him out to the warren of streets, not breathing easily until we were back in a public square. As the noontime sun shone upon us, Goran laughed and said, "That was fun! I wish Saeran had given us more to do!"

"Fun?" I almost shouted. "That man was going to draw his knife on you!"

"Nonsense." Goran stared at me as if I had sprouted wings. "He enjoyed the bargaining."

"He said you were an insulting dog, and he'd rather pluck your fleas than hear another word from you!"

Goran only laughed. "That was a *game*. We were working our own Common Play back there, the man and I. You should have scribbled down the words to teach our friends when we get back home."

I shook my head, but his enthusiasm was infectious. "Why did you ever waste your time on a stage?" I asked. "Clearly you could have made a fortune in some market town."

"I'm just lucky, Keara-ti." He smiled as he jangled the copper coins in his pocket. "And so are you, for I'll share my fortune with you today. What do you fancy? Boiled sweets? Toffee apples? A pear tart or fig pudding?"

My mouth watered. The Darkers had good food, and plenty

of it, but they did not waste many resources on sweets. "Fig pudding," I said, remembering a treat Mother had made years before in celebration of Robina's wedding. Morva and I had licked the wooden spoon that Mother used to stir the stuff, and we had laughed ourselves silly, whispering that the sweetness of the pudding might actually be enough to tame even Robina's temper.

"Fig pudding it is, then," Goran said.

I don't think that Caw himself could have winged his way more directly to the narrow street where old women offered up sweets for sale. Fig pudding for me and a custard tart for Goran. Pear cider washed down the treats, and there were still a half dozen coins waiting to be spent. As the sun sank closer to the rooftops, we wandered through Barleytown, laughing and telling stories to pass the time. At last the air began to chill, and our breath ghosted before us.

"We'd best meet up with the others," I said, but I could not keep reluctance from my tone. We Travelers might have been fortunate to have found the darkhold weeks before. We were certainly privileged to have been trusted and taken in. But I had treasured the day just spent in Barleytown, back in a town, alone with my one true friend and free from constant lessons and the never-ending feeling that I was being watched.

Even if the cost of the day had been separation from my darkbeast. Even if I longed to tell Caw all that we had done.

Goran pointed down an alleyway. "We can take that shortcut to the godhouse."

"How do you *know* that?"

"Didn't you see the building before? When we passed the man who was grilling sausages?"

"The man—"

"Around the corner from the cooper?"

"The cooper?" I had no memory of a man selling buckets and barrels.

Goran sighed in exasperation. "This way."

Part of me resented the quick pace he set. He was hurrying to get back to Wynda, I told myself. He was tired of spending the day with me. He would be grateful when he was back with the others.

Of course if Caw were there, my darkbeast would make some wry observation, telling me I was foolish and needy and vain. Goran was merely rushing because we had been told to gather as the sun set.

After all, *I* was the one who wore Goran's bracelet. *I* was the one he had chosen as his friend. Not Wynda. Not anyone else. Me.

I hurried to match him, step for step. One turn. Another. A third, almost invisible in the twilight shadows.

And then we stood before Venerius's godhouse. Its wooden columns lurked in the gloom like giant trees standing sentinel on the edge of a forest. It was too dark for me to make out the slate roof, the tiles layered like leaves above the round building. A pair of torches flickered beside the yawning mouth of a door. The flames picked out a wooden carving of a dog, a hound, carved from the trunk of a chestnut tree.

We had no godhouse for Venerius back in Silver Hollow. My home village had been too small for such a luxury. But I had memorized the god's symbols when I was learning my first words. I had seen other examples of the hunter's godhouse along the road as I journeyed with the Travelers.

It was customary for local hunters to gather inside the godhouse after a good day in the woods, offering up the liver and heart from their successful pursuit of game. Between the hunters and we Darkers who were gathering at our appointed time, I expected to see a clutch of people outside Venerius's place of worship. I expected to feel the thrum of excitement. I expected to hear the whisper of prayers, fervent gratitude for a good day's hunt. I expected to smell fresh blood, the scent of the kill.

But I never expected to see a dozen Inquisitors ranged in a semicircle before the godhouse, iron chains held at the ready.

PART TWO

Pride

I was nine years old, and Mother had asked me to collect our bread from the communal ovens. I was proud to have the new task. Robina had collected the bread when I was very young. Morva had done it for the past three years.

I gathered half a dozen chestnut loaves, sniffing each as I added it to my stack. Morva never brought home enough to last the week, to tide us over until the next baking day. She said she could not carry all the chestnut, not if she brought the wheat home too.

I was better at carrying than Morva was. I was the best at carrying of anyone my age, in all of Silver Hollow.

Goodwife Weaver watched as I tried to balance the six loaves. "Your stomach is giving orders to your eyes, little one."

"I can carry them all," I said, sticking out my chest like the

plumed rooster that scratched around the dirt in front of our cottage.

"Take care that you do," Goody Weaver said. "There won't be replacements if you lose them."

I threw my shoulders back to prove that the stern woman had nothing to worry about. I knew that each family came to the oven once a week. Each could take what they needed, but no more. Each could linger as long as they liked, but could not return. That was the way baking day was done; the requirements were older than the Family Rule itself.

I suspected I had made a mistake as soon as I left the oven. Six loaves were difficult to balance. The hard crust of one slipped against another. My fingers were too short to grasp them easily; I had to lean all of the bread against my chest.

That was fine, though. I could anchor the stack with my chin. I could deliver all six loaves, something that neither Morva nor Robina had ever managed. Even though I could not turn my head to see where I was on the path.

I counted the steps from the oven to our cottage. I thought I waited long enough to turn off the main course. I thought I gauged the angle precisely, taking the quickest route to our front door. I thought I cleared the edge of our neighbor's trough, the deep basin that held water for their two cows and their shaggy horse.

But I banged my hip into the sharp wooden corner of the trough. All six loaves went flying—four of them landing in the water, one finding the perfect center of the mud puddle that oozed beneath the slow-dripping container. I caught one loaf, the smallest one, the one that had sat a little too close to the fire and was singed just on one side.

That was the way my father liked his bread. I had chosen that loaf just for him, because this week—for the first time ever—we were going to have enough chestnut bread for everyone.

I tried to save them. When I stepped closer to the water, though, I slipped a little, splashing mud over the single loaf on the ground. I still thought I could salvage it, brush it off, at least let us eat the nutty, crunchy inside, but then I slipped again, and my right foot came down squarely in the middle of the crust.

I had to tuck Father's loaf under my arm. It shifted, and I almost dropped it. By the time the bread was secure, the four loaves in the trough had started to puff, to expand, to drift across the water like clouds across a summer sky.

I stared in disbelief until Mother came to the doorway and ordered me into the cottage. She took one look at the small, singed loaf in my hands and asked me what I had possibly been thinking.

"I thought that I could carry six!"

"Six? Why would you think that? Did Robina ever manage six at one time? Did Morva?"

"But I am better than they are! I can do more than they can!"

Mother glared at the miserable little loaf; it looked even worse in my otherwise-empty hands. "Take your pride to your darkbeast!"

She barely remembered to pluck the bread from my fingers before she tightened the leash around my wrist, the bond I was required to wear when I offered up my failings to Caw.

"I thought you were bringing me a treat," *Caw chided.* "Bread as dark as I am."

I glared at my darkbeast. "Father likes it that way."

"You'll be hungry for decent bread by next baking day. Even a loaf of plain wheat bread will look good by then."

"I had a plan! I am better at getting bread than my sisters ever dreamed of being!"

"And how has that worked for you?"

My belly rumbled, as if it were hinting at lean times ahead. "I thought I was going to help everyone. I thought I would make things better for all of us, share enough bread to please everyone all week long."

"Everyone?" *Caw cocked his head at an angle.* "And who prefers the chestnut bread, above all else?"

I knew what he was getting at, but I refused to give him the satisfaction of an answer. "Lots of people like chestnut bread."

"Who in this house?"

"Mother likes it. My sisters, and Father, they'll eat a chunk or two."

"And who else?"

I hung my head, knowing I had to admit the truth. "Me. Chestnut bread is my favorite." *Caw's head bobbed, as if he agreed with me. I knew I had to say the rest of it.* "I took too many loaves of chestnut *bread because I was thinking of myself. I thought I could carry them when I knew my sisters could not." My voice faded to a whisper. "I was prideful."*

Caw waited, but I could think of nothing more to say, nothing more to offer up. At last he fluttered his wings against his cage. "All right, then. Your longing for bread by the end of the week will teach you more than I can, in any case. I take your pride. Forget it. It is mine."

The familiar sparkle filled my body, the thrum of darkbeast magic released into my blood. For the first time since I'd watched the chestnut loaves fall, I felt good. I believed that all might turn out well in the end, even if I spent a good part of the next week hungry.

I started to slip the leash off my wrist. Caw hopped close and tilted his head at a becoming angle. "But that loaf in the mud?" he whispered. "Could you bring it to me? What's a little muck and mire to a darkbeast like myself?"

I waited until after midnight, so that Mother would not see, would not be angry with me for bringing filth into her good, clean home. And Caw gulped down every last bite of the nasty stuff, gloating silently in the dark.

Chapter Six

*B*ut *Barleytown is too small to have a godhouse for each of the Twelve.*

That was the first thought that crossed my mind as I stared at the assembled Inquisitors. After all, we weren't in Lutecia, where each of the gods had a dedicated home, where hundreds of supporting priests and Inquisitors gathered each and every day.

No. Someone had called all these Inquisitors here, summoned them to the cobbled road in front of the building dedicated to Venerius.

I glanced around, suddenly fearful for the other Darkers who had spent the day roaming the streets of Barleytown, collecting their own supplies for the darkhold. If only I could warn them before they, too, stumbled on the Inquisitors. If only I could tell my companions to flee, to seek refuge in the streets of the town, to find their own way back to the isolated clearing in the woods where they could be safe from certain doom.

Even then, I did not understand. Even then, my memory snagged on the only Inquisitor I had ever spoken with, the one who had stopped me in Rivermeet months before. I remembered how Taggart had paid off that man with hard-won silver coins— more money than expected, more money than was fair, but a simple transaction. A simple bribe.

Nothing like the challenge that faced us now. For now, all the other Darkers were standing *with* the Inquisitors.

Saeran was there, her hood thrown back so that her icy hair glinted in the torchlight. Wynda stood beside her, a curious smile twisting her lips. As I gaped, I realized that each and every one of our Darker companions stood in the shadows of Venerius's tall wooden columns. They were calm. Confident. Clearly allied with the dozen Inquisitors.

Goran and I had been betrayed. I suddenly understood all of the questions I had answered in the caverns, all the times the Darkers had asked me if I knew anyone else who had spared a darkbeast. Saeran and her people had sprung a trap on us three Travelers, and she had hoped to drag others down with us.

"Goran," I whispered.

"I see," he said, and his fingers clutched around mine, slipping past the darkbeast bracelet.

That tiny motion was enough to free the Inquisitors. They descended upon us, white robes billowing.

I told myself to flee. I told myself to escape through the alleys of Barleytown, to run while I still could.

But my feet would not obey me. My limbs remembered years of lessons from Mother, from the priests of all the Twelve. Inquisitors were sacred to all the gods and goddesses. Inquisitors knew what was right in all things. Inquisitors must be obeyed.

And I remembered something else, something Goran had taught me months before in Rivermeet: Inquisitors *always* succeed.

My friend had said the words then. And clearly both of us remembered them now. We froze as the robed figures looped heavy manacles around our wrists. They fastened massive iron locks to chains tightened around our waists. They strung links between our feet.

Wynda darted forward. Her hand flew faster than Venerius's own golden shaft, and my cheek stung with the force of her slap. She laughed and pulled her arm back, ready to strike me again. "Leave off," I shouted, unable to duck away, unable to free myself from her assault.

Desperate, still not fully comprehending the danger I was in,

I looked to Saeran. "Please," I said, and I raised my heavy arms toward her, pleading for aid. "There must be some misunderstanding. You must not realize—"

For answer, Saeran reached into the shadows on the porch of Venerius's godhouse. She lifted up a curious contraption—a metal mask, hinged on one side so that it could go around a prisoner's head. An evil-looking spike jutted forward where tender lips and tongue would be. A rough bell sat on the top, jangling ominously as Saeran brandished the device.

"Branks!" Goran hissed.

I'd heard of the branks before. Scolds and gossips were forced to wear them—people who offended the Twelve with their speech. I swallowed hard and imagined the metal spike against my tongue, sharp as swordleaf and bitter as mudroyal. I rolled my lips closed, determined not to give Saeran a reason to force me into the thing.

The woman narrowed her eyes and nodded. We'd reached an understanding. For now.

I suddenly understood that none of the people whom we had met in the clearing was actually a Darker, had actually spared his or her own darkbeast.

What had Caw said when we first arrived at the compound? They felt *different*.

How different, I was only beginning to fathom. How had the adults pretended to be bonded with their creatures? How had the Darkers—no, not Darkers. Never Darkers. How had Saeran's people lived such lies in the caves beneath the woods?

I looked toward Goran, to see if he had gleaned all that I now grasped. His face was very pale, whiter even than it had been that morning, when Aurelius's Inquisitor had walked toward us in the square. Was that man facing us now? I craned my neck, trying to distinguish individual faces beneath the terrifying snowy hoods. I was unable, though, to make out any specific features inside the shadowy garments.

By now townspeople were gathering, lured by this odd disturbance on a cold winter night. Whispers grew to shouts. I heard the word "Inquisitor" slithering through the crowd. And somehow, impossibly, "darkbeast."

Saeran must have planted knowledge among the people, whispering the truth during the long day that we had all spent in Barleytown. These folk knew that Goran and I had spared our darkbeasts. Our twelfth namedays had come and gone, and we had refused to slay our constant companions.

Someone threw a rotten pear, and it smashed against Goran's shoulder. He muttered a curse, the sort of word that would have earned him a scowl from Taggart if we had been back among the Travelers.

Taggart.

My belly tightened at the thought of the old man. He had

declined to come with us, staying behind at the darkhold. Had he known we were going to be betrayed?

No. Of course not. He would never have let me, let his own grandson, stroll off into danger.

Even as a bruised and slimy apple crashed against my arm, my heart beat a little faster. Back at the darkhold, Taggart would figure out that something was wrong. He would realize we were not returning at the expected hour. He would do something to free us, something to engineer our escape, the way he had when Goran first spared Wart, when we fled from the Primate's Guard in Lutecia.

A fistful of rotten hay thudded against my black tunic. Just as well—the stench was enough to wipe any hint of sudden hopefulness from my face.

Goran and I might have been injured then and there. The crowd was restless; they were eager for something to brighten the long winter night. I caught a glimpse of one woman, her face twisted as she called Goran a horrible name. It took me a moment to place her, to realize that she was the older woman we had seen by the well, the one who had stood by herself, who had seemed so isolated and alone. She was just one of the crowd now, one of the entire township of Barleytown intent on attacking Goran and me.

Before the crowd could dissolve into a lawless mob, one of the Inquisitors stepped forward. I could just make out a spray of white stitches across his chest—an exquisitely detailed fly, its pair of wings picked out with threads that glimmered in the torchlight. The Inquisitor was sworn to Bestius, then. To the god of dark-beasts.

As I swallowed hard, the man raised a hand for silence. The crowd's response was immediate; they were better primed than any audience the Travelers had ever met. Goran and I were providing finer entertainment than any revel.

Even as my knees started to tremble, I forced myself to think, *Taggart will come. Taggart and Caw together.* The words echoed so loud inside my skull I thought Goran might even be able to hear them.

"Good people of Barleytown!" the Inquisitor proclaimed, and his voice was higher than I expected, reedy in the nighttime air. The townsfolk, though, did not seem to care if he was a great performer. They surged closer, as if they were about to hear the finest Holy Play ever staged. "Behold a pair of traitors, the likes of which you've never seen before."

There were angry murmurs, and I suspected Goran and I would have been showered with more refuse if the Inquisitor had not been standing so close to both of us. Even so, I caught several men spitting and raising their right hands in defiant gestures, as if they would cast us out from their midst even before the Inquisitor finished having his say.

My breath grew ragged with fear, but I forced myself to think again. My fingers threaded through the chains that encircled my wrists. I found Goran's darkbeast bracelet, and I fingered one of the knots.

Taggart will come. Taggart and Caw together.

The Inquisitor went on. "Good people of Barleytown, you are watched over by all the Twelve. You are protected by the Twelve. Loyal servants to the Twelve have gathered here to preserve you, to keep you safe and sound beneath the Wolf Moon."

The squeaky voice paused long enough to gesture toward Saeran and Wynda, toward all the so-called Darkers. Saeran sank into a deep curtsy, turning her face to the side, more modest than Madrina, the mother of all the gods. A part of me was astonished that she was not a Traveler, for she was a finer performer than any woman I had seen upon the Great Road.

When she rose up from her curtsy, she glared at Goran and me. Her hatred was like a tangible thing, a burning rope that tugged across the twilit street. I fingered another of my bracelet's knots.

Taggart will come. Taggart and Caw together.

I had to believe my silent chant. I had nothing else to give me hope.

The Inquisitor droned on, complimenting the people of Barleytown as if they had done something brilliant by capturing

Goran and me. He announced that we would be taken east, to Lutecia. That we would be shown justice in Bestius's godhouse, before the Primate himself. That the Twelve would have no mercy.

I found another knot.

Taggart will come. Taggart and Caw together.

The moon had risen by the time we left the freezing streets of Barleytown. A small herd of horses was tied up on the eastern side of the village, nearly a score of beasts, each pawing the ground, snorting from wide nostrils. Every animal was fitted out with a gleaming bridle, with supple reins. I was not surprised to pick out sigils of all the gods on their tack—Venerius's chestnut hound, Madrina's golden cow, Pondera's brindle cat.

No, I was not surprised to see that the fine beasts were dedicated to the Twelve. I *was* surprised though, by the rough cart that was lashed behind a pair of matched grays. And I was astonished by how hard it was to keep my balance as I was thrust onto the tumbrel. And I was amazed by how sore my iron-weighted arms became, and my knees, and every bony bump of my spine, as the cart began to grind its way along the Western Road.

My fingers fumbled past the bracelet's knots, as if I were reading carved letters on a wall.

Taggart will come. Taggart and Caw together.

Saeran rode beside us, apparently content to have left behind the majority of her so-called Darkers. I wondered what the others would do, where they would go now that their work was done. Now that Goran and I had been caught like mice in a trap. Surely the pretend Darkers had no reason to return to the caves. They were free to rejoin their true families, free from their supposed darkbeasts.

As hatred kindled inside my chest, I saw Wynda cut her horse between Saeran and the cart. Goran's face softened just a shade. He still did not understand, not in his heart of hearts. He still did not grasp how thoroughly we had been betrayed. Some part of him—even a tiny sliver at the bottom of his soul—wanted to believe that Wynda remained a friend, an ally.

I longed to kick him, to warn him, to tell him never to trust anyone again.

Instead Wynda conveyed the message for me. She leaned close and tangled her gloved fingers in Goran's onyx-dark hair. Even then I saw the faint light of hope flicker deep within his eyes. He swallowed hard and whispered, "Wynda. Friend."

She tightened her grasp. "I'm not your friend, fool. I was never your friend!"

"But in the sheep pen . . . when we were feeding the lambs . . ."

"I was hoping to learn of other heretics like you. Other idiots we could lure to our caverns before turning them over to the Inquisitors, like proper folk do."

Goran looked stunned. "I thought . . ."

I could not let him fumble for more words. I could not let him embarrass himself in front of that viper. I spat, "Why didn't you just hand us over to the Inquisitors straightaway?"

She laughed at me like I was a mewling babe. "A cow gives more milk with sweet hay than with briars. We thought to discover all of your lying, cheating companions. Don't worry, darkling scum. You'll be left to the Inquisitors soon enough and they'll complete the job that we began."

"But Wynda," Goran choked out, as if he could not comprehend her words.

She tightened her fingers, which were still knotted in his hair. "Enough! You disgust me!" Droplets of her spittle fell on Goran's cheek, but there was nothing he could do to clean himself.

Saeran clucked at the back of her throat, clearly summoning Wynda to her side. For a moment, it seemed that the girl would not obey the older woman, would not fall in line. In the end, however, she satisfied herself with tugging Goran's hair one last time, and then she fell back into the ranks of the other riders.

Goran sniffed beside me, and I carefully avoided meeting his eyes. It was enough to count the knots on the bracelet he had given me.

Taggart will come. Taggart and Caw together.

The night was endless. My belly cried out for food, even though I was not certain I could keep anything down. My throat was parched. My iron bonds grew heavier with each jarring foot-step of the grays.

As the moon climbed, the night grew even colder. Even in my exhausted misery, I was grateful for the cloak I wore, for the black wool that managed to shield me a little from the chill.

Goran's garment was even warmer, made of thicker stuff. He pulled closer to me as the cart lurched on, standing tall beside me. After a long time he settled his hands on the side of the cart, fold-ing his fingers around the wood with the careful precision of the Primate holding his scepter.

It was a Traveler's trick. I knew that. By placing his body next to something large, something sturdy—the cart—Goran assumed the mass and security of that object.

It was a trick, but it was a good one.

I placed my hand next to his. Our chains clanked together, but our arms were close; we shared our heat in the sharp, moonlit night. I felt my spine grow straighter. My shoulders thrust back, and I raised my chin. I did my best as a Traveler to depict the very essence of a proud woman, embracing my fate bravely no matter what might happen next.

The faintest of grins flickered across Goran's lips. He knew what I had done, and he approved. I flexed my wrist so that the bracelet became visible beneath my bonds.

Taggart will come. Taggart and Caw together.

I could not say how many hours we lurched along the Western Road. My eyes grew sandy, but I fought to stay awake. I lost the feeling in my feet, yet I managed—barely—to keep my balance. My fingers turned to ice, but I would not relinquish the posture Goran had set for us both.

The sky started to lighten before us, softening from black to indigo to the gray of a pigeon's breast. Recolta tripped over the horizon, disappearing as the light grew stronger. One of the Inquisitors issued a sharp order, and the entire company came to a halt. I could make out the shadows of a village up ahead, the outline of Pondera's godhouse welcoming all weary travelers with food and water, with a place to rest our heads.

Before we could ride into the settlement, though, there was a clatter of hooves on the road behind us.

"*Keara!*" I heard inside my head, and I nearly cried out with joy. Caw was at hand, close enough to speak inside my mind. Somehow, miraculously, Taggart had already caught up with us, had already devised a plot to rescue Goran and me from the Inquisitors.

The old man must have traveled with Wart as well; Goran had clearly been shocked to full wakefulness by speaking with his own darkbeast. Following my comrade's cue, I relinquished my grip on the tumbrel. I set my teeth against my own exhaustion, and I turned to look back on the road we had just traveled. I ordered myself to stand even taller, to look every bit the part of a conquering warrior queen.

And yet the sight I saw nearly drove me to my knees.

Taggart had come. Taggart and Caw together.

The Traveler was bound at the wrists, lashed to a horse. He was escorted by a pair of burly soldiers, the most rugged Primate's Guards ever to set foot outside Lutecia. Tied to Taggart's horse was a cage, cruel iron bars filled with a trio of hulking black shadows. Caw and Wart and Flick, all left bare to the freezing air.

Taggart, Caw, Wart, and Flick together. Joining Goran and me in absolute defeat.

Chapter Seven

At first I had paid close attention during our eastward journey, watching for a chance to escape. But there was never a possibility of freedom. The Inquisitors kept all three of us humans bound in chains, locked to the sides of our sturdy horse cart.

They kept our darkbeasts from us, caged away so that I could not take comfort from the satin touch of Caw's feathers beneath my fingertips. At least my raven was close enough that he and I could talk, silently, from mind to mind.

He wasted no time filling me in on all that he had learned.

The handful of people who had been left behind at the darkhold had moved quickly, revealing their true purpose almost before our group had disappeared into the woods. *That Saeran,* Caw said. *"She is sworn directly to the Primate to help the Inquisitors in all their duties. She has a special bond to Bestius, a special goal of tracking down those who spare their darkbeasts."*

I barely remembered to keep my protest silent. *"But how could she move so quickly to set up the false Darkers? We only fled Lutecia at the Hunter's Moon!"*

"They built the darkhold years before. There are others they have snared there. Others who gave up friends, companions, lured by an apparent community of allies. We never would have been snared by the Inquisitors or by soldiers loyal to the Primate. We were far too wary for that. We were only caught because we thought we had found friends." Caw shuddered, shaking out his feathers. *"Once we fled Lutecia in the fall, Saeran only needed to sow her false trail, spread rumors until one landed on fertile ground. Until one reached Taggart."*

I cast a worried glance at the old man. He was slumped in a corner of the cart, his head bouncing as the horses pulled us over ruts in the road. *"How could he have been so easily fooled?"*

Caw made a clicking sound deep in his throat. *"When a man hears the same things many times, from many different sources . . . At least one of them must have been trusted. Must have been an old ally, turned by Saeran long ago."*

I shook my head in frustration. In the end, Taggart would have been more suspicious if his head had been clearer, if he had not fallen ill with grippe. I should have helped him more, insisted on finding the proper herbs, demanded that he eat properly.

Caw interrupted my medley of remorse. *"They were too clever for all of us. How could we suspect that they would create such an elaborate false display? That entire darkhold. All that food . . ."*

"And all those people," I said, thinking of the children I had sat with, week after week, reciting my lessons.

But that, of course, was why they had done it. The false Darkers had been brilliant, perfect in every step of the lying revel they had played out beneath the forest.

The Travelers could have learned a lot from the false Darkers, a lot about living a lie. But even that, even the constant, consistent presentation, was not Saeran's greatest victory. *"The darkbeasts!"* I said. *"How did they work the darkbeasts?"*

But Caw did not want to speak of his fellow animals. He sent me wordless images of a dozen priests bound to Bestius. He let me sense the ancient ritual of mudroyal and ladysilk, the process somehow twisted to bind adults to darkbeasts. I mourned the corruption of innocent darkbeasts in miserable silence.

League after league, we jolted on toward Lutecia. And even as my despair grew, even as I was buffeted by anger and sorrow and fear, I felt a tiny flame of another emotion. At first I did not recognize it. But then its taste flooded my mind.

Gratitude.

Even in the midst of this disaster, I offered up a whispered prayer to Clementius. The god of mercy had arranged for our capture the evening *after* a full moon—the evening after a traditional nameday celebration. Nearly a month must pass before Bestius's priests could demand that we execute our darkbeasts.

Within the week, we arrived back in Lutecia. The first time I had ever glimpsed the Primate's Pearl, I had been startled by the city's beauty. The Silver River split a dozen times on the broad plain that led to the sea. Each of those branches divided a dozen more, until Lutecia was spread out upon countless tiny islands. Upon first viewing, the entire city glinted in sunlight, rare and delicate and precious.

I'd learned the truth, though, when I had fled from the Primate's theater competition months before. I had discovered the Pearl's rotten core—narrow alleys and worm-eaten wood, stinking stagnant canals.

We passed through Bestius's Gate, one of twelve that led to Lutecia's heart. With every step through the jumbled streets, an Inquisitor shouted: "Behold the Lost! Behold the Lost, brought back to the refuge of all the Twelve!"

Messenger birds had clearly been sent from Barleytown. Citizens of Lutecia pressed close to our cart. There was a hum of expectation in the air, sharper than any buzz that had ever anticipated the Travelers. As if joined by one mind, the crowd took up the Inquisitor's proclamation. "Behold the Lost!" they whispered. "Behold the Lost!"

They pointed at us captives as if we were creatures from a dream. Caw might have been Mortana's own snow-white raven, for all the fascination of the onlookers. The crowd laughed at Taggart, jeering at his disheveled beard, at the thin crust of drool that had hardened around his lips. They cried out to Goran, demanding to know what he'd done, how he had strayed. And they mocked me outright, pointing at Caw, shouting that my darkbeast should be long dead and rotting, offered up on a nameday past.

I saw white-robed figures at the back of the crowd—more Inquisitors fanning the flames. The religious enforcers were spreading our story before we ever made it past the Primate's Theater, past the Garden of Madrina, past any of the places I recognized from my earlier stay in the Primate's capital city. I was dazed by the twisting streets, confused by the jumble of buildings that crouched, row after row after row.

But I had no trouble recognizing our ultimate destination.

Godhouses were the same the entire world over. Buildings dedicated to Bestius were always low, square spaces. The walls were always black as roasted mardock root—stained dark by herbal washes in villages like Silver Hollow, but plated with thin sheets of onyx here in the richest city in all of Duodecia.

As the wagon creaked to a stop in front of Bestius's godhouse, the crowd drew even closer. They caught their collective breath as if they knew what spectacle awaited them. The result was a strange silence, all the more eerie because my ears were full of the wagon's creaking, dulled by the lonesome music that had taunted me all the way from Barleytown.

And in the midst of that silence, in the center of all that hopeful expectation, a whisper from my past wormed through my memory. "The Inquisitor uses knives on all the Lost," it said. "And brands." The voice chanted, "He leaves his mark on bodies, as well as souls." And perhaps the worst words were the last: "And then he prays for them, repeating his words over and over and over."

Goran had told me that months before. At the time, I had feared for his life when he took my place with an Inquisitor devoted to Patrius, the father of all the Twelve. Taggart had forced Goran to accept punishment in my stead. I had fretted for an entire day before Goran was returned to the Travelers' troupe, exhausted, hands raw from hard work, but otherwise unharmed.

Physically unharmed. Goran had seen terrible things while he labored for the Inquisitors. Terrible things inflicted on the Lost.

Lost. Like all three of us now.

A handful of men pushed their way into the bed of the cart. Their hands were rough on my arms, and they were no gentler with Goran or Taggart. We were half dragged, half carried out of the cart, onto the paved road. My legs trembled beneath me, scarcely able to support my weight.

In fact, I started to shudder uncontrollably as the doors to Bestius's godhouse shot open. A new Inquisitor was framed on the threshold. I blinked hard. I could not believe that a single man could be so tall, that one person could have shoulders so wide. He looked as if he were an ox made human—broad and bulky and absolutely unable to be moved. His huge body seemed even larger because of the staff he carried—a massive span of wood like the trunk of an oak tree.

His voice tolled out like the largest bell in Duodecia. "Who approaches Bestius's godhouse?"

"It is me," said the Barleytown Inquisitor. My captor's voice had always sounded reedy. Now, though, it broke on the third word, crumbling in front of the greater force before him. I understood the terror that frayed his eager reply. I could not imagine speaking words myself. I could not fathom being judged by the new Inquisitor.

"*I*," said Caw, in the trembling silence of my mind.

I barely managed to think a wordless question toward him.

"*I. The Inquisitor should have said, 'It is I.' Perhaps that's only a matter of grammar, but the Twelve have a right to expect perfection in those who serve them.*"

Caw actually sniffed in disdain. I had never imagined a raven sniffing before, but I found myself oddly proud of his superior knowledge, of his perfect understanding of the rules of speech. I threw back my shoulders and raised my chin, grateful that Caw was my darkbeast, that he and I had been magically bonded for so many years.

"There," he said, and I grasped the strong tone of approval in his voice. *"That's the attitude I expect from you. Stand straight now. Nothing bad will happen to us tonight."*

He had no way of knowing that. No way to be sure. But because my darkbeast said the words, I believed them to be true. Caw was offering me hope for the first time in a week. If he was smart enough to correct an Inquisitor's grammar, strong enough to sit tall on his iron perch, the least I could do was follow his example. I held my hands before me as if *I* had chosen to adorn them with iron, as if *I* had decided to make manacles a fashionable addition to my travel-stained clothes.

"Excellent," Caw whispered inside my skull. That one word gave me the courage to draw a complete breath, perhaps the first since we had passed through Bestius's gate. I grabbed another when I saw that Goran was following my lead, that he had taken his own proud stance. For the first time in hours I dared to flick my fingers against my knotted darkbeast bracelet, ignoring the iron embrace of my chains.

Caw's encouragement was even enough to hold me steady

when I realized that Taggart was *not* following suit. The old man sagged in the grip of the men who had dragged us from the cart. His eyes were glazed, as if he saw nothing of Lutecia, nothing of the godhouse that hulked before us. Whatever strength he had regained in the darkhold beneath the forest, it was gone now, chased away along the brutal, rutted road.

My captors, of course, had not been idle while Caw and I carried on our silent conversation. The Barleytown Inquisitor had presented us prisoners, noting that we were traitors and heretics all, traveling throughout Duodecia with our darkbeasts well after our twelfth namedays.

I waited for the massive new Inquisitor to summon me forward, to demand my name. Instead he merely crashed his massive staff against the onyx steps. "Bestius welcomes all," he bellowed. "Even the Lost."

Those words were apparently the cue for all our captors to gather around. They took no chances—each of us daring traitors and heretics was surrounded by four full-grown, able-bodied, white-robed figures. I craned my neck, desperate to keep Caw within my sight. When I glimpsed Wynda lifting his cage free from the wagon, I could not help myself—I cried out, "Let him be!"

"Silence!" demanded the new Inquisitor. He enforced his command with another thunderous crash of his staff. My ears rang, and I wondered that the stone threshold did not crack. "The Lost will not speak unless spoken to!"

As if to emphasize the command, the minor Inquisitors around me tugged my chains. My arms were yanked hard to the right, and I started to shout out a protest. The only thing that kept me silent was the look on Goran's face. That, and the slight shake of his head. The silent message that we were better off yielding now, giving in for the short term.

Any further decision was taken from me as the three of us prisoners were forced up the godhouse steps. The giant Inquisitor yielded cramped passage for us to enter the cold darkness dedicated to the god of darkbeasts. Saeran and Wynda followed behind, as proud as cats bringing home mice from the fields.

I squeezed my eyes shut, then opened them wide, willing my vision to adapt quickly to the gloom. A night-black altar filled the center of the square, mirroring the onyx walls. In the center of the stone surface was a quartet of braziers, each filled with burning incense. Curls of scented smoke spiraled to the ceiling.

The smell hurtled me back to my nameday, to the last time I had worshipped in Bestius's godhouse. Children had chanted outside then: "Kill the darkbeast! Kill the darkbeast!" Their cries had been filled with religious fervor. I knew the rhythm of the words well. I had chanted them often enough myself, for other girls becoming women. For other darkbeasts.

Before it was my turn. Before it was my darkbeast in question.

Now it was deadly silent inside the godhouse. The walls must be very thick, or the crowd outside had drifted away as soon as the thrill of our arrival was past.

The Inquisitors who had dragged us down the Western Road clearly knew what was expected of them. They pulled our chains, forcing us to walk before the altar. One of them pushed sharply between my shoulder blades, emphasizing the desired direction.

Across the floor. Down a tight spiral of stairs. Across another room, this one underground. Down a long hallway, lit only by a handful of smoky lanterns. We were always followed by the false Darkers who had betrayed us.

Part of me panicked at the earth I knew was packed above my head. I thought about the Silver River, about the watery paths that cut back and forth through Lutecia. Could we truly be safe underground here?

Before I could dwell on my fears, though, our captors stopped before a wall of iron bars. A cage, I slowly realized. The Inquisitors were placing us inside an iron cage.

The door creaked open, heavy and ominous. Taggart was pushed in first. He stumbled over the raised threshold, barely reaching out to protect his head as he fell against the far wall. Goran swallowed a wordless cry and rushed forward to help his grandfather.

I wanted to resist. I wanted to dig my heels into the stone floor. I wanted to catch my fingers against the bars, to push back, to make the Inquisitors work for the prize of imprisoning me.

Even so, I knew that I was helpless. The Inquisitors would eventually succeed in forcing me into the cage. If I resisted, they might hurt me, badly. And they might punish me in other ways. They might search me. They might take my bracelet, which was now conveniently hidden beneath the iron bonds around my wrists.

It was better for me to square my shoulders. Better to glare at them down my nose. Better to force my fists to relax at my side, to order my fingers to be straight and proud.

The door clanged shut behind me. The noise was strangely muffled by the earthen corridor, as if we were encased in a bushel of lacemallow. I steeled myself to turn around, to face my captors like a proud, unbroken villager of Silver Hollow.

I nearly crumpled, though, when I saw Wynda approach the bars that shut me in like an animal. She hefted an iron cage before her. Caw. And Flick and Wart, too. Our beloved darkbeasts were locked away as thoroughly as we were. Their enclosure was too small; Caw could barely ruffle his wings. The iron bars were very close together; the container was designed to keep even Flick from escaping.

With a truly evil laugh, Wynda set the cage on the flagstones—beyond my reach, even if I smashed my face against my own iron bars.

"Please," I pleaded.

I longed for the feel of my darkbeast. I longed for the clutch of his talons on the fabric of my clothes. I longed for the weight of him, the rustle of his wingtips, the slight scent of dust on his tail feathers, and the way I automatically raised my shoulder to give him a level perch.

"Not now," Caw chided. *"At least they're not refusing to feed me."*

"Yet."

"Be brave, Keara-ti. If only till the false Darkers leave."

Wynda stepped back from the cell. Her glare was vicious as she kicked at the darkbeasts in the cage, but she did not turn it over. Not here, in Bestius's own godhouse. For a moment, however, I saw her jaw work, and I realized that she intended to spit—but whether at me or at Goran or Taggart or at the darkbeasts I could not be certain.

Before she could hawk up the mess in her mouth, though, Saeran folded bony fingers around the girl's elbow. "Come," the older woman said. Wynda obeyed, but I could read reluctance in every step.

"Well," Caw said, casting his head at a variety of angles as he

tried to take in our cell. *"Shall I teach you all how to make yourselves at home in a cage?"*

Now that our captors had disappeared down the long hallway, I lost the rigid certainty that had held me straight. My muscles rippled, and my knees threatened to turn to porridge. Caw whistled inside my thoughts, long and low. *"None of that, now, Keara-ti."* I heard familiar chastisement behind his words even as my breath shuddered in and out. *"I take your fear. Forget it. It is mine."*

Chapter Eight

But Caw never really took my fear.

Certainly he made me feel a little braver about being stranded in a cage with two other humans. He made me slightly less nervous when the heavy door clanged shut at the far end of the hallway. He helped me to sleep during the long, lonely stretch that might have been night or day or night again.

But in my heart, I was still afraid when I awoke. I still waited for the Inquisitors to produce their knives and brands. I cowered, imagining the punishments I had heard about all the days of my life.

At least Goran spared me a beating, our first full day in the godhouse.

The Inquisitors set us to work with nothing more than a spoonful of slimy porridge in our bellies. Our task was to polish the massive onyx altar in the center of the round godhouse room. We were required to finish before the sun reached its peak outside, before Bestius opened his doors for the faithful to pray in the afternoon. The work would have been challenging under any circumstances. It was made nearly impossible by the iron chains we still wore around our wrists.

Taggart was set to labor on the single piece of stone that made the top of the table. Goran and I were forced to our knees, crouching beside the vertical black panels. Each piece of stone was joined to its neighbor with a gritty dark mortar, some substance that seemed to collect grease and dust like a lodestone. Hundreds of dedicated worshippers must have visited Bestius's godhouse the day before, touching the altar as they offered up their prayers. Thousands of fingers must have caressed the stone, leaving behind filthy prints.

I caught my tongue between my teeth to concentrate better while I worked. The darkbeasts sat in their cage in the center of the altar, almost as if they were in training for their ultimate sacrifice. Goran had been forced to carry the cage when we were chivied to our morning duties. I was grateful that Caw had accepted the indignity without complaint. Now he watched our work with an appraising eye. *"You missed a spot there."*

"I can scrub an onyx tile without your help, thank you very much."
I let some of my fear flow into my silent, sarcastic words. I much preferred speaking with my darkbeast aloud, but I wouldn't risk that with an Inquisitor standing a scarce arm's length behind me. Especially not the oxlike man who had greeted us the night before.

Even here, inside Bestius's sacred godhouse, the Inquisitor kept his hood drawn close about his head. I did not need to see his face, though, as he bellowed, "You! There! You missed a spot!" His massive finger pointed to the smudge I had overlooked.

I chanted a few lines of the Family Rule inside my head, just to drown out Caw's chortle.

I wanted to ask Goran if this was the way all Inquisitors behaved. I wanted to know if Bestius's godhouse was the same as Patrius's, if laboring for our Inquisitors was like working for the white-robed man who had taken Goran in Rivermeet. I wanted to find out whether polishing Bestius's onyx was the same as polishing Patrius's silver.

I had no chance to speak, though. No opportunity for idle chatter. Apparently satisfied that I was scrubbing properly, the Inquisitor barked out another command, as he'd already done a hundred times that morning. "From the beginning," he shouted. "The sigils of the Twelve."

I filled my lungs, fighting not to cough when I breathed in the sharp stink of the cleaning solution on my rag. "Patrius," I

started, in perfect unison with Goran and Taggart. "A white stag."
We'd already fallen into a rhythm: name a god, stroke up the onyx.
Name an animal, stroke down. "Madrina," we chanted to the
music of our manacles. "A golden cow." The other symbols tripped
off my tongue, and we concluded in perfect unison: "Venerius. A
chestnut hound."

The Inquisitor nodded with each recitation, but he was already
filling his lungs before we delivered our final reply. I braced myself.
He was going to make us go through the list yet again. This was
worse than any of the facts we had repeated back in Saeran's caves.
At least there Goran and I had been surrounded by other people.
There we had been granted the illusion that we belonged to a
community as we chanted through the lists.

"You, girl," the Inquisitor barked, and I nearly fell from the
surprise of him breaking his pattern. "What food did Madrina
serve Patrius at their first meeting?"

"Marshmint tea," I said immediately. I took little pride in
knowing the answer. Mother had sold endless amounts of marshmint to new brides who wanted to greet their husbands in the
ancient way.

The Inquisitor stepped closer, his massive shoulders blocking
out my view of the sanctuary. "And under what Moon did Aurelius
bless the goldsmiths?"

"Thunder," I squeaked, almost forgetting to rub at the altar. I might not have known the answer if my nameday had not fallen under the same moon.

Where were these new questions coming from? Would they be repeated a dozen dozen times, like the list of the sigils? And why was *I* being required to answer alone? What about Goran and Taggart?

I glanced at Caw, to see if he understood what was happening. He merely bobbed his head, though, a typical maneuver. If I hadn't known him as well I did, I would not have realized he was directing my attention to a spot on the edge of the altar. I darted my rag toward the white mark, scrubbing hard before the giant Inquisitor could call me to task. I tried to ignore the way my metal bonds chafed at my wrists.

My white-robed tormentor moved closer behind me. As I watched him from the corner of my eye, my scalp prickled. He plucked a riding crop from his belt and flipped the knotted leather against his meaty palm. The noise was loud enough that I jumped.

"Work, girl," he intoned. "Be grateful for the chance to honor Bestius!"

"Blessed be his name," I said, for I had already learned to offer up that little prayer whenever the god's name was said aloud in this house of worship. All three of us humans had. Caw nodded, as if he were personally accepting my blessing, and I redoubled my efforts at scrubbing the onyx plane before me.

"Where did Recolta first deliver the gift of wheat to all her people?"

Recolta, the goddess of the harvest. I should know the answer. My breath came faster as I realized I had no idea.

The Inquisitor stepped still closer, slapping his crop against his palm once again. "Recolta!" he snapped, as if I might not have heard him the first time.

"I—" My mind spun from city to city, places big enough to boast the presence of a goddess. Could it be Lutecia, here in the north? That made little sense; the northern fields were not known for their wheat harvest. Austeria, then? But what could connect Recolta to the southern port? There were dozens of towns where she might have first appeared, hundreds of villages.

The Inquisitor loomed over me, close enough that I could feel the whoosh of air as he primed the riding crop against his palm. "Recolta, girl! Do you not honor the Twelve?"

Caw's voice cut through the panic inside my head. *"Wart says, 'Millers Gate.'"*

Wart? Why would Wart know anything about the goddess of the harvest?

It wasn't slow-thinking Wart, though, who had provided the answer, I was stunned to realize. It was Goran. Goran, speaking through his darkbeast to mine.

Behind me the Inquisitor flung back his riding crop. My

shoulders tensed, bracing for the blow, even as I shouted, "Millers Gate! It was Millers Gate!"

"Very well," the Inquisitor said, and the menace in his voice chilled my spine. Nevertheless, my fingers traced the circuit of my darkbeast bracelet beneath my bonds, automatically counting off the knots. The motion soothed me, and I finally drew a full breath.

But the Inquisitor was not finished. As if to prove that he had no favorites, the man lurched around the altar, moving to stand behind Taggart. Once again he tapped his riding crop against his free hand. Once again he fired off a series of questions.

Taggart, though, seemed to know no answers, despite his years spent performing the Holy Plays. For that must have been where Goran gleaned his answer for me—from the revel of *Recolta and the Golden Grain*. Taggart, however, had apparently forgotten all the Travelers' texts. He merely stared at the rag beneath his gnarled fingers, offering no reply when the Inquisitor demanded to know Mortana's favorite fruit.

I longed to help him, to share the answer, but I did not know myself. *"Caw? What is it? Tell Flick what to say!"*

But Caw remained silent, apparently as ignorant as I. Goran must not have known either; otherwise he would surely have helped his grandfather.

The Inquisitor whipped his riding crop through the air, and

the leather sliced across Taggart's shoulders. The old man tightened his fingers on his rag, but he did not cry out.

"Mortana's favorite fruit?" The Inquisitor bellowed. When Taggart remained silent, the riding crop fell again. "Mortana's favorite fruit?" the Inquisitor demanded again, emphasizing each word with another slash. Taggart caught his breath against the pain, raising his manacled hands in defense, but the Inquisitor showed no mercy. "Mortana's—"

"He doesn't know!" Goran shouted from the far side of the altar. "He can't tell you, because he doesn't know!"

The Inquisitor raised his weapon, as if he were going to flay Taggart on the very surface of the altar. Rather than strike the old man, though, he pounced on Goran, forcing the boy to lean against the newly shined altar. "Did I ask for your opinion?" The Inquisitor's question hung in the air like poisonous smoke above a fire.

"No," Goran said. He paused before he added, "Honored lord."

I wondered what had prompted him to speak the honorific. Under other circumstances, I would have expected any nudge toward politeness to come from Taggart. But the old Traveler remained frozen at the altar, his hands spread wide upon the onyx. His every muscle was drawn taut, as if he were using his last drop of energy to stay upright.

That was when I noticed Caw bobbing his head inside his

cage. Caw. My wry and disrespectful darkbeast was apparently using the placid Wart to advise my human companion in the ways of polite address.

"If you please, honored lord," Goran said. "Could you instruct us in the ways of the Twelve? Will you teach us Mortana's favorite fruit?"

Goran pitched his voice perfectly—not sarcastic, not rebellious.

I should not have been surprised. He was accustomed to performing before crowds. He was skilled in reading people, in determining just how much of a dramatic flair to sift over his words. The Inquisitor was merely another audience, another listener to be lulled with the magic of the Travelers' revels.

And Goran's gamble paid off. The Inquisitor squared his broad shoulders and intoned, "Mortana's favorite fruit is darkapple."

"Darkapple," Goran repeated. "Mortana's favorite fruit is darkapple."

From another boy, the words might have sounded mocking. From another boy, the repetition might have been a challenge, a dare. But Goran managed to lace his recitation with respect. With awe. With gratitude.

The Inquisitor nodded and then grated out a warning. "Careful, boy. You've left a smudge there."

Goran bent back to his polishing, and the interrogation went on. We were drilled on the gods, on their preferences, on their unique stories. When one of us knew the answer, we shared by way of our darkbeasts. When we were all ignorant, we begged forgiveness of the honored lord who towered over us.

And all the while my fingers grew red from the astringent solution that I rubbed on the altar. My throat burned at the evil smell. My eyes watered from the fumes, and my wrists chafed beneath my bonds. But every time I thought that I must rest, that I must climb to my feet to stretch my legs or ease my back, Caw managed to catch my eye. He tilted his head. He ruffled his feathers, even in his tiny space.

And his continued high spirits reminded me that there was hope. I had spared his life back in Silver Hollow, and we had journeyed this far together. There was always hope.

And so we finished our first morning in Bestius's godhouse, bringing the altar to shining perfection just as the Inquisitors cast open the doors for the public to enter. Of course our captors quickly found other tasks for us Lost to perform.

That first week we were kept completely separate from other worshipers, from other Lost. We swept the endless underground hallways using soft-bristled brooms that could not possibly gather every last mote of dust, at least not to the Inquisitors' expectations. We polished the iron bars on our cage, rubbing them with rags until they gleamed dully in the torchlight. We pared mountains of apples, pears, and turnips, and we punched down hundreds of loaves of sharp rye bread—the food for all of Bestius's Inquisitors and priests in Lutecia.

Goran was the one who figured out how to keep track of the passage of days, using the chains around his wrists. Each link counted for one sunrise. He had a strip of dark green cloth, torn from the raiment provided by the so-called Darkers before our ill-fated journey to Barleytown. Each evening, after we ate whatever passed for supper, Goran moved the cloth from one link to the next. We could count from his right thumb and know that we had spent four days, five days, six, then seven, all locked in Bestius's godhouse.

Throughout it all, I wore my darkbeast bracelet. It was like a secret bond with Goran, a hidden promise that our friendship would remain strong no matter what dangers we faced. My fingers frequently found the knots without my conscious thought. At night, when we collapsed onto the dank floor of our cell, I would sometimes see Goran's eyes stray to the twist of black fur on my wrist. A smile would ghost over his lips, and for just a heartbeat our fears were eased. We had a connection that stretched farther than the godhouse, beyond the Inquisitors' tireless bullying.

And the Inquisitors *were* tireless. I had expected them to favor Bestius, as we were in the house of the god of darkbeasts. But our white-robed tormentors demanded answers about all the Twelve.

I learned more details than I had ever thought possible about the gods, about what they loved and what they hated. Every night I dreamed the answers in my sleep, the words cutting deeper and deeper through the bedrock of my nightmares.

It was bad for me, and for Goran, too. But it was worst for Taggart.

Something had broken inside the old man. He seemed well enough physically. His lungs were finally clear, and his fever had faded. He shuffled from room to room in the godhouse, completing his tasks without additional punishment. He ate every bite of food that was placed before him, even the provisions that were moldy or stale, and he drank every cup of musty water that the Inquisitors spared.

But the creature who walked and cleaned and ate and drank was nothing like the old man I had known. There was no fire in his eyes. No spirit of challenge.

I confided my fears to Caw in the dark one night, thinking my words to his cage outside our cell. *"He is no longer the man he was. Remember the way he led the Travelers? The way he always took joy in life on the road?"*

"There's precious little joy to be found here," Caw reasoned. *"Less joy, even, than treats."*

I wished that I could reach Caw, that I could give him the solitary scrap of apple peel I had hidden inside my cuff. It was a sorry excuse for the sweets he preferred, but it would have been better than nothing.

"Perhaps tomorrow, Keara-ti. perhaps you'll have a chance to share your treasure then."

I tested his words for sarcasm, but I could find none. He seemed genuinely happy, positively thrilled to anticipate such a simple treat.

"Hush, Keara-ti," Caw said as I fought the sudden urge to weep. *"Sleep. All will be well in the morning."*

But alas, my darkbeast was wrong. The morning brought only a new terror.

Chapter Nine

I had somehow managed to drift into deep sleep, the sort of slumber where even dreams dared not follow. The sound of the iron lock on our cage barely roused me. The Inquisitors' torches, though, got my attention—especially when one of the flaming brands came a mere handbreadth from my face.

"There," said one of my captors. His voice rumbled like an avalanche I had once heard back in Silver Hollow. It was the ox man, the giant who had greeted us upon our arrival at Bestius's godhouse. He was the most frequent of our keepers, but I had not grown used to his massive size, to his bellowing voice. "We're supposed to take that one."

Apparently, *I* was "that one." As I roused, two Inquisitors flanked me, their steely fingers closing around my arms. As always, their faces were shielded by their hoods. Ox Man I knew. The other one stank of onions.

"Wait!" I protested, looking around furiously. Why weren't they taking Goran and Taggart as well? Despite my protest, the Inquisitors marched me forward, forcing me out of the cell. "Just a—I need my darkbeast. Caw!" I grabbed for his cage.

"The bird will wait for you," Onion Breath said without sympathy. He tugged on my arm, as if to emphasize my need to hurry. Before I could argue, the men had rushed me down the corridor, past the metal door, and deeper into the godhouse than I had ever been before.

"*Caw!*" I thought, the single syllable bursting forth like a shout.

"*Go, Keara-ti,*" my darkbeast thought. "*Go, and I will—*"

The Inquisitors hustled me out of range before I could hear what Caw would do. They forced me through the hallways rapidly, barely letting my feet touch the floor. We climbed stairs. We rushed down corridors. We rounded impossibly tight corners.

And, finally, we arrived before an incredible, intricately carved wooden door.

Torches stood on either side of the masterpiece, guttering in the breeze created by our sudden arrival. I squinted to make out the magnificent shapes—spiders and lizards and snakes and rats.

Darkbeasts, all executed by some master craftsman so that each individual claw, every separate scale and tooth, stood out like the parts of moving, breathing creatures. I blinked in astonishment, and when I opened my eyes, I could make out ornate letters at the top. B-E-S-T-I-U-S.

Ox Man raised a fist and pounded on the frame beside the door. "Come!"

The voice was loud. Solid. As if the speaker were accustomed to being obeyed. My breath caught in my throat, and I tried not to panic.

Ox Man and Onion Breath opened the door and pushed me into the space beyond.

I could not have said what I was expecting after that incredible carved door. A molten pool of onyx, perhaps. A shimmering vat of the stinking liquid we used to clean the altar. An array of torture implements far more frightening than the manacles that ringed my wrists, than the riding crops tucked into the belts of the Inquisitors behind me.

Whatever I had expected, I was wrong.

There was a man inside the room—that much I knew from the shouted command. And he was an Inquisitor. At least he was clad in flawless white robes.

But this Inquisitor broke the rules. His hood was pushed back so that I could see his face.

He was young—not much older than my sister's husband, Lastor, back in Silver Hollow. His blond hair was combed neatly, setting off his high cheekbones, his grass-green eyes. He held himself with a certain power, a definite pride.

He was seated on a high-backed onyx chair behind a table capped with the same substance. Nodding once at the men beside me, he said, "Thank you, brothers." There was that tone again, that certainty that he was in control. Ox Man and Onion Breath bobbed their heads, and their fingers finally relaxed on my arms. I knew I would have bruises by nightfall. The man behind the table said to my escort, "You may leave us."

Both men bowed and left the room, closing the magnificent wooden door behind them. I swallowed hard and raised my chin as I met the young Inquisitor's incredible green eyes.

My wrists rubbed against my manacles as my fingers twisted toward my bracelet. The fleeting touch of fur sent steel down my spine. After all, the night that Goran had given it to me, I had proven myself stronger than I had ever imagined, conquering the snowbanks in the forest. I set my jaw, newly determined to match the man, prideful gaze for prideful gaze, at least until I found out why he had forced me here.

"Keara of Silver Hollow," he said.

"Honored lord." I pushed the words past the pounding of my heart.

"You may call me Paton."

"Yes, hon—Lord Paton."

"No 'lord,'" he said, and his thin lips twisted into a tolerant smile. "I have given up my worldly titles to serve my master, Bestius, blessed be his name. I am merely Paton now."

"But who are you?"

I blurted out the question without thinking of consequences. I truly wanted to know. Who could this man be—young, but able to order the other Inquisitors, even the one as large as an ox? Able to throw back his hood and show his face? Able to pin me with those dangerous emerald eyes?

"I am the Inquisitor Ducis for Bestius, blessed be his name."

The Inquisitor Ducis. The man in charge of every single Inquisitor devoted to the god of darkbeasts, throughout all of Duodecia. One of twelve robed men who managed the rehabilitation of all the Lost in the primacy.

And he thought it was important to speak with *me*.

He continued to stare with that penetrating gaze. As if he knew the direction of my thoughts, he leaned back in his chair, tenting his fingers in front of his chest. I *had* to look away.

Behind Paton stretched ranks of shelves, carved into the very stone of the walls. Each was filled with carefully crafted statuettes, carvings that matched the glorious door through which I had passed. Even from across the room, I caught my breath at the beauty of the forms, at the perfection of the creatures captured in stone. I could make out the individual scales on the lizard that crouched beside the Inquisitor Ducis's head. A rat had a dozen separate whiskers, each as fine as the hairs on my head. A buzzard cocked its head at me, the flesh of its naked neck puckered in the torchlight.

Paton leaned forward, forcing my attention away from the animals. "What do you know about them, Keara?"

For a moment I thought he meant the onyx creatures, the ones in plain sight behind him. But there was no reason for him to question me about carved animals. The Inquisitor Ducis must have some other mission, some other goal. I recovered quickly enough to gasp, "About who?"

Paton's face became grave. His eyes snagged mine again, and I could not have looked away if Caw himself had flown into the room. "The Darkers." I made some noise of protest, which only made Paton wave a long-fingered hand. "The heretics who refuse to kill their darkbeasts," he elaborated.

My heart pounded so hard that my fingers grew numb inside their bonds of iron. "We never found them, my l— Paton. We only found Saeran, in the woods."

He nodded. "Aye. You only found my people. The ones who are faithful to Bestius, blessed be his name."

"Blessed be his name," I hastened to echo, hoping to stay on the good side of the Inquisitor Ducis.

He was asking about true rebels. About Brigid—the old woman who had assisted Taggart and Goran and me as we made our escape from Lutecia. Brigid, who had risked everything to give us food and water and silver coins, to find a boat so we could flee.

I cleared my throat. "I do not know any true Darkers. Only the false ones we found within the woods."

Paton's tone was surprisingly mild, but he did not blink as he asked, "Why should I believe you, Keara?"

"I would not lie!"

For answer, he laughed. The sound was low, almost like a purring cat. He spread the fingers of one hand over the onyx surface of his table. "The Lost always lie."

My voice trembled like sheepleaf in a winter gale. Nevertheless, I struggled to convince him. "I am not Lost, my lord. Not with this."

"Paton," he reminded me. "Not 'my lord.' Bestius would not have it any other way. Blessed be his name."

"Paton," I whispered.

He stood in one smooth motion, moving quickly enough that I staggered back a step. "Very well, Keara. Perhaps you need some time to recall all you know."

I locked my knees and ordered my legs to stop their trembling. They did not obey, but I was able to draw a full breath as

Paton walked around his desk, moving with the easy grace of a man who has done something a thousand times. "Take a while," he said. "Study the creatures of Bestius, blessed be his name. When I return, perhaps you will remember more."

He stared at me for a long moment then, his gaze as sharp as swordleaf. I wanted to ask what he saw, who he thought I was. What he thought I knew. I wanted to find out why he had taken me from my companions, why he believed I was the one most likely to give up true Darkers. I wanted to learn how long he would keep me here, how many hours or days or weeks he would keep me separated from Caw.

I said nothing, though. I was certain he would give no answers until I was prepared to share my own knowledge with him. Instead he merely nodded once, and then he closed the door behind him. I swallowed hard as a key turned in the lock.

Of course I tried the latch as soon as Paton left, but it would not budge. I was alone, with nothing but the onyx darkbeasts behind me for company. I tried to ignore their blank stares as I considered the Inquisitor Ducis's bargain.

All I had to do was give up Brigid's name. I only needed to tell the Inquisitors where she lived, in the darkest, dankest alley of fair Lutecia. I only needed to betray the impoverished old woman who had risked everything for me, and for Goran and Taggart. For Caw.

She might not live there still. She might have found a new home, a new hovel in the city's back streets. My words might not harm her in the least.

But my words *might* cause her death. Hers, and that of any other Darkers she knew in the Primate's Pearl.

Frustrated, I turned toward the shelves. There was a raven there. On the top shelf, far to my left. Automatically I reached out to run my fingers over his feathers, trying to ignore the weight of my bonds. I had not realized that I expected the stone body to be warm, the feathers to flutter against my touch, but of course the bird was only stone. I pulled my fingers back as if they'd been burned. I'd been a fool to imagine anything else.

Fighting my disappointment, I touched a toad that huddled on a lower shelf. It could have been Wart's twin. I rapidly discovered that the model was attached to the shelf, but I should not have been surprised. Paton would not leave me in a room where I could use onyx darkbeasts like weapons. He would never take the chance that I would throw statues, attacking him upon his return.

I tried to think of what Goran would do if he were in my place.

He would try each of the statues, just to be certain. He would attempt to find one he could pry free.

I set about testing the figures, digging in with my fingers, pushing against the wall with my feet, using my entire body to try to break off even the smallest wedge of stone. I worked methodically, starting with the lowest shelf, then working up to the one at knee height, then the one at my waist.

Finally I was testing the animals at the very upper limits of my reach. The pointed snail shell was as immobile as all the others. The vole. The starling.

Nothing. I could not pry any of the statues loose. I was stuck here, utterly defenseless.

And that was when I heard the key turn in the door's lock.

Paton was back. I was going to have to give up Brigid or suffer whatever penalty the Inquisitor Ducis might choose. I fingered the knots on my darkbeast bracelet and turned to face my doom.

Chapter Ten

Paton, though, did not walk into the room.

Instead, the newcomer was a boy. He was a handspan taller than I was, with long arms and a deep chest that promised he would be a sturdy man. He wore a simple brown tunic and breeches, as if he were a servant momentarily on leave from the kitchens or the stables. His hair was tousled, blond strands glinting in the light from the oil lamps on either side of the door. His eyebrows peaked as he realized that I stood inside the chamber. Confusion spread across his features, and his mouth opened in a perfect O of surprise.

But it was his eyes that captured my attention. Eyes as green as grass. As sharp as emeralds.

This boy was not Paton, but he was certainly some relation.

"Who are you?" he demanded.

I pulled myself to my full height. "I might ask the same of you!" Perhaps it was his rough clothes that gave me the courage to challenge him. From the look of surprise that flashed across his features, he was not accustomed to being questioned.

"I am Dillon, son of Hendor, Princeps of Duodecia."

Princeps. Heir to the Primate. The boy who would take the throne when his father died.

I dropped into a curtsy, hoping that my studies with the Travelers had allowed me to master the maneuver. Of course, I had never worn chains when I performed with the Travelers. But I tried to incline my head at the proper angle, and I did my best to bend my knees to a respectful depth.

Dillon waved his hand, as if I annoyed him. "None of that. Not here in the godhouse of Bestius-blessed-be-his-name." He delivered the honorific phrase as if he could not wait to rush on to his next sentence. "But I *did* ask you a question. Who are you?"

"I am Keara, of Silver Hollow."

I expected his eyes to grow wide, his face to blanch as he realized he was speaking to one of the primacy's greatest villains. Instead he merely nodded. "I heard you were in the godhouse."

I knew I should stay quiet. I should treat Princeps Dillon with the honor and respect owed his status. I should wait for him to speak to me, to ask me questions, and I should not dare to address him first. Nevertheless, I could not refrain from asking, "Why are you here?"

"I often study in my brother's room." His brother. Paton. That explained why they shared the same hair, the same eyes. The same twist to their thin lips.

I responded before I realized it would be smarter to stay silent. "Why isn't *he* Princeps? He's older than you are."

Dillon's mouth twisted into a frown. "Do you doubt the truth of what I say?"

"Of course not, Your Highness," I said, even though I had done precisely that. "Begging your pardon, Your Highness. But what is there to study here?" I thought about adding another "Your Highness," but I bobbed an additional curtsy instead.

"I'm studying the maquettes." His voice was grim.

"Maquettes?" I had never heard the word before.

Dillon gestured to the onyx statues behind me. "The models for the darkbeasts. They were made by Howell, you know."

"Howell?"

Dillon shifted his feet, settling into a wider stance, like a soldier reporting for duty. He clasped his hands behind him and threw his shoulders back. "Howell of Lutecia. The finest sculptor in the history of Duodecia, born some time before the reign of First Primate Kerwen, died in the twenty-third year of Kerwen's reign. At the command of the Primate, he created the maquettes for Bestius-blessed-be-his-name so that priests could identify perfect specimens when they breed their darkbeasts. The maquettes are still used to determine which animals are good enough to bind to children with ladysilk and mudroyal."

I stared at the Princeps in shock. He was quoting from something, rattling off the words as if they were some ancient revel.

But the words had no rhythm, no rhyme. How could he have memorized so much? Goran's trick of placing the words would never work—not when there were so many specific ones to recite. How had the Princeps done that? And what else did he know?

Even as I marveled at his ability, I remembered one of the first lessons I had ever learned from Taggart: Details make the story. If I could remember details as well as Dillon could, I would be able to craft thousands of new revels. I tried to keep awe from my voice as I said, "Begging your pardon, Your Highness, but why are *you* studying them? As Princeps, you'll never need to breed a darkbeast."

Dillon swallowed hard. "I'm studying them because I *can*. Because I must set aside my studies after my nameday. After the Hunger Moon, when I slay my darkbeast."

Nameday. Hunger Moon. Dillon was telling me he was still officially a child—for six more weeks.

Reflexively I glanced at his wrist. Sure enough, he bore an

aging tax tattoo, the purple ink fading as he neared the end of a year of payment. He would need to visit a titheman to forfeit his head tax before he sacrificed his darkbeast.

My belly tightened, and I thought of how the titheman had terrified me back in Silver Hollow. Everything about him had been intimidating—his casket of coins, and his armed guard, and his demands that Mother turn over so many hard-won coppers. I had longed to flee the white-haired old man.

Dillon, of course, would never need to worry about scavenging a handful of money on *his* nameday. He would never be threatened with going to Aurelius's godhouse, with begging the god of wealth for a loan to tide him over for the year.

In fact, now that I thought about it, it was outrageous that Dillon would pay the same twelve coins I had paid. He was the *Princeps*. He had strolled in the Primate's gardens; he had probably seen the invaluable snails that were crushed to make dye for the tax tattoos. Any fool could see that Dillon should pay more for his annual tax than I had done.

My fingers traveled to the intricate knotwork around my wrist, and I raised my chin with pride. I had met the Primate's demands; Mother and I had, together. They had nearly bankrupted us, but we had done what was required. That was more honorable than any prince counting out spare pocket change to meet his obligations.

Dillon had no way of knowing what I was thinking, but he stepped back when he met my eyes. He gestured toward the carved door that had been open all the while. "Come along. We've spoken long enough that I'll have to study the maquettes another time. Luncheon will be laid out, soon enough."

Luncheon. As if I were accustomed to feasting with all the noble folk of Duodecia. I stammered, "I—I don't think I'm supposed to leave here. Paton told me to wait for him."

"You'll be a long time, then. My brother just received a summons to the palace. Our father demanded to see him immediately, something to do with the Austerian Inquisitors, I think. That is why *I* was free to study Howell's maquettes." Dillon watched me hesitate as I weighed the consequences of escaping from Paton's study. "Well, if you *want* to stay . . . ," he said at last, fishing a key out of his pocket.

"No!" I said. I lowered my voice when I realized I had shouted. "No," I repeated more meekly. "I'll come with you."

Anything was better than waiting in that study. Better than imagining the torture Paton would apply when he returned. Better than dwelling on the lengths the Inquisitor Ducis would go to extract my knowledge about Brigid.

Dillon stepped aside, allowing me to pass before him into the hall. He closed the door behind us and locked it carefully. "Where have they been holding you? Which level?"

"I don't know. It's far from here. We walked through several corridors." Dillon started to look annoyed, so I rushed to give him more information. "We're underground and behind a metal door. There's a long hallway. The bars to the cell are iron, and we polish them every morning."

Dillon's face grew grim. "Follow me," he said.

And then he led me through the stone corridors beneath Bestius's godhouse. He seemed familiar with every twist, every turn. Of course, a boy who had memorized all those words about Howell the sculptor could probably memorize maps as well. Who knew how long Paton had given Dillon free reign through the godhouse?

Once, we came across a priest, a man of middling height, clad in the traditional black robes. His panicked obedience could not be disguised—he gasped as he recognized Dillon, and then he clenched his fingers into a fist, pounding his own chest before saluting like a soldier.

Dillon scarcely acknowledged the gesture.

By the time we reached my holding pen, we had passed an Inquisitor and three more priests. Each had offered up a fervent salute. Besides the men, a pair of serving girls had practically collapsed in the hallway, burying their faces in their skirts.

I began to suspect that my curtsy had not been sufficient, manacles or not.

Two robed guards stood at the entrance to the prison cells. Dillon accepted their salutes and then demanded that they open the door.

"Begging your pardon, Princeps," one of the Inquisitors said. "We're not to let anyone in or out. Not without a written order from Paton himself."

Dillon glared as he pulled himself to his full height. "Do you think I'd lie about my own brother's instructions, man?"

The Inquisitor bobbed into a bow. His voice ratcheted higher as he said, "Please, Your Highness. I'm only saying—"

"You're only saying that you will ignore your Princeps when he makes the most simple of demands."

"No, Your Highness!"

"Excellent," Dillon said. "I was certain you would understand."

I heard the man swallow. I saw his hands shake. The smell of his sweat was acrid in the hallway. Nevertheless, he extracted a key from his robes. The metal grated as the guard worked the lock.

Dillon merely nodded, as if he had known his orders would be accepted all along. I started to walk through the doorway, but Dillon's fingers clamped around my arm. He jutted his chin toward the Inquisitors. "Go ahead, man. Get the prisoners."

"Y—Your Highness?"

Dillon bit off each syllable, as if they were brittle flatbread. "Go. Get. The. Pri-son-ers."

"Your Highness, the Inquisitor Ducis has ordered them held—"

"The Inquisitor Ducis has changed his mind. And he has sent me here to deliver his message. Would you like to explain, in person, why you are not able to comply with such a simple command?"

The robed guards ducked through the doorway, scurrying down the hallway like rats swarming a tithing barn.

"What are you doing?" I whispered, barely making the words louder than my breath.

"Whatever I want," Dillon said, matching my tone. "The one advantage of being Princeps is that I don't have to justify myself to common Inquisitors."

Common Inquisitors? And that was the *one* advantage? I could think of many others. But I wasn't about to argue my point there. Not then. Not with the guards returning.

Goran stumbled before them, his eyes wide with surprise. He clutched the cage that held our darkbeasts. As soon as Caw saw me, he shouted, *"Keara-ti!"* His breath caught in his throat, making a sound like a purr crossed with a moan. *"How have you rescued us, Keara-ti?"*

I had to answer truthfully. *"I don't know."* I glanced at Dillon's emerald-hard eyes. *"I'm not sure I have."*

Before I could add further explanation, Goran reached my

side, and Taggart shuffled up a moment later. The old man was in worse shape than he'd been that morning. There was no color in his cheeks, and his lips were gray, as if he'd drunk too strong a dose of middlewort tea. I reached for his arm, trying to lend him my strength as he stumbled forward. His skin felt like dusty parchment.

"Come along," Dillon said with the same snap of authority he had used on the Inquisitors. "We don't have all day."

He led the way through the corridors—the dark stone ones we'd come to know so well. But then he took us to a stairwell, a twisting set of steps built inside the godhouse's thick walls. As we climbed, Goran wedged his shoulder under Taggart's armpit, half carrying his grandfather up each uneven step. I took the darkbeasts' cage and followed, ignoring Caw's frantic questions. I had no answers I could share. The pair of Inquisitors pushed close behind.

We emerged into a hallway aboveground. Narrow windows were set high within the whitewashed walls. Noontime sun streamed through, bright enough to make my eyes water after so many days of torches and oil lamps. Dillon marched us to the end of the corridor. He used his key on a heavy wooden door, and I began to suspect that its iron teeth fit every lock in the building.

Goran and Taggart stumbled into the room that Dillon revealed. I followed much more cautiously, bracing my fingers on the doorjamb.

The walls of the small chamber were stark white, featureless except for a frieze of tiny black darkbeasts painted at eye level. A window was set across the room—so high in the wall that I could never reach it, even if I stood on Goran's shoulders.

A mattress filled most of the floor, along with a stack of threadbare blankets. A clay pitcher crouched on a narrow shelf, next to a shallow basin. The room smelled of stale straw and dust, but it was a thousand times more comfortable than the stone chamber we had left behind. My eyes filled with tears, and I turned to Dillon to thank him.

I was surprised to find the Princeps standing so close to me. His gaze was locked on the cage in my hand, as if he were trying to read the secrets of all the Twelve in the rainbow glint of daylight on my darkbeast's feathers. My motion, though, broke Dillon's concentration, and his jaw hardened as he looked at me.

His voice was gruff as he said, "You are in the priests' dormitory now. Your guards will bring you food." He nodded toward the pitcher. "Let them know if you need more water."

It took me three tries to speak. "Thank you. Why are you doing this?"

"I'm Princeps," he said, as if that explained all the world. Before I could push him for more, he stepped back. "Take your rest today. Tomorrow you'll be back at work for the glory of Bestius."

"Blessed be his name," we prisoners chorused, along with the Inquisitors. Dillon caught up with us by the last syllable.

The robed guards stepped outside, taking their positions at either side of the door. Dillon paused with his hand on the frame. Once again his attention seemed snagged by Caw. He reached inside his tunic and brought out his key, the one that had let us into this haven. Sure enough, it fit into the darkbeasts' cage.

With a flick of the Princeps's wrist, Caw and the others were free. I raised my shoulder, giving my raven a perfect perch. A skitter of black, Flick, disappeared into the folds of Taggart's garments. Goran scooped up Wart with a wordless cry of joy.

It felt good to have Caw where he belonged. Right. For the first time in days, I felt as if I could draw a full breath.

"Thank you," I said to Dillon, and my voice broke across the words. There was so much else I wanted to share with him. So much I wanted to say.

Instead I flinched as the oaken door swung shut. The grate of the key in the lock was like teeth scraping darkapple pits, and a shiver rippled down my spine.

"*Well,*" Caw said. "*He seems a nice enough boy. Perhaps he'll bring us treats the next time he comes to visit.*"

Chapter Eleven

I don't know what surprised us prisoners more—that Paton did not raid our room during the night, or that Dillon *did* show up the following morning. With early sunlight leaking through our room's high window, I appreciated the fact that the Princeps sent away our Inquisitor guards. He did not hesitate as he faced down their grim concern; rather, he merely issued an imperious command that he would be responsible for us all morning.

Caw was grateful for the apple dumplings that the Princeps distributed after our white-robed captors shuffled down the hall. Goran, though, appreciated nothing. He sat on the edge of his mattress, eating his food in silence, watching Dillon with a wary eye.

And Taggart seemed unaware of Dillon's presence altogether.

I closed the old man's fingers around his apple treat, reminding him to eat it, every bite. I made sure that he saw my darkbeast bracelet. I thought the reminder of Goran, of Goran's mother, might be enough to call him back to himself. I even thought about asking him to produce his darkbeast, to offer a bite or two to Flick. But then I decided it was not wise to call attention to the reason all three of us humans were prisoners in the godhouse. No reason to remind Dillon that we had all spared our darkbeasts, all risked the eternal anger of Bestius. Blessed be his name.

When I had finished my dumpling and surreptitiously licked my fingers clean, Dillon said, "The Inquisitor Ducis is in conference with the Primate. He was not able to issue commands for your work this morning. I volunteered to guide your labors."

My belly tightened reflexively, and I shifted enough that my chains jangled around my wrists. Dillon obviously noticed; his eyes darted toward my bonds. Without a word, though, he gestured for us to follow him out the door.

Caw stretched his wings and made a chirping sound at the back of his throat. "Of course," Dillon said, as if he understood the raven's meaning. "You may bring your darkbeasts."

"First treats. And now companionship. Things are turning around for us, Keara-ti. You were wise to find this one."

"I did not find him," I admitted. *"He found me."*

Nevertheless, Caw settled on my shoulder, chirruping happily as we headed back to the stone staircase. His good cheer matched my own until I heard Goran demand, "Where are you taking us?"

Dillon's voice hardened to match my friend's sharp tone. "Anywhere I please."

"Your Highness," I said, hoping to soothe the Princeps, even as I reminded my fellow Traveler of Dillon's rank.

Goran cut me off before I could continue. "Taggart and I will take our chances with the Inquisitors," he said. He turned around and closed his fingers on his grandfather's arm. I wondered if Taggart could even stay on his feet without the contact.

Dillon's rock-hard eyes narrowed. "They'll send you to work in the breeding room. And force you to recite."

"At least we'll know *they're* acting in the service of the Twelve." Goran's tone was defiant.

I whirled on him, moving quickly enough that Caw needed to tighten his talons to maintain his perch. "Why are you doing this?" I hissed.

"Why are *you*?" Goran countered. "Keara, you don't know this boy. You don't know why he has befriended us. Can you be so easily bought with a straw mattress and an apple dumpling?"

And a well-lit room, I wanted to add. And water, and warmth, and an uninterrupted night of sleep—all topped off with a release from our Inquisitor guards. But rather than make a logical response, I heard angry words crackle from my mouth. "And you weren't bought by Wynda? By a winning smile and the chance to sit beside her at table?"

Goran looked as if I had slapped him. "It wasn't *my* fault we ended up with the—" He stopped that excuse, though, before it was halfway born. I understood why. The only way to finish was to cast blame onto Taggart. And Travelers' loyalty—not to mention family ties—would never allow that.

Dillon sighed in exaggerated boredom. "If the two of you want to speak in circles all day, you can do that in the breeding room. With the Inquisitors watching over you, riding crops in hand. No need for me to stand here and listen."

Again, the breeding room. I had no idea what horror lurked there, but Dillon made it sound dire indeed. And if it was worse than the other duties we had undertaken in the godhouse . . .

Pretending I was a Traveler performing on a stage, I turned back to the stone staircase. I wanted to settle my hand on the iron railing, make a grand show of noble grace, but my manacles prevented that. I had to settle for holding my head high, pretending to be a proud girl of high birth. I barely lowered my chin a hairbreadth, to indicate that Dillon could now lead us to his secret destination.

The Princeps nodded once himself, and then he started down the steps, moving with the confidence of his birthright. He was obviously certain we would follow.

And he was right. We followed, despite Goran's muttered complaint. Despite Taggart's wordless shuffle. Despite Caw whispering inside my skull, *"I don't think we're likely to find any more apple dumplings down there in the dark."*

"Don't you start too."

"What? I'm only looking out for your best interest!"

"You're only looking out for your own belly," I snapped.

By then Dillon was leading us into a tangle of hallways. I tried to remember the twists and turns, but I was quickly lost inside the warren, as lost as I had been in Saeran's false darkhold. Caw must have become aware of my stuttering heartbeat, because his tone was serious as he said, *"I do wonder what a Princeps wants with a group of ragtag Lost. Goran might not have expressed himself with the eloquence expected of a Traveler, but he raises a good point. You know nothing of the game that Dillon plays."*

Goran I could ignore. Caw's admonition, though, made me truly nervous.

"Should we have gone to the breeding room, then?"

"I'm not inclined to go voluntarily to any place held out as a threat. Besides, we're here now. Nothing to be done for it. But speak to this boy. Find out what he wants. And why he's willing to go against the Inquisitor Ducis to get it."

I nodded, but I had no time to put Caw's plan into action. Instead I drew up short as Dillon stopped in front of a door, identical to a dozen others we had already passed on this hallway. There was no lock—instead he merely worked the latch, pushing hard to send the oaken panels crashing back on their hinges.

I caught my breath.

I don't know what I expected. Perhaps a score of Inquisitors baying for our blood. Maybe the Inquisitor Ducis himself, sitting behind a desk, furious that we had left our cell. Possibly Saeran and Wynda, ready to mock us for our gullibility, for our earlier failure.

Instead I found a pile of wool.

No. Not a pile. A mountain. There were hundreds of fleeces piled high. Each had been washed and skirted, trimmed for use. They shimmered with an eerie whiteness, with the perfection of the Inquisitors' robes. Staring at them made my eyes ache.

Dillon nodded toward a basket that contained carding paddles. "You'd best get started."

"Us?" Goran said. "And what about you?"

"Goran!" I berated him, shocked at his tone.

Dillon seemed unperturbed, though, as he pointed to Goran's manacles. "*You* are the ones being held prisoner, not I. Now, Keara? If you'll come with me?"

"No!" Goran looked as if Dillon had struck him. "You can't take her! We stay together!"

For answer, the Princeps merely looked at me calmly and repeated, "Keara?"

I could have refused. I could have said that I needed to stay with Goran and Taggart. I needed to help my ailing elder. I needed to make sure they both knew how to card. I could have dug in my heels like a stubborn sheep.

But a part of me was curious. I *wanted* to follow Dillon, to see why he was singling me out.

Goran gasped as I turned toward the door. I could not tell if he was annoyed, or if he truly feared for my safety. I made myself meet his eyes. "Help Taggart," I said. "He needs you."

Goran started to say something, but he discarded the words. Tried others. Failed again. His eyes settled on my manacles, on the chains that momentarily obscured the bracelet he had given me.

But Goran was not the one who made decisions here in the godhouse. He was not the one who had the power to dismiss our Inquisitor guards. He could not offer up the easy job of carding, providing respite from the Inquisitors' forced hard labor.

And so I followed Dillon.

Chapter Twelve

We did not have far to go—only to the end of the hallway and down a narrow flight of stairs, straight ones that descended a single level. The steps were tucked into shadows; I would have missed them if Dillon had not led the way. He lifted a torch from its cresset on the wall and gestured for me to precede him.

"Can you sense anything?" I asked Caw.

"Goran is very angry with you."

"That's not what I meant!"

"I know."

Before I could press Caw for more useful information, Dillon gestured again. "Afraid?" he asked. I heard the dare beneath his words, saw it in his faint smile.

"Never," I answered, squaring my shoulders and taking the first step.

Dillon chuckled.

I reached the bottom of the steps only to find that we stood in yet another stone room. The floor here was rough, as if the ancient flagstones had somehow buckled. A draft raised the tiny hairs on my arms. The room was cool, noticeably colder than the one that held the fleeces. The light from Dillon's flickering torch barely reached the corners as he shoved the brand into a rusty bracket.

All that, I registered in a heartbeat. It took me a moment longer to identify the sound in the room—and that was because I wasn't expecting it. Not here. Not this far underground.

The rush of running water.

I looked at Dillon in surprise. He had taken that commanding stance again, the same as in Paton's study, feet planted, hands clasped behind his back. He intoned, "Twelve subterranean rivers cut through the city of Lutecia. Tributaries of the Silver, each aquifer is located at an average depth of twenty ells. The water remains fresh, even at the edges of the city closest to the sea due to the steady outward flow and the filtering effect of the earth."

"How do you do that?" I asked.

"What?"

"How do you memorize so many words? It's incredible! I mean, I know that Travelers learn more lines than that, but they have set pieces to help them remember. They move about the stage to trigger different scenes. And all of the revels rhyme. You don't have any of that with the things that you recite."

I could hardly believe it, but Dillon, son of Hendor, Princeps of all Duodecia, looked embarrassed. "Janna drills me until I know the words."

"Janna?"

"She's a clerk in my father's library. She's responsible for placing all the scrolls in their proper drawers."

"A clerk?" The admission astonished me. I had imagined Dillon working with the finest scholars in the land. I expected Hendor to have philosophers to train his son, the most brilliant experts gathered from the farthest reaches of the primacy.

But this Janna was a clerk? A common household servant?

Dillon blushed, as if he were also aware of the discrepancy between reality and expectation. "She takes the time to explore new subjects with me. She explains when I do not understand. She knows every scroll in my father's collection, and she guides me from one to the next. She makes sure I memorize the important things."

Important things. Like the twelve subterranean rivers of Lutecia.

I turned back to the trough. As I studied the channel, I could make out figures carved into the stone. They weren't letters, at least none that I recognized. The shapes shimmered, right at the edge of the flowing water. Their lower halves were worn, obviously eroded from the passage of water.

I could make out a star with a dozen rays extending from a central circle. I leaned closer to interpret the other signs that followed. Four vertical lines separated by arrows. At the end, a square.

"What are those?" I asked, pointing.

Dillon frowned. "I don't know."

So. Janna had not taught him everything.

The shapes seemed to call me, to draw me forward. I caught my breath as I approached the stone basin. The torch cast long, eerie shadows on the wall. I reached out shaking fingers and was rewarded with an icy shock. "It's freezing!" I exclaimed, jumping back.

"Technically, no," Dillon said. "There is no ice."

"I merely meant—"

He cut me off. "The temperature sets the Tincture."

"The Tincture?" I knew the word, of course. Mother brewed dozens of tinctures from her herbs. But I could not think of one that required icy water to work properly, much less something that would be useful here in the godhouse of Bestius. Blessed be his name.

Dillon nodded toward a massive basket in the corner of the room, just beyond the spray from the underground stream.

I realized that the woven container was filled with grease wool, freshly shorn fleeces. One quick breath assured me that these had not been cleaned like the ones in the chamber above. They still smelled of grass and manure and the natural oil that kept sheep dry in rainy weather.

A stone jar stood beside the basket. I recognized its shape—Mother used one like it, but much smaller, to store her most valuable herbs. The inside of the lid would be wrapped with fine-woven linen and bound with the pith of river reeds to keep air from drying out the precious contents.

Ignoring my awkward manacles, I reached toward the jar, giving Dillon a questioning look. When he granted a permissive nod, I flexed my fingers and opened the jar.

I took a deep breath. "Hyssop," I said. "And rackweed. And silvermist. All traditional purifiers."

Dillon grinned. "They said you know herblore."

"They?" I stiffened at the thought that he had talked about me with someone else.

He ignored my question. Instead he nodded toward the jar again. "There's one more ingredient."

I closed my eyes and breathed deeply. "Hyssop," I repeated. "Rackweed, silvermist, and . . ." I trailed off. I took pride in my ability to sort herbs, and I could sense one more in the mixture, but I had no idea what it might be.

"*Saltbite*," Caw said.

"Saltbite?"

I was shocked that Caw knew an herb I'd never heard of. My darkbeast, though, was not the one who answered me.

"Saltbite," Dillon confirmed with a broad smile, and he crossed the room to join me. Despite the rough floor, his steps were smooth, graceful. As he moved, he reached into a hidden pocket in his breeches. He pulled out a leather sack and glanced over his shoulder, as if to make sure we were alone.

Only after he was certain that no one had followed us down the narrow staircase did Dillon dip the bag into the jar. He made short work of scooping out a handful of herbs, of tying them securely in the sack. I could see a design printed on the leather—the arms of the Primate, crossed with a single crimson bar. I'd learned enough with the Travelers that I knew the bar indicated property belonging to the Primate's heir. To the Princeps.

Dillon turned to me with a crooked grin, bowing slightly. "Saltbite," he repeated. "Worth a Primate's ransom. It grows only on a single island, far across the Eastern Sea. No man has ventured there in the lifetime of my father or my grandfather or his father before him. Take it. Make sure Paton does not find this on your person."

I pulled my hands back. "I can't do that!"

"Of course you can. It's a gift."

"Not if I must keep it hidden."

"You keep other gifts hidden."

He nodded toward my wrist, and I felt my cheeks flush. One of the knots on the darkbeast bracelet had slipped free from beneath my manacles. How had Dillon noticed the thing? And how did he know it had been a gift?

As if he could read my mind, he said, "You look at Goran every time you touch it."

Flustered, I refused to acknowledge what he said. Instead I argued, "You've stolen these herbs. They belong to the Inquisitor Ducis. You don't have the right to give them to me."

Dillon produced the master key that hung at his waist. "Paton would not have given me this key if he did not intend for me to use it. Besides, the saltbite mixture belongs to my father, to the Primate. He is the one who distributes it to the Inquisitor Ducis. He is the one who controls the herb, and as his heir, I can give this bit to you." He shoved the pouch toward me again. The scarlet bar blazed out like a warning. "Must I command you to take it?"

My heart clenched.

Dillon was right about one thing. I *did* know herblore. I knew about all the ingredients in the secret mixture—all but saltbite. And a part of me was desperate to learn more about that new herb, to touch it, to breathe its scent again, to taste a tiny bit upon the tip of my tongue. I was my mother's daughter. I wanted to learn.

"But what does it do?" I asked. I was surprised to hear the longing in my voice.

Dillon answered as if he'd been called to recite before his tutor. "Saltbite is a trefoil herb, growing close to the ground. It favors sites that receive full sunlight and an adequate sea breeze, but it will not flourish without fresh running water upon its roots. The stems become woody when exposed to excessive sunshine. The seeds are poisonous to most fish and all birds if eaten before the berries are fully ripe. When saltbite is combined with other herbs in a cold-water tincture, it purifies wool, strengthening the fibers and sanctifying the material in a manner unique to the station of Inquisitors."

"*Saltbite keeps wool from staining,*" Caw clarified, his wry voice contrasting completely with Dillon's lecturing tone.

"And how do you know about it?"

I meant the question for my darkbeast, but Dillon was the one who answered. "I told you. Janna has taught me many things." He looked at me earnestly. "Please," he said, and the reciting scholar disappeared completely. In his place stood a real boy with his own form of longing written on his face. "Take it. I want you to have it."

I reached out for the saltbite mix. I hefted the leather bag on my palm. It was not an ordinary pouch—the leather was coated with wax and doubled over at the top, designed to protect the herbs from exposure to water.

Dillon had planned his gift well. I stashed it in the folds of my tunic.

"Thank you," I said. And then, because those words did not seem adequate for such a valuable present, I tried to offer up a bit of heartfelt understanding. I asked, "You love your studies with Janna, don't you?"

Dillon sighed and shifted his feet. I was surprised to recognize the expression on his face—it was the feeling in my heart whenever I thought of losing Caw. But Dillon's voice was hard as he said, "No Primate has time to waste on browsing moldering books."

"You *had* the time. What changed?"

He grimaced. "Three years ago my oldest brother died. Lorcan was riding in a pageant, honoring Patrius with the Sea Offerings. He'd been gifted with a new horse, a massive white stallion. The beast was spooked by the first call of the Sea Horns, and it reared. Lorcan leaped free, but he slashed his hand on one of the Horns. Everyone knows they bear a poison for which there is no cure."

Not everyone. *I* had not known that. I had never heard of Sea Horns, or even the Sea Offerings. In fact, I only vaguely remembered hearing that the Primate's eldest son had died. Such news had meant little to a nine-year-old child in distant Silver Hollow.

Unaware of my thoughts, Dillon continued his tale. "Paton

became the Princeps then. But six months ago, the gods spoke to him and told him he was chosen by Bestius."

"Blessed be his name," I said quickly, remembering the weight of the godhouse above me. Even though there were no Inquisitors nearby, I dared not forget to honor the god here in his very home. Even as I spoke the honorific phrase, I wondered how Bestius had chosen his Inquisitor Ducis. What had the gods said to Paton to make his destiny clear?

Dillon, though, did not join me in honoring the god of dark-beasts. Instead he repeated bitterly, "Bestius. Paton swore his allegiance, knowing he must renounce his claim to Princeps. And that left me to serve as my father's heir."

"But why *wouldn't* you want to be Princeps?"

"One day I'll be responsible for all that happens in Duodecia. And I'll never have time to read the scrolls in my library. Never have time to write books. I'll never have time to study the customs of my land, to debate the meaning of the past, to learn the millions of things I want to learn."

The longing in his voice made something ache deep inside my chest. "But you're here now," I reminded him. "You're learning about Bestius."

No "blessed be his name." Not from either of us this time.

"Not about Bestius. I'm learning how to be the Princeps. Paton is teaching me, whenever he has a moment to spare.

Whenever he's not trotting off to meet with other Inquisitors, to do my father's bidding as Inquisitor Ducis." He sighed. "This was all my brother's idea, but I'm beginning to think he only suggested it so that he could control me. He wanted to keep me from reading, from studying, from doing what I want during the last few weeks before my nameday."

Finally I understood why Dillon had released me from Paton's study. Why he had moved my companions and me into the priests' quarters. Why he had given me the precious gift of herbs. He longed to strike out against his older brother. He wished for some revenge, for some fair exchange after all that he had given up.

"Poor, pitiful Princeps."

"Caw!" My darkbeast obviously did not feel as sorry for Dillon as I did.

But I actually understood a little of the grief beneath Dillon's words. After all, I had longed for something beyond my birthright. I had yearned for the Travelers, been lured to their revels, even when Mother had ordered me to stay in our safe, secure cottage. I had left the only home I'd ever known because I wanted something different, something more.

Dillon could not leave his home. He could not forsake his destiny. He was trapped—and if rescuing a few Lost was the only form of rebellion he could make, I was happy to be the instrument of his revenge.

I settled tentative fingers on the back of Dillon's hand, trying to ignore the heavy shift of my manacles. "I'm sorry," I said. "I wish things could be different."

"Wishes and dreams are like stitches and seams," Dillon muttered.

The line was from one of the Common Plays, *The Tailor and the Trout*. I struggled to remember the next rhyme, to complete the couplet that Dillon had begun so casually. The words would not come to me though. I was certain Goran knew them. Goran and Taggart both.

Goran and Taggart. Who were laboring in the room above us, at the top of the stairs.

"I wondered when you would remember them," Caw said.

"I never forgot them!" My reply was sharper than I intended because I felt guilty. Because I *had* forgotten them. At least for a moment. At least while I listened to Dillon's story, while I learned about his heart's desire.

The torch chose that moment to flicker wildly, as if it were reacting to my lie.

"Why is there such a draft in here?" I asked.

Dillon shrugged. "The water flows through the trough with a little clearance. The draft comes from upstream."

"Why did you bring me here?"

He shrugged again. "I heard you had herb knowledge, so

Saeran told Paton. I wanted to share this. I thought you might like to learn."

To learn—the way he loved to do. And he was right—I *was* fascinated by the herbs, by the water that ran underground, by everything made more mysterious by the way the torchlight now leaped high and low. "I did," I said. "I *do*. But I should help Goran and Taggart. There's a lot of wool to card."

One more trademark Dillon shrug. "It hardly matters if you get it done."

"But the Inquisitors! They expect us to complete our tasks! If we fail, there will be consequences."

"Ultimately the Inquisitors answer to the Primate. And I'm the Primate's heir. That is enough to protect you."

"But Paton—"

"Paton will answer to me." Five words, but they conveyed more information than the text of an entire revel. Anger. Resentment. And most of all—determination. Dillon was determined to make Paton pay for plucking him from the life he had led, the life he had loved.

As I turned toward the stairs, I realized that I had my true work laid out for me. I needed to figure out a way for Paton's payment to include freedom. Freedom for Goran and Wart. For Taggart and Flick. For Caw. And for me.

PART THREE

Outrage

My first memory, or a scene retold by Caw over the years . . .

I was a child, just past my first nameday. My sisters danced around me, teasing me with their mobility while I was trapped by my short, chubby legs. They watched me try to take a step. Again. Again. Each time, they laughed when I fell hard on my bottom.

I wailed, enraged by their teasing, surprised by the sharp hurt of falling. Mother scooped me up and shook her head, saying, "We don't cry. Take it to your darkbeast."

She wrestled me into the corner of the room, swatting at my bare legs as I kicked to be free from her. She dropped me in front of Caw's cage and slipped a rag leash around my chubby wrist. I tugged and wailed some more, but my mother only repeated, "Take it to your darkbeast."

I pulled and cried and flailed until I was so tired I could no longer move. Only when I had collapsed on the floor, one wrist secured to Caw's cage, did the raven come over to look at me.

Mother had leashed me to his cage in the past. She'd said those curious words: "Take it to your darkbeast." But I did not understand what she meant. I did not comprehend what Caw was.

And Caw, for his part, had never made his purpose clear. He had thought feelings to me—cool rushes of comfort, warm explosions of affection. But he had never placed words inside my head. He had never spoken.

Now, as I sniffled beside his cage, he cocked his head to one side, completing a thorough study of me with one shiny eye. He bobbed his head and spread his wings, letting the firelight catch them and turn them iridescent green.

I reached through the cage for his feathers, gulping in surprise when he let me catch him. For the first time ever, he spoke. "Children can be cruel. They want you to fall because they think it's funny."

I stared at Caw, too young to form a response in words. I could not state my surprise at his voice. I had no way to explain my indignation at my sisters' treatment.

Nevertheless, Caw seemed to understand what I was thinking. "Practice where they cannot see you," *he said.* "Stand. Find your balance. Take one step and then another. The next time they tease you, you will be able to chase them. You will catch them, and they won't tease you about walking again."

I was silent, thinking about the bird's words. After a pause, he said, "I take your outrage. Forget it. It is mine."

As he said the words, a glorious feeling drifted over my body. It started at the base of my neck, and it flowed down my spine, through my arms and legs, then up to the crown of my head. It felt like I was turning into sunlight—warm and golden, like the hot apple cider that Mother sometimes poured into my mug for a special winter drink.

I wanted that feeling to last forever. I wanted to feel Caw's calm assurance, his certainty, his acceptance of me despite all my flaws, all my weaknesses. Even though I did not fully understand my desire, I promised myself I would do whatever it took to get my darkbeast to take my failings for all the days of my life.

That night, in my crib, I stood. I lifted my hands from the carved wood until I could feel the balance Caw had described. I concentrated, and I took a step. Another. Concentrating hard, I slid over the side of the crib, stretching until I reached the floor. I practiced walking until I could cross the room without falling.

The next day, my sisters teased me, but I stood up and walked away. I looked back and found Mother nodding, sunshine glinting off the silver pin that held her long black braid. She gave me one of her rare smiles, and I knew that I had been a good girl, the best that I could ever be, all thanks to my darkbeast. All thanks to Caw.

Chapter Thirteen

I don't trust him." Goran's jaw was set as he lugged a heavy basket across the room.

"You don't *like* him," I said. "That's different."

We had been arguing about Dillon for hours. I never should have told Goran about the saltbite. At least our fighting helped to pass the time.

A week ago, when Inquisitor Ducis Paton had returned from his meeting with the Austerians, he had been outraged by what Dillon had done, freeing us from the underground cells and lightening our workload. Paton had ordered us out of the priests' quarters. He had commanded that we be wrapped in extra chains, that we be placed on half rations. He had ranted and raved and condemned all of our Inquisitor guards to punishment nearly as severe as our own.

Dillon had faced him down, though, calmly stating that he had acted as he thought best. Paton's green eyes had bulged in outrage at his younger brother's insubordination, and then he had ordered Dillon down to his study.

I had no way of knowing what words were exchanged by the brothers in front of Howell's maquettes. But my Traveler friends and I were not returned to our underground cell. We received no more chains, and we maintained full rations.

Nevertheless, the Inquisitor Ducis won on one count. We were pulled from the easy task of carding soft, clean wool. We were sent to the breeding room.

Upon description, our tasks here seemed simple enough. We were supposed to muck out the cages of the darkbeasts that the priests bred, clearing away soiled straw, leaving behind fresh bedding and food. For a girl raised in a village filled with sheep, the breeding room should have been easy.

But I quickly learned that more darkbeasts died in the breeding room than ever saw the light of day.

Darkbeasts needed to be perfect. They needed to match up to the standards of Howell's maquettes without any variation, without any flaws. Bestius's priests were merciless as they inspected their creatures. If a rat's whiskers were too long, it was designated

for destruction. If a toad's back had too many warts, it was sacrificed. A lizard with a twisted tail was useless to the priests. Flawed
darkbeasts were an affront to the Twelve.

The priests culled their collection every morning, reviewing
the maturing animals with dispassionate eyes. Executions were
performed on the spot—the priests carried daggers forged specially for the purpose.

But holy men could not be bothered with cleaning up their
messes. They could not be concerned with the crushed and broken
animals they left behind. That was a job for the Lost. That was a
special torment for Goran and me.

More than once I wondered if the priests had selected this
punishment due to the nature of our crime. We Darkers had
come to love our darkbeasts, had come to honor them as unique
creatures with strong personalities of their own. What penalty
could be worse than cleaning up the ranks of destroyed, imper-
fect animals?

But we were not only there to clean up death. We were
intended to feed all the darkbeasts that survived the day's culling.
Ordinarily I would not have minded distributing food—at least
not to most of the animals. But with every cage I passed, with
every breeding box I walked by, I dreaded the next day's culling. I
worried that another of my charges would be judged flawed, that
another execution would be completed the following day.

I offered a bit of dried-out bread to a jet-black mouse, clicking my tongue against the roof of my mouth to encourage the little animal to eat. Nervous around me, her sides heaved in and out, and I could make out the stripes of her ribs beneath her skin. She needed to eat. She needed to put on weight so that she could match Howell's ideal.

I wished that I could remove my manacles—I suspected that they only made the poor beastie more nervous. Helpless to free myself, I settled for holding my breath and willing the creature to take the bread. Caw hopped closer, seeming to take interest in my labor for the first time that day.

"Is that a bite of seedcake?"

"It's bread. And it's not for you."

Caw huffed, but he made no attempt to take the mouse's treat. Instead he cocked his head toward Goran, who was sluicing out ferret cages. I could smell the animals' musk from across the room.

"Trust him," Goran said through gritted teeth, still talking about Dillon. "Like him. It's all the same. I don't think he truly means to help us."

"How can you say that?" I protested. "We're wearing clean clothes, aren't we? And last night we slept on a mattress, in a room above ground."

"And food," Caw added helpfully. *"The Princeps has made sure we eat three times a day."*

Goran still scowled, so I repeated Caw's words before I pulled out my sharpest argument. "And what about Taggart? You have to agree that Dillon helped him."

Dillon had given Taggart a new woolen cloak, one thick enough to cushion the Traveler's old bones. He had insisted that the old man was not well enough to leave his room, arguing to Paton that if Taggart could not walk unassisted, then he could not labor in the breeding room.

The night before, the Princeps had even brought a tisane to our chamber, a brew that was supposed to bring the old Traveler back to himself. I had sipped the drink before administering it. It turned out to be a simple mixture of drymoss and carter's root, something Mother might have brewed if she had known about our need. Taken over a fortnight, it would calm Taggart's mind. Restore him.

We hoped.

I sighed and closed the last of the mouse cages. I could finally move on to some other creature. Some animal less afraid of me. Some creature more robust, more likely to pass the priests' next inspection.

I turned down the next row and found a dozen low, woven cages. The sign stamped on the lid was clear enough—snakes.

I shivered. Even though I knew I was supposed to honor all darkbeasts, I had always disliked snakes. They slithered places they weren't supposed to go. They stole eggs. I could clearly remember Vala Traveler winding Slither around her forearm, warming the pathetic creature until it could hunt for its own breakfast.

Gritting my teeth, I lifted the lid of the nearest cage. A branch was jammed into the space, spreading from corner to corner. The darkbeast was twined about the limb, knotted around itself a half dozen times. It flicked its tongue toward me, and I could not tell if it was threatening or merely greeting me.

I kept my eyes on it warily as I hurried to collect the debris at the bottom of the cage. I could smell the rot of decaying leaves and the sharp whiff of droppings. My manacles rubbed hard against my wrists as my fingers closed around more debris—something crumbling, like bark. Something hard, like a rock. Something sharp, like . . .

I screamed as I pulled my hand out of the muck. My fingers clutched a quill, long and sharp. The shaft was snapped in two, held together with only a handful of midnight-black barbs. The entire feather was stiff, as if it had been soaked in blood. It was the nightmare I had imagined, ever since I first learned I was expected to execute Caw. It must have belonged to a bird that the priests had rejected, a bird that had been turned into prey for the dark-beast snake that glared at me from its branch.

I started sobbing.

Goran was at my side faster than I would have thought possible. "It's all right, Keara," he said, taking the horrible feather from me. "It's all right."

I tried to gulp in air, but I only gave myself a case of hiccups on top of my horrible struggle to breathe.

"Keara-ti," Goran crooned. "Don't look at it. Don't, Keara-ti. Don't look."

I heard Goran. I understood his words. But I could not do as he instructed. I could not tear my gaze away from the thing that had once been a living, breathing bird. Like Caw.

"*Not like me at all,*" my darkbeast said. He had taken flight at my scream, flapping awkwardly to huddle on the floor. Now he took a cautious step toward the ragged thing Goran had thrown to the flagstones. "*My feathers are much larger than that. And better groomed, too. I would never let so much dust accumulate between the barbs.*" He cocked his head, studying the offending item with first one eye, then the other. "*I don't believe that thing even came from a raven. It's from a common crow at best.*"

"What difference does that make?" I moaned.

"*Well!*" Caw said, and he ruffled his chest feathers until he seemed twice his normal size. "*We have been together all this time, and you still think I am nothing more than a common crow!*"

"I—" I tried to explain.

"*You think I'm just another puny black bird? Don't you realize that I am twice the size of a common crow?*"

"Yes, but—"

"And do you not see the glory that is my beak?" He turned his head to the side so that I could admire the sleek black protrusion that was much larger than any crow's.

"Of course. I—"

"And my tail! Don't you recognize elegance when it sits beside you—feathers that come to a fine point, instead of a boring fan?"

"Caw, I—"

"And you completely ignore my ruff!" He puffed out his chest, making all the feathers stand on end. The effect was impressive—he looked as if he wore a mane, like the lions rumored to roam the Great Desert far to the west. As I watched, Caw shook his shoulders, rippling his feathers all the way down to his wedge-shaped tail. He looked so regal, so impressive, and so positively disdainful that I had compared him to the poor snake prey that I had to laugh.

Goran sat back on his heels, relief clear on his face. "Won't let you get a word in edgewise, will he?" He dug in his pockets, and I'm pretty sure he would have offered Caw a treat if he had found anything remotely satisfying.

I sniffed away my tears. "I'm sorry," I said. "I just keep thinking about what they'll make us do. I keep thinking that you and I—and Taggart, too—will be forced to place our offerings on the altar upstairs. We'll give gifts to the very priests who keep us here, and then we'll kill our darkbeasts, and there isn't anything we can say or do to change that."

"I'm not so sure about that," Caw remonstrated. *"Now, if I were a common* crow, *you might be helpless, but with a* raven *by your side..."* He bobbed his head as if he were ready to take on Inquisitors, the Primate's Guard, and anyone else who made me unhappy.

Goran could not know what my darkbeast said, but he added his own consolation. "Don't be so certain, Keara-ti. You can't give up hope."

I took a deep breath. If we lost hope, then we truly had *nothing* left. "I won't," I promised. "I haven't."

And I wasn't lying. Sitting in this miserable chamber, surrounded by debris from the handful of surviving darkbeasts that were destined to be sent all over Duodecia, only to be sacrificed in little more than twelve years ... The breeding room actually made me firmer in my resolve than I had ever been.

I moved closer to Goran, lowering my voice so that I barely breathed the words. "We'll get out of here. We'll never tell the Inquisitors about the Darkers."

Goran nodded, smiling encouragement.

As if my vow had summoned our white-robed captors, the door to the breeding room opened. One of our guards stepped over the threshold. Of course I could not see his face within his snow-white robes, but I knew the instant he registered the stench of the snake's cage because he took a half step back. Nevertheless, his voice was firm as he said, "Time to answer questions, you Lost curs. Step outside."

"Some of my best friends have been lost curs," Caw said, settling on my shoulder and smoothing his feathers to a satin gleam. *"Those poor dogs are always so grateful when I set them straight. They have long memories, dogs do. They bring treats to those who aid them."*

I would have smiled, but I was already walking past the Inquisitor. The last thing I wanted was for him to draw out our questioning because he thought I was not serious enough.

Without waiting to be commanded, Goran and I knelt on the hard stone floor of the hallway and folded our chained hands in front of our hearts. We knew that the Inquisitors expected us to humble ourselves before the Twelve. They intended us to offer up the pain in our knees, the ache in our backs. And, of course, the never-ending stream of answers about the gods.

"What is the favorite food of Aurelius?"

Goran and I answered in unison. "Aurelius's favorite food is kidney pie."

"What is the favorite food of Bestius, blessed be his name?"

"Bestius's, blessed be his name, favorite food is sorrel soup."

"What is the favorite food of Clementius?"

And so it went, question after question after question. We completed reciting the gods' favorite foods. Their desired beverages. Their preferred scents. And then we moved on to the clothing preferred by each of the Twelve.

"What clothing is worn by Madrina?"

"Madrina's clothing is a linen kirtle."

"What clothing is worn by Marius?"

"Marius's clothing is a bronze cuirass."

"Where is the home of the Darkers?"

"The Darkers' home is—" We both started to answer routinely, and then we choked to a stop.

This was how the Inquisitors worked. They made their presence so familiar, so constant, that everyone was lulled into acceptance of their power. We knew they were stronger than we were. We knew they had the full force of the Primate behind them. They had a right to make us speak, a right to make us betray a friend.

The Inquisitor demanded, "Where can the Darkers be found?"

Neither Goran nor I responded.

The Inquisitor let annoyance sharpen his voice. "Where are the Darkers?"

Silence.

"Who are the other traitors?"

Silence, but I felt a rogue giggle rise in my chest. The Inquisitor sounded so impatient, so frustrated. I could almost imagine him as a child, stamping his feet, throwing himself onto the floor, pounding and screaming because we were not giving him what he wanted.

"You think this is amusing, Keara of Silver Hollow?"

"No, honored lord."

"But you are laughing, Keara of Silver Hollow?"

That domineering tone terrified me. And yet, at the same time, I felt my giggle rounding out to a laugh. An impossible, utterly inappropriate laugh. As if to calm me, Caw spoke inside my head. *"This would be a better time to think of sad things, Keara-ti."*

But my silence had stretched on too long. I had pushed the Inquisitor past all forbearance. He snatched the riding crop from his woven belt and commanded, "Extend your hands, Keara of Silver Hollow. Palms up."

I wanted to disobey. I wanted to tell the Inquisitor that he had no right to punish me. I wanted to take his quirt and throw it down the hall—better yet, open the door to the breeding room and toss the braided leather into the smelliest pile of debris.

Goran, though, shook his head beside me. Just a tiny gesture; I probably would not have noticed, if my gaze had not darted toward the oaken door.

But Goran was right. It was a bad idea to further antagonize the Inquisitors. It was only a matter of time before they escalated their punishment from the riding crop to something more hurtful—the knives or brands I'd dreaded since first hearing about the white-robed enforcers. I should be grateful I was getting off so lightly.

I extended my hands, and I was proud to see they did not shake.

The Inquisitor slashed down with his small whip. For a heartbeat, I felt nothing, and then my hands flared with pain. I curled my fingers closed by reflex and shut my eyes, but the Inquisitor merely commanded, "Again."

I had no choice but to open my palms. The crop flew again, bit again. A third time. Four. With each stroke outrage blossomed inside my chest, and I had to fight to keep from shouting out my fury.

Five blows. Six.

"Enough!" The single word echoed down the hallway. Swallowing hard, I tasted salty copper, and I realized I had bitten my lip. Caw tightened his talons on my shoulder, offering silent encouragement and support. I marveled that he had not flown away, as any lesser bird would have done. Certainly as any *crow* would have done.

I opened my eyes and blinked away tears. Dillon, Princeps of Duodecia, towered above me. For a moment I nearly failed to recognize him. He had shed his brown homespun. Now he wore the crimson and gold of the primacy, the colors of his father. An expertly tailored tunic made him look as tall as a full-grown man—an image only enhanced by the cloak that swept from his shoulders, surrounding him in a pool of finely woven wool.

"Enough," he repeated, and the one word sounded like a complete lecture about the nature of command.

"Your Highness," the Inquisitor said, and there was a tight band of anger beneath the politeness of the title. "These Lost must be instructed—"

"I forbid you to beat these Lost."

"Your Highness?" Now the Inquisitor was awash in disbelief. "You certainly cannot mean—"

"I mean precisely what I said." Dillon's voice was hard as onyx. "These Lost are under my protection."

"Brother, this time you go too far."

I jumped at the words. I knew what I would see before I turned around. I knew the high cheekbones. I knew the blond hair, glinting against the pushed-back Inquisitor's hood. I knew the green eyes, hard as glass. I knew Paton, the Inquisitor Ducis.

I followed Dillon's eyes as he looked over my shoulder. "Do not test your Princeps, *brother*," Dillon said, matching Paton's tone precisely.

"You're in my godhouse, boy. You presume too much."

"I am not a boy!"

"Did I miss your nameday? Have you slain your darkbeast, child?" Paton's laugh was harsh.

"You're the one who made me Princeps, Paton. You walked away from the title. Now I yield to no man but my father."

"You insolent pup! I should turn you over my knee and spank you here!"

Dillon stiffened, and for a moment I thought he would throw himself at his brother. Automatically I gauged their strength. Paton had the greater reach, the greater weight, more years of experience. But Dillon was not encumbered by Inquisitor robes. And he had the fire of rage in his belly.

The fire of rage, but not of stupidity. He swallowed hard and planted his feet, as if he were about to recite. "No, Paton. I will not fight you like a child, scrapping in the nursery. This matter goes to the heart of Duodecia. To the core of the Twelve."

"Ah," Paton said, pulling a sarcastic smile. "So says the scholar."

"My *studies* say the Princeps trumps any Inquisitor. Even an Inquisitor Ducis."

"Then let us bring your *studies* before Father. Let the Primate decide." Paton set the words between them as if he were drawing his sharpest sword from its scabbard.

Dillon swallowed hard. "Let the Primate decide."

"At the start of the Snow Moon," Paton said.

"The Snow Moon," Dillon agreed.

Three days hence.

Paton turned to the hooded Inquisitor who had watched the

entire exchange, crop held at the ready. "Carry on." He gestured toward me, toward my red-striped hands.

"No," Dillon said, in a voice that brooked no argument. "The Lost are protected until the Primate decides."

Paton let a slow smile spread across his lips. He nodded to the Inquisitor, waving for the man to put aside his quirt. "Fine. We'll spare them three days. But after that, they'd best be ready to taste the true power of Bestius, blessed be his name. After the Snow Moon." Slowly, calculatedly, he reached across and ruffled his brother's hair, as if Dillon were his friend. As if Dillon were a child.

The Inquisitor Ducis strode off before Dillon could slap his hand away. I stared at my feet, wondering who had truly won the encounter.

Chapter Fourteen

He's doing this for us, Goran."

The three of us Lost stood in an anteroom, somewhere deep in the Primate's palace. We were clad in identical clothes—simple black tunics, matching breeches. Our feet were cased in plain boots. Dillon had ordered our iron chains removed before we left the godhouse. He had replaced them with simple golden restraints, the narrowest of cuffs around our wrists. The bonds were merely symbolic; we could shrug them off any time we chose. I had tucked my darkbeast bracelet beneath mine, wincing as the knots pressed into bruises.

"You're wrong, Keara." Taggart's voice was rusty, and he paused to clear his throat. While I resented his entering my argument with Goran, I was secretly thrilled to see how steadily the old Traveler stood. For the first time in weeks, his spine was straight. His eyes were clear. Dillon's potion of drymoss and carter's root had finally taken effect.

Taggart went on. "Dillon has not helped us because he is our friend. He is using us, as surely as the Inquisitor Ducis was. We are pawns in their games. Either one will sacrifice us the instant he sees a possible gain."

That wasn't true. Dillon had risked something for me. He had given me the pouch of saltbite.

"Did he give it to you? Or did he take it from Paton?"

I bristled. *"They're the same thing, Caw."*

"Ah," he said. *"My mistake."*

I waited for Caw to say something more. He never admitted his failings that easily. Now, though, he lapsed into infuriating silence, taking advantage of our waiting to preen the feathers of his right wing. I resisted the urge to shrug him off my shoulder.

Instead I touched my fingers to the waxed pouch hidden deep in a pocket of my tunic. Aside from my darkbeast bracelet, the saltbite was my only possession in all the world.

"Listen!" Goran said. I caught my breath, but it was still several heartbeats before I made out what he had already heard. Booted feet, marching down the corridor.

Goran stepped to my side. His fingers closed around mine,

squeezing gently. "Be of good faith, friend, be of good cheer. The Twelve will protect us, so go without fear."

Another Travelers' couplet, a quote from a Common Play. Before I could conjure up the next line, Taggart came to stand behind us. Flick scrambled up to sit on his shoulder as the old man clapped his hands on both our shoulders. "Be ready, children. Be ready for anything."

I shouldn't have been surprised to see the Primate's Guard. The handpicked soldiers were personally responsible for the safety of the Primate. Each was sworn to Marius, the god of soldiers, to give his life for his lord. Rumor said that every man carried a dozen weapons at all times, although I could not make out more than four each, even on the captain of the squad that hurried us into the hall. After the first few steps, I stopped trying to spot hidden blades. It was enough to know that I was at the mercy of these men.

My heart pounded as they marched us through the palace. The corridors were filled with more wealth than I could have imagined when I lived back in Silver Hollow—tapestries threaded with gold and silver, mosaic floors set with precious stones. The ceilings were painted with detailed maps of every land the Primate ruled, from the bustling port of Austeria to the river-wrapped islets of Lutecia.

All too soon, though, my attention was forced from the finery around me. The Guards marched us through a pair of intricately carved double doors. My belly tightened as I remembered the last carved door I had passed—the one in Bestius's godhouse. The one that had brought me to Paton. To Dillon. Ultimately, here.

But now we entered no quiet study. Instead, we were in the Primate's throne room. We, and half the population of Lutecia, or so it seemed. The room was filled with men and women of every description. Inquisitors lined the walls, their white robes shimmering in the shadows. Noblemen wore their finest silks and satins; ladies displayed their most striking gowns.

Against the far wall, centered between two massive onyx columns, sat a throne. The chair seemed like a living thing, crouching at the top of four gilded steps. A carpet ran to the bottom of the stairs, a rich weaving of crimson tufted with gold thread that cut through the crowd, too precious to defile with ordinary feet.

For just an instant it seemed as if we were back at the cath, at the massive theatrical competition the Travelers had joined on the Primate's nameday. But at the cath I had never seen the Primate. He had been sheltered inside a tent, hidden behind his Guard and the judges and the press of the crowd.

Now, for the first time, I saw Primate Hendor in all his glory.

Even though he was seated, I could tell that he was tall. His broad chest was covered by a golden cuirass, the armor only adding to his bulk. In one hand, he held an orb, a perfect sphere that bore the telltale swirls of its legendary twelve component parts.

In the other, the Primate held a scepter, a baton fashioned from a dozen rods. Stylized fire emerged from the top, melting all the pieces into one whole. Binding all the primacy together.

But throne and armor and orb and scepter were not the things that held my gaze. Instead I was pinned by a pair of emerald eyes. Hard as stone. Sharp as glass. Bright as a springtime field. The eyes of Dillon. Of Paton. Of Primate Hendor.

The Primate's Guard stopped ten paces from the throne. As one, each man pounded his chest, extending his hand in the open salute to his lord. Goran and Taggart and I were Travelers at heart; we understood a cue when we saw one. I dropped into the deepest curtsy I had ever managed, and both men bowed until their foreheads touched their bent knees.

Only when we stood did I see Dillon and Paton.

The Princeps stood at his father's right hand. He was clad in black that matched our own—sleek and simple, with only the faintest hint of gold embroidery at his throat and wrists. At his feet sat a golden cage. Squinting, I made out the shape of a jet-black mouse. That would be his darkbeast, then.

"Squeak," Caw confirmed. *"Hardly two bites of meat on him."*

"Caw!"

Despite my darkbeast's hungry greed, Dillon's strategy was sound. No one could blame a child for bringing his darkbeast to such an important confrontation. Nevertheless, the mouse reminded the Primate—and the crowd—that Dillon was Hendor's youngest son. Perhaps the creature planted a seed that Paton sought unfair advantage. Just maybe the mouse would equate with mercy as Hendor pronounced his judgment.

The Inquisitor Ducis stood opposite his brother, to his father's left. He wore the expected shimmering robes of his station. Bestius's sigil, a fly, was picked out across his chest in exquisite embroidered detail. Even here, outside the godhouse, Paton broke with tradition and wore his hood pushed back, his face bare for all to see.

He was relaxed, composed. His thin lips were pressed into a tolerant smile, as if he had already calculated and dismissed the value of his brother's darkbeast. The Inquisitor Ducis was the very model of confidence.

"Well met, my sons," Primate Hendor said, and his voice silenced even the slightest murmur from the crowd. He waved one commanding hand at the captain of the Guard, and the soldiers melted to the sides of the chamber. Even at rest, though, they looked as if they were prepared to scale a castle wall.

The Primate settled his orb on a specially constructed stand before he leaned back on his throne. He rested his scepter across his right thigh and said, "Let us begin. Princeps? You requested this meeting. You may make your argument first."

Without hesitation, Dillon assumed his scholarly stance,

clasping his hands behind him. His shoulders were back. His chin was high. But I caught him dart a glance to his right, to a woman clad in rough-spun brown skirts. I could not say how old she was—her face was smooth, but her hair was as white as an Inquisitor's robe. Her hands were clasped before her, and I noted the ink stains on her fingers.

Janna," Caw supplied. The woman who had taught Dillon all he knew about arguing, about persuading. The woman whose guidance he would leave behind when he slew Squeak and became a man.

Dillon cleared his throat and began. "Honored Father, you have bestowed upon me the title of Princeps, the designation that I will be your heir when you walk among the Twelve, may that day be long in the future. All who live in Duodecia know the power of the Primate, the supremacy of one man over all the politics of state, over the worship of the Twelve. The Primate is the unquestioned Defender of our Faith, the leader in all things secular and spiritual."

"He's laying it on a bit thick, isn't he?"

"Hush, Caw!"

Dillon needed to make clear that he was not challenging his father's authority in any way, that he was not seeking current control of the throne. He needed to confirm the absolute command that Hendor had over all his people.

The Princeps continued. "Our forefather, First Primate Kerwen, laid a foundation for ruling Duodecia. He crafted a structure that has served us well for generations. Wise Kerwen appointed a dozen Inquisitors Ducis, one to guide the worship of each of the Twelve. He sent those men forth from this very room, appointing them to their unique godhouses."

Dillon seemed to gain strength from reciting his family history. His voice reached the high arches of the ceiling as he proclaimed, "But Kerwen made another appointment, early in his reign. Kerwen named his Princeps, his successor and his heir. Kerwen designated who would hold the ultimate power of the primacy after his own death. I stand before you, Father, as the loyal descendant of Kerwen. I stand before you as the humble Princeps to your rule."

"Do humble men wear gold at their throats and wrists?"

"Hush, Caw!"

Dillon's golden accents merely underscored the fact that he had set aside more substantial worldly wealth. He had chosen wisely, demonstrating that he was not intent on material gain. His only purpose today was to clarify power for the good of all Duodecia.

Dillon drew a deep breath to continue. He had laid out the background of his argument—none of what he had said so far was in dispute. Now it was time to press the difficult part of his case.

"Inquisitors Ducis. Princeps. But who prevails when a conflict arises between them? Who takes precedence, in matters of discipline? Malvin of Austeria, writing seventeen years after Kerwen took the throne, said that the Princeps is the fruit of the Primate, the same in every way as the tree from which he grows. In *The Arguments*, Malvin wrote, 'Whosoever speaketh ill of thine Princeps—'"

"*Speaketh? Thine? Is there no modern rendition he can quote? He'll make the Primate fall asleep if he's not careful.*"

"*Hush, Caw!*"

Dillon finished quoting *The Arguments*. I sneaked a glance at the Primate's face. He'd understood the archaic language, certainly, but my Traveler's senses told me the man was losing interest in the proceeding. He shifted the scepter on his knee and moved his wrist to a more comfortable angle atop the orb.

Dillon, though, seemed unaware that he was losing ground. He expanded his chest and quoted from Ungus of Hollowdale. I could not say when Ungus lived, and I had no idea where Hollowdale rested on a map. But I was certain, within a single sentence, that Ungus of Hollowdale was one of the most pretentious, self-aggrandizing men ever to write a text.

"*Perhaps you'll wake me when it's over?*"

"*Hush, Caw!*"

Dillon's argument got worse from there. Of course, he

exhibited astonishing recall, quoting dozens of obscure texts. He never hesitated as he recited the words of ancient scholars. He obviously knew his material.

But the words he quoted became longer. The arguments grew more obtuse. Even those of us who wanted him to win grew lost in the archaic language.

And then the worst thing possible happened. Primate Hendor yawned.

A polite man would have hidden his reaction. He would have clenched the muscles of his throat and tightened his lips to swallow silently. He would have opened his eyes widely, exaggerating his interest to cover the moment when his attention had flagged. He would have leaned forward, paying even greater heed to what he had missed.

But Primate Hendor was ruler of all Duodecia. He had no need to be polite. He could say and do whatever he desired.

And so he yawned openly, not bothering to disguise the motion.

Dillon blanched. He cast a wild glance at Janna, but she had no way to save him. Instead the Princeps was forced to clear his throat, swallow hard, and hastily conclude, "For all those reasons and more—which I will spare you unless you ask—the Princeps's word should hold more sway than that of any Inquisitor Ducis. My suit should be granted over that of my brother Paton, and these three Lost souls should be released into my command."

Caw shifted on my shoulder, and I braced myself to hear my darkbeast's sarcastic comment. He said nothing, though. As if he knew the argument was already lost.

Primate Hendor scowled as Dillon completed a perfect bow. His eyes were still narrowed as he turned to Paton. "And you, Inquisitor Ducis? Do you have a host of philosophers to quote in your support?"

"No, Primate," Paton said brightly. "I would not dare to compete with the Princeps at the sport he holds most dear."

A quick glance at Dillon revealed high color blossoming on his cheeks.

"He should take his anger to his darkbeast," Caw said. And before I could reply, he continued, *"I know. I know. 'Hush, Caw.' You need not say it, I've said it for you."*

Paton continued, seemingly unaware of the discomfort he had brought to his blood brother. "When the Princeps challenged me to this debate, I thought I might make my argument in a different way. With the Primate's indulgence . . ."

Paton waited for his father to deliver one curt nod before he extended his white-clad arm toward the threshold of the throne room. The doors sprang open before his gesture was completed—someone had clearly been waiting on the other side.

No. Not some*one*. Many people. Many people, clad in exotic costumes—feathers and shells, mirrors and pearls. Several of the folk wore elaborate masks—that one was dressed as Mortana, that other as Clementius. I caught a glimpse of all the godly sigils I knew too well.

The assembled crowd of nobles exclaimed at the newcomers, surprise giving way to delighted laughter. Of course the court was pleased. Of course the court was amused. They were about to be entertained by Travelers.

And then, when I thought that the contrast with Dillon's boring speech could not be any greater, I heard a voice that chilled my bones. A voice that I had thought I would never hear again. A voice that was all the more outrageous because it had once belonged to a friend.

"Greetings, Honored Primate, and thank you for your gracious welcome. My name is Vala Traveler, and my people speak today for the Inquisitor Ducis."

Chapter Fifteen

Goran yelped and took a full step forward before Taggart settled a hand on his shoulder with a sharp word of warning. Most eyes in the room went to my friend and his grandfather, speculating on the surprise pasted across their faces. Whispers began to spread as people realized that Goran and Taggart knew Vala, that they had once been part of the same troupe.

No one looked at me, though. No one searched for my reaction.

No. That was not true. One person looked to see what I would say.

Vala.

She had been my friend once, the person I had shared all

my secrets with. We had slept beside cooking fires, heads on a single pack that served as a pillow. We had roamed the streets of riverside towns, crying the revels, gathering people to watch our shows. We had giggled behind our hands, playing pranks on Goran. We had called each other Vala-ti and Keara-ti, gloried in the easy friendship of children on the Great Road, roaming all of Duodecia.

But that had changed when Vala killed her darkbeast, Slither. That had changed when Vala lost the easy grace she had always had upon the stage, when she struggled to find words to convince a hostile audience.

That had changed when Vala discovered that I had saved my darkbeast, that my twelfth nameday had come and gone, and Caw still sat upon my shoulder.

Everything had changed.

And at the same time, nothing was different at all. Vala still had hair as dark as Caw's wings, with wide black eyes to match. Her brows still tilted at an exotic angle. She still had the snow white skin of a princess.

And she still had a voice that could charm an audience to silence.

"Greetings, honored Primate. Greetings, honored court. We thank you for your presence; we'll try to keep this short."

A new Common Play, then. The Travelers must have spent the

past three days working like a hive of bees. When I had lived with them, Taggart had written all the revels. He'd always had a glib hand with rhyme; rhythm and words seemed to pump together within his blood. I wondered who had written these newest words. Who had risen to the challenge Paton had set? Who had chosen the costumes, the masks?

But within moments, I stopped wondering. I was too busy listening, my belly twisting as I realized the tale the Travelers told.

There were three Lost, depicted with all the ancient formulas for villains. Tangled hair reached to the Travelers' waists. They wore mottled masks, with huge noses curving over liver-colored lips. Ragged leashes cinched their wrists, visible reminders of the darkbeasts who had failed at their tasks, who had neglected to take away the failings of such evil wrongdoers.

But these were no simple villains, no stock characters plucked from the annals of all the Common Plays.

For one of these villains went by the name of Taggart. He had a beard that matched his matted hair, and he wore a flimsy neckpiece of rusty iron whirls. A massive lizard had been stitched out of black wool and pinned to his back, its head curling up to nearly cover the player's head.

There was a Goran, too. He stomped about like a spoiled child, wearing short breeches hiked up to the middle of his chest. He delivered his lines in a squeaky voice, made all the more tremulous because of the weighty toad strapped to his back.

And there was a Keara.

My namesake wore filthy rags made of homespun so rough that the poor Traveler already displayed itchy welts on her arms and legs. She spoke her words with a finger permanently hooked into her lower lip, forcing an annoying lisp, a complete exaggeration of the way courtiers assumed that villagers spoke.

I gaped, remembering a morning months before when Vala had coached me, in Rivermeet. Then, an Inquisitor had demanded that I be held accountable for failing to invoke the Twelve before I ate. Vala—my friend in those days—had shown me how to act as if I were an idiot, as if I were beyond judgment.

The Villain-Keara used all those affectations and more. Her costume was stuffed with extra cloth so that she appeared monstrously fat, and she constantly snatched food from the other characters, cramming it into her mouth, spilling crumbs and drooling. The raven on her back was so gigantic that the Traveler could scarcely move.

But somehow she managed. Somehow they all did.

They acted out a version of our story. We lied, we stole, we cheated, all in the service of our bloated darkbeasts. We disrupted the cath, and we fled Lutecia. We arrived at Saeran's enclave in the woods, challenging beautiful brave souls who fought to keep

Duodecia safe for moral, upright folk. And we found ourselves back in Lutecia, confined in Bestius's godhouse, where Paton was the only man brave enough to restrain our villainy.

My cheeks burned with outrage. Was that how others truly viewed me? Was that what Vala had seen in the days, weeks, months that I had thought she was my friend? No wonder she had become so hateful, so filled with anger and with spite.

I shrank closer to Goran and Taggart. Tears of shame rose hot in my eyes, spilled down my cheeks. Without conscious thought, my fingers found the knots on my darkbeast bracelet, and they danced from one to the next, spinning the round of ferret fur, desperate to find comfort.

I could feel the eyes of the watching nobles in the throne room. I could sense the hatred on every face. Once, I dared to look at Dillon, but he was standing next to Janna, shrunken and defeated. All his hard work, all his studies and memorization and recitation—they were nothing in the face of the story the Travelers told.

For the players were not merely mocking us Lost. The Travelers were targeting the Princeps.

Dillon had argued for mercy. He had proposed treating us Lost like erring students, like well-intentioned people who could now be schooled on how we had made mistakes. With his carefully chosen quotations from ancient philosophers, the Princeps had explained that we Lost could be honored and respected, despite our many wrongs.

But the Travelers made clear that we three had no hope of redemption. We were monsters—we and Dillon and anyone else who had ever thought to give us succor.

Through it all, Vala Traveler spoke the words of the narration. Her voice rang out strong and clear, echoing off the ceiling of the throne room. She bore witness before the Primate, reminding all the watching court that Goran and Taggart and I were not only grotesque, but we were heretics. We were traitors.

I stole a glance at Taggart. The old man's features twisted with a braid of emotion. There was horror, honest revulsion at the images presented. And there was pity for desperate, jealous Vala, for all of us who would suffer for her wrath. And there was—most surprisingly of all—pride.

For Taggart was the man who had taught these Travelers. He had nurtured them for all the years that they learned their game. He had instructed them on how to hold their heads, how to wave their hands, how to wring out each drop of emotion from the audience they addressed.

And while Taggart had never imagined using his training for this purpose, while he had never considered a story as broad as the one they now told, an attack so vicious, I could see that a part of him was prideful at the foundation he had laid.

Steeling myself, I turned back to see how the Travelers would end their show.

We villains were in Bestius's godhouse now. I cringed as I watched Traveler-Inquisitors quiz us on our knowledge of the Twelve. Of course, we monsters knew nothing of the gods— we could not recite their names, much less their attributes. We stumbled over the most obvious facts, ignorant and utterly uncaring. The audience laughed at our clumsy attempts, at our showing ignorance worse than the laziest child's.

Nevertheless, the Traveler-Inquisitors mercifully tried to aid the revel's villains. They administered fair punishments. They provided kind instruction to guide the mind. They assigned measured labors to fortify the body.

Labors.

Polishing Bestius's altar—wittily represented by four Travelers who wore shimmering onyx-colored cloaks. Sweeping the corridors—signified by other performers standing shoulder to shoulder. Cleaning the darkbeast breeding pens—depicted as sparkling containers of gold and silver, never stinking, never mired in the broken bodies of murdered animals.

In every case, of course, the villains failed at their tasks. We were too stupid, too lazy, too headstrong to meet Bestius's most simple demand.

It was all so obvious, so clear. Even though I *knew* the truth, I found myself lulled by the revel, drawn along by the story as I had always been by the Travelers' offerings. I somehow separated the monstrous Keara from myself. I somehow ignored the horrifying raven that sprawled before me. I somehow slipped into the magic of the rhyme, the glamour of the performance. Reluctant, unwilling, I fell under Vala Traveler's spell.

"Pay attention!" Caw's words jolted through my mind; he was shouting louder than I had ever heard him shout before.

Villain-Goran and Villain-Taggart were huddled before a mountain of brilliant fleeces—a length of whitest silk stretched between two poles. They fumbled with oversized paddles, accomplishing nothing but tangling the wool they carded.

Soon, though, no one watched as the pair comically wrapped themselves tighter and tighter in the white silk banner. Rather, Villain-Keara commanded every eye.

I gaped as my monster self knelt before a simple jar. The container was emblazoned with the Primate's seal, the image of an eagle picked out in glaring gold so that none could miss it.

Villain-Keara studied the jar. Like an animal, she sniffed it. She tasted it. She put her ear to it, as if she believed it could speak. The audience laughed, of course, for who could be so foolish that she did not know the purpose of an ordinary jar? At last Villain-Keara sat on the jar, smashing it into six pieces. More laughter rose as the monster-me rubbed her sore bottom.

But the laughter stopped when Villain-Keara reached into the wreckage of the container. When Villain-Keara seized a leather pouch. When Villain-Keara displayed her trophy for all to see.

For the leather pouch was emblazoned with the same mark as the jar—Primate Hendor's personal seal. The Traveler who represented me turned about slowly, fighting to raise her arm past the raven that threatened to consume her. Only after she was certain that everyone had seen the treasure did she deliver a careful line, enunciating every syllable so that no one could miss the significance of what had just happened.

"What have I discovered here? What have I just found? Precious herbs of Hendor, say! I'll steal them, though I'm bound."

The Villain-Keara rattled her Lost chains loudly as she stashed her leather bag deep inside her costume. The motion made her overbalance, and the raven on her back drove her to her knees. The Traveler, well trained in meeting audience expectations, shouted out a curse, taking Bestius's name in vain.

At the blasphemy, the crowd fell silent, and every eye turned toward the Primate, toward the living incarnation of all the Twelve. Primate Hendor's eyes blazed like copper pots left too long in the fire. His mouth worked, but he could not summon words. He clambered to his feet, raising an arm that shook with fury. An arm that directed attention away from the Villain-Keara.

An arm that brought every eye in the room to rest on *me*. "Bring me that heretic thief!"

For a heartbeat, nothing happened. No one moved. No one spoke. No one breathed.

And then the room exploded.

"They lie!" shouted Dillon. "That's not what happened!"

"Darkers, now!" came another voice, a woman's voice, high and piercing in the chaos.

"To the Primate!" bellowed the Guard, all their voices raised as one, and they plunged into the throng.

Travelers scattered, flinging masks and costumes in their wake. Noblemen scrambled for their weapons, for the stylish, useless blades that graced their courtly finery. Caw launched himself from my shoulder, flying straight for a bevy of perfectly groomed women, who screamed and scattered at his approach.

Goran was the first of us Lost to recover. He clutched at my wrist, pulling me down to the floor. In the same motion, he grabbed at a fleeing courtier's cloak, tugging the blue garment free before its owner knew what had happened. Goran tossed the cloth to me, and I reflexively covered my stark black tunic.

Another scramble, and Goran had a green cloak to toss over Taggart's shoulders. A third, and he was wrapped in his own camouflage of silver.

By then Caw was circling above me, repeating his most raucous cry in a blatant attempt to add to the insanity. I stumbled forward, desperate to reach the place where Dillon had stood. The Princeps had not been implicated in the Travelers' version of my theft, but I could not believe he was safe here. Not now. Not when he had shouted about the revel's lies. Not when someone had spied on us, learning the truth of what had happened in that distant chamber. Not when someone had twisted reality to enrage the Primate.

Frantic, I caught a flash of golden hair, and I staggered a few steps to my right. Someone stepped on my cloak, and I felt the fabric rip. I could not hear it though. I could not hear anything above the bellows and the screams.

Another flash—the black of Dillon's tunic. But before I could reach him, iron fingers clamped down on my arms. I twisted like a fresh-hooked fish, but I had no hope of breaking free. I filled my lungs, ready to shout the Princeps's name, ready to plead for my life, ready to say anything, do anything, just to survive one more heartbeat.

"*Yield!*" cried Caw from some vantage point above me.

"*I can't,*" I shouted silently, knowing he would never hear me above the throng if I tried to speak aloud. How terrible must the fight be, if even my darkbeast counseled surrender? Yielding would mean the Primate's Guard. Yielding would mean death.

That realization gave me the strength to thrash even more

desperately. My captor shifted behind me. He levered one arm against my throat, crushing my windpipe as he pinned me to his chest. My feet left the floor, and I tried to kick backward, tried to plant the soles of my boots against his shins. My legs tangled in the blue cloak though. My heartbeat pounded in my ears. A red wash sifted over my vision. I twisted, turned, tried to bend myself double at the waist.

"Stop!" Caw shouted. *"They're Darkers! You are held by Darker friends!"*

I barely grasped his meaning as the throne room faded to black.

Chapter Sixteen

Someone was striking my belly, over and over and over again. My jaws clicked shut, and I bit my tongue. My head was hanging upside down, and I started to choke as bile rose in my throat.

"Stop," I moaned. "Leave me be."

"She's awake."

The pounding stopped. I was flipped over, steadied on my feet. My head whirled, and I realized I had been carried on the shoulder of a man. A man clad in the crimson and gold of the Primate's Guard. I bit back a scream.

"Thank the kind man," Caw chided.

"I—" My throat ached fiercely. I swallowed hard, but that only made the pain peak.

"We don't have time for this."

I squinted, trying to discern who had spoken. I could not make the faces around me focus. There. That woman. Brown robes. Smooth face. Cloud-white hair. Ink stains on the fingers that she snapped in front of my nose.

"Janna," Caw prompted, and I remembered he had given me her name in the throne room. I realized something I should have thought of then. My darkbeast had never seen the library clerk. He'd had no way to recognize her among all the people in Lutecia. He'd had no way to know her name.

"And Sleek," Caw said. That was when I saw the jet-black garter snake wrapped around Janna's forearm. The creature shot out its forked tongue, sampling the air between us. I yelped and took a step back, only to find myself against the solid chest of the Primate's Guard.

Janna had clearly spared her darkbeast. The library clerk must be a Darker. And Sleek must have spoken to Caw in the silent way of all darkbeasts, identifying his partner to my raven even before the chaos broke out in the throne room.

Snake or not, Sleek would be my friend. I would make him as welcome as Wart. As Flick. As Caw.

"And while you're meeting our companions, say hello to Nessan." The Primate's Guard whose beefy hand was the only thing holding me upright. *"And his darkbeast, Chirp."* The largest cricket I

had ever seen waved antennae at me before disappearing beneath the soldier's breastplate.

"I don't—" And this time it was a little easier to force words past the ache in my throat.

"Can you walk, Keara-ti?" I whirled around at Goran's familiar voice. It was rushed and annoyed, but transparently tinged with relief. He was standing behind the Primate's Guard—*Nessan*, I reminded myself. The silver cloak Goran had appropriated was now shredded, but my friend still wore his finery with a Traveler's cocky pride. Caw flew from his shoulder to mine. Some of my confusion flowed away as my darkbeast settled on his familiar perch.

I nodded. "I—I think so."

"Very well." Taggart. I blinked hard, and I could see him in the shadows, nearly lost in the green cloak Goran had stolen. "By now they will have realized we are not in the throne room. These passages will not stay safe. Janna?"

The white-haired woman nodded grimly. "We can reach the waterway from here. But do not bring your stolen finery. We dare not leave it where we're going; it would only focus unwelcome attention. Hurry."

And hurry we did.

We peeled off our cloaks, tossing them into a tangled pile of blue and green and silver. Nessan made short work of stripping off our golden bonds. Janna gathered our shed belongings and dashed down a hallway. From the flicker of orange light, I realized she must have tossed them into a hypocaust, into one of the heated tunnels that coursed beneath the palace, providing winter comfort. The cloaks would give way to the flames in short order. The gold chains would be left behind though. I could only hope we were far away when some lucky servant discovered the unexpected prize.

Caw filled me in on the details I'd missed after Nessan choked me into unconsciousness. Vala had shouted that I must be searched, that I had the stolen saltbite on my person. Guards had sprung forward, eager to execute her command. As the revel collapsed around us, Janna had summoned our allies, calling Darkers to her aid. Nessan had answered the call, plunging into the crowd to capture me and to guide Goran and Taggart to the servants' hallways behind the throne.

Goran and Taggart, of course, had listened to their darkbeasts. They had gone without a fight. Caw was shadowy on details, but there was at least one other Darker who had helped us fight through the crowd, who had contrived to disguise our escape.

Three Darkers, all in the heart of the Primate's court. More, perhaps, whom Caw had not identified.

But only Nessan and Janna were with us now. Nessan and Janna and Chirp and Sleek, all running for their lives.

Torches were scarce in the servants' hallways. That made no difference to Janna, though. She moved steadily, picking up her pace when it became clear that my strength had returned, that I would not slow the group any more than I already had. Before long, she gathered us close, barely voicing a whisper. "The library is on the other side of this curtain. We must reach the far wall and the staircase to the lower levels."

She paused just long enough for us to nod, and then she slid the heavy tapestry back on its iron rod.

Light streamed into the corridor. It was brilliant, blinding after our passage through near-absolute darkness. I dashed instant tears from my cheeks, trying to force my eyes to stay open. Janna was already leading the way into the library.

If I had not known better, I would have thought the room was a godhouse. It would have been a confusing one, though, with the white marble columns that belonged to Patrius topped with intricate capitals, like those of Aurelius. Janna chivied us into a rectangular chamber, and I thought the space might be dedicated to Mortana, the goddess of death. But then we reached a wooden door, a carved threshold that spoke of Venerius. Before I could catch my breath, we had passed into a round chamber, a room clearly devoted to Pondera.

And so it was as I glanced around—here was a sign of Recolta, there a symbol of Tempestia. Bestius. Marius. Madrina.

The library was home to all the Twelve.

Windows were set high in the stone walls, great fields of mullioned glass that allowed winter sunlight to spill like cold milk across the floor. Shelves were cut into the rock beneath the windows, between the signs of the Twelve. Some held scrolls—hundreds and hundreds of rolls of parchment, stacked one on top of the other. Others held books—great leather covers decorated with jewels, bound with precious metal. A half dozen richly illustrated volumes were displayed on the gigantic round table in the center of the chamber.

Janna ignored those treasures, though. She did not spare a glance for the sigils of the Twelve. Instead she headed straight for a malachite column, for the mottled green associated with Clementius. All of us followed, obedient as ducklings.

Behind the column a breath of cool air brushed my cheek. The breeze rose near my feet, from a flight of stairs that disappeared into the floor. Janna said, "Hurry, now. To the bottom. All the way down."

Taggart nodded, springing down the steps with a vigor that belied his lingering illness in Bestius's godhouse. Goran followed close behind. I raised my hand to my shoulder, offering Caw a steadier perch on my wrist before I plunged into the darkness. My foot was on the topmost step when I heard a shout.

"Janna!"

I knew the voice without turning around. I knew the emerald eyes that would be flashing at the library clerk. I knew the thin lips that would be twisted into a frown.

"Your Highness." The woman wove a thousand emotions into the spoken title.

I could not help but turn to face Dillon, to see him one last time. He stood precisely as I had pictured him. No, not precisely. I had not realized he would cradle a golden cage against his chest. I never imagined he would bring his darkbeast as he hunted us down.

"I knew you would come here," the Princeps said, directing his words to Janna. He barely spared a glance at Nessan. It was a sign of how upset he must have been that he did not think to question what one of his father's sworn guards was doing here, in the library, when chaos reigned in the throne room and beyond. "I had to find you," Dillon said. "I had to tell you that I'm sorry."

"You owe me no apology, Your Highness." Her voice was kind.

"I knew the words, Janna. I knew the stories. I could not make the Primate understand, though. I could not give life to the ancient scholars."

A fond smile flickered at Janna's lips. "Few people love the old ones as you do, Your Highness. Besides, after the Travelers appeared, you never had a chance."

Dillon shook his head. "I owed you better, Janna. You and the

Lost. All the . . . Darkers." His tone hardened. "I heard you. You summoned rebels in the very throne room of the Primate."

Janna's tone was resolute. "Your Highness—"

But she did not have a chance to finish, to offer up any excuse, any explanation. Instead, Nessan surged past her. I barely glimpsed the soldier plucking something from his wide belt. He flicked his wrists, and then I realized he had cast a net. Filaments as thin as spider silk settled over Dillon. The Princeps bellowed and fought to free himself, but his arms were quickly bound by his sides.

"Traitor!" Dillon shouted. "You are sworn to the Primate! Sworn to me! Release me at once!"

Nessan grunted as he wrestled the Princeps toward the floor. It was scarcely a match. In fact it would not have been a struggle at all, if Nessan had not tried to be gentle. He said through gritted teeth, "I cannot do that, lord."

Dillon continued to thrash ineffectively. "To me!" he shouted. "Guards—"

Nessan produced a dagger from somewhere. Faster than the flicker of a snake's tongue, he reversed the blade, bringing it down hard behind the Princeps's ear. Dillon collapsed immediately.

Janna wailed, "You were wrong to do that!"

The guard grimaced as he used a thumb to peel back Dillon's eyelids. He must have been satisfied with what he saw, because he pulled the Princeps into a seated position. "We've come too far to have him call the entire Guard now."

"But when they find him here, they'll know where you have gone. The Route will be compromised."

Nessan nodded toward the stairwell. "Then they must not find him." He hefted the Princeps onto his shoulder. "Come. You said yourself that we haven't much time."

"Nessan, you can't."

Instead of answering, the Guard looked at me. "You, girl. Take the Princeps's darkbeast." He nodded at Squeak's cage. I was frozen, though, staring in disbelief. The Primate's Guard had raised arms against the Princeps, against the boy he was sworn to protect. Nessan stared at me with the intensity of a man who was putting his life on the line. "Now!" he said, and while his voice was barely a whisper, it had the power of a shout.

I scrambled for the cage. Janna was still fussing, but Nessan hurried us both down the stairs. I sneaked one glance and realized that he carried Dillon across his shoulders. He was kidnapping the Princeps. In effect, we all were.

I lost track of the steps in the dark. Only when my foot crashed against a stone floor did I realize I had reached the last one. I turned to speak a warning, but Janna seemed to know the way; she edged to the side as soon as she found the rough floor. Nessan, though, swore when he reached the bottom. He grunted once, and I heard cloth snag against the wall. Dillon, I realized. Nessan must have set down his burden.

Goran whispered, "Keara? Are you all right? What happened? What took so long?"

Before I could answer, there was the sound of stone striking stone. A spark leaped, and I realized that Nessan had used a flint. One sharp breath, and I smelled pitch. A flame leaped out of the darkness, and I discovered another hidden weapon of the Primate's Guard—a hand-size torch.

Nessan held the fire above his head, pressing an ear to Dillon's chest.

"The Princeps!" Taggart said, barely swallowing a shout. He whirled on Janna. "What in the name of all the Twelve were you thinking?"

"Ask this ox." She nearly spat at Nessan.

The Guard rolled his shoulders. "It was take him, or be discovered."

Taggart gaped in disbelief. "The Primate will never let this go unanswered."

Nessan merely shook his head. "I'm telling you, we had no choice. I know the Guard. I know what they would do once this cub raised an alarm."

As if in answer, Dillon moaned. Janna said, "He's coming around." She fought to free his hands from Nessan's nets, chafing

his wrists. All the while, she shot murderous glances at the soldier.

"We'd best go, then," Taggart said. "Before he shouts again."

"Go where?" Goran's voice cut through Janna's simultaneous protest. I could tell that he was angry, frightened. And I realized that I would have been furious myself, but I already knew the answer to his question.

Taggart settled a hand on Goran's shoulder and drew him toward the far wall. "There," he said.

As if in confirmation of my thoughts, Nessan's torch guttered in a draft. It flickered as the torch had done when Dillon gave me the saltbite. Even in the dim light, I had no trouble finding the trough at Goran's feet. I could make out the twelve-rayed sun carved into the side. Six lines marched to the right of the sun, separated by arrows. The sequence of strange shapes ended with a square, drawn with harder edges than the one I had seen in Bestius's godhouse. The stone channel was as deep as a tub for washing; I could easily submerge myself without touching the bottom. It was wide, too—my shoulders would not brush the sides. The water rushed through, flowing as fast the Silver River after spring melt.

"I'm not going to like this," Caw said.

"None of us will." I answered him aloud, before I realized that my words would be nonsense to the others. No one cared, though. No one was listening to me.

Instead Taggart was explaining everything to Goran. "It's a type of map. We're starting at the sun, and we're going to the square. The lines indicate how many passages to take, how many legs of the trip. At the end of each section, you'll reach a crossing and turn in the direction of the arrow. Memorize it all, now."

Tentatively Goran dipped his hand into the water. He did not say that it was freezing or that Wart would be battered. He did not say that he was afraid. But I hoped he thought all those things. Because I did.

"Let's go," Taggart said. "We have wasted enough time."

Perhaps Goran had learned obedience as a Traveler. Maybe he listened because Taggart was his grandfather. He might have obeyed because he had nowhere else to go. In any case, he climbed onto the edge of the trough. He traced the six lines with his fingers, along with the arrows between them. He looked across the room, caught my gaze for a dozen heartbeats.

And then he slipped into the stream, feet-first, with his face toward the ceiling, as if that posture might protect him from underwater danger.

"Goran-tu!" I cried. But he was already gone.

Taggart went next. Quickly. Silently.

I climbed onto the trough. "Come, Caw," I said. I tucked him beneath my tunic before he could protest, before I could think about how terrified he must be.

"Take the Princeps's darkbeast," Nessan said, and he gestured for Janna to give me Squeak. I started to take the mouse out of his golden cage, to place him into the folds of cloth beside Caw. Nessan shook his head though. "We can't leave the cage here. We can't leave anything behind to show how we've escaped."

"What about Dillon?" I asked.

"I'll get him through."

How? I wanted to ask. In the dark? In the water? Scrambling to change direction at the crossings?

I saw that Janna had the same questions, the same hopeless, helpless concerns. Nessan shook his head. "I'm the Primate's Guard, and I promise you the Princeps will survive." His eyes brooked no rebellion as he tested my grip on the golden cage. "Now go. We are out of time."

I had no more arguments. I could offer no more excuses. I closed my eyes and thought some vague prayer to all the Twelve, barely resisting the urge to run my fingers over the knots of Goran's darkbeast bracelet. Before I could acknowledge the fear that slammed around my heart, I cast a brief mental warning to Caw.

And then I slipped beneath the water.

Chapter Seventeen

The water was cold, colder than I ever imagined. It shocked my body and my mind, bringing tears to my eyes. It rushed me along a stone channel in the dark, even as I fought the urge to go back to the known, to return to the library and the Primate's palace, and everything else that was familiar to me.

To go back to Vala.

I was still reeling from my outrage at the Travelers' performance for the Primate. Of course, I knew there was no going back. The library wasn't safe. And Vala was not my friend, would never be my friend again. Vala hated me—me and Caw and Goran and Taggart, and every aspect of the Travelers' life we had shared.

Now, as my feet breached the water in front of me, my chest

began to ache. My lungs demanded that I open my mouth, that I breathe. I kept one hand over Caw, where he huddled inside my tunic. The other clutched at the golden cage. I fought the urge to use my fingers to push against the stone tunnel. My eyes popped open as I fought against the water.

And so I saw the light. It was gray and cold, shining from above.

The tremendous force of the water lessened, and I was able to get my legs under me. I stood, breaking the surface of the stream, and I gulped down great breaths of fresh air. Eddies rippled about my knees, curls of water that streamed in from my left, sweeping across the pool where I now crouched. I turned my face upward, and I could make out a shaft carved into the stone, through which shone a single beam of dusty daylight.

My teeth started to chatter, and I fumbled in my soaked tunic. Caw was curled against my belly. My fingers shook as I used one hand to pull out my darkbeast, the other to raise up Squeak's golden cage. I exposed the animals to the soft light, to the air, and, by reflex, I offered up a prayer to Bestius that they be spared.

Bestius. The god of darkbeasts. The god whose Inquisitor Ducis most wanted us captured and killed.

"This was not your best idea," Caw said after he had shaken all his feathers.

"This was not my idea at all." Even though I whispered, my voice echoed in the stone enclosure. I winced and looked above, hoping I was not attracting unwelcome attention. Where were we? Still beneath the Palace? Somewhere under the city streets?

Squeak made a tiny sound, living up to his name. "Is he all right?" I asked Caw, barely voicing the question.

"He'd prefer to be in a granary," Caw replied. *"Or at least with the Princeps."*

Dillon. Dillon, who would be carried through that horrible watery passage by Nessan. Who might be on his way even now. I could not linger here. I could not occupy the space they would need to stand, to catch their breath.

I closed my eyes and tried to remember the carvings on the side of the trough. Six vertical lines—we had accomplished the watercourse associated with the first one—then an arrow pointing to the left.

I turned in that direction. The tunnel was dark, dropping almost immediately into a channel that would leave no room for my head to surface. The light from the shaft above me did not penetrate farther than my arm could reach.

"Come on," I said, returning Caw to my sodden garment. I filled my lungs and ducked beneath the surface.

Almost before the water started to batter me, my thoughts returned to Vala. I could not believe she had performed in that revel. I could not believe she had narrated the text about me as a villain, as a thief.

A thief. How had the Travelers known about the saltbite? Dillon would not have told a soul, not when he was the one who had actually filled my pouch with the herb. And Goran and Taggart had been working in the room above us. They would have known if anyone had spied on the lower chamber.

Still without an answer, I reached another crossing. Again, I could stand and squint in the gray light. I could release Caw, raise up Squeak in his cage, give them both a chance to catch their breath. I turned to the right as the arrow had indicated and prepared to submerge myself again. Before I could move, though, Caw said, "*Inventory.*"

"What?"

"*Inventory. The Inquisitor Ducis must have inventoried the saltbite. It is precious stuff—he likely weighed the container every day. Especially if he knew the Princeps had shown an interest in it. And you, with your history of studying herbs . . .*"

I shuddered, unable to tell if I was reacting to the cold or to the notion that I had been caught by Paton's suspicious calculation. My fingers clutched at the waist of my sodden robes. The leather pouch was still there, safe where I had tucked it when Dillon ordered me to change into my black garments.

I placed Caw there as well. None of us was getting closer to our journey's end as long as I stood at the crossroads. I warned my darkbeast, and then I slipped into the next watery passage.

Three more times we surfaced. Each space allowed me to stand. Each had a distant light from above. Each allowed me to catch my breath, to free the darkbeasts, to brace myself for another section. And each submersion in the water washed my mind a little more clear, made me more certain that Caw was right, that Dillon and I had walked into a trap with the saltbite.

I was exhausted by the time we reached the final tunnel. I had lost all feeling in my toes, and my fingers felt as if they were swaddled in new-shorn wool. My teeth were chattering so loudly I thought all the Primate's Guards could hear me—wherever they were, far above me, far behind.

I searched for the glow of light overhead, resisting the urge to open my mouth, to breathe in water. I fought to pull myself along the stone trough, just a little farther, just a little faster.

As my lungs began to ache, my brain shouted a series of warnings. I had somehow missed the square. I must turn around. I must go back to the last crossing, fight against the current, battle for my life. I planted my fingers against the sides of the stone channel, trying to catch myself, trying to stop, but I had too much momentum.

Just as panic started to paint my thoughts red, I made out the faintest glimmer of light ahead. I kicked off the walls one last time. I pulled myself along, trying to ignore the crimson fog that pressed around my eyes. The haze made me dizzy and sick. I needed to open my mouth and breathe.

And then there were strong hands beneath my arms. I heard Goran's voice, reminding me to fill my lungs, slowly, deeply, over and over again. Taggart was freeing Caw, was exclaiming over the golden cage and the midnight-black mouse that huddled inside like a lifeless stone.

A rough blanket settled over my shoulders. Goran's quick hands rubbed my arms through the fabric, scratching me, making the blood flow, warming me enough that my teeth stopped clattering in my jaws.

I looked around, still too dazed to speak. We were in a stone chamber, a single room that was roughly the shape of a square. The stone channel where I had swum cut across the space, heading toward a gap in the far wall. Shadows on the wall to my right hinted at a doorway, at stairs that disappeared into the gloom. The only light came from an air shaft, another gray column like the ones at the crossroads of the waterway.

I thought about climbing to my feet, about checking out the rest of the room. But that would require shifting beneath my blanket. I would need to expose my flesh to the air. I would need to summon strength, energy, determination. And all of that was beyond me.

Instead I whispered, "Caw."

My darkbeast fluttered his wings, offering the barest confirmation that he had survived our watery journey. I collected him from the cold floor and folded him close to my chest, taking comfort in the wordless thoughts he planted deep within my mind.

I was still trying to remember how to put together words into sentences when Nessan came through the passage. The soldier emerged from the water without any aid, scrambling for his own purchase, finding his balance unassisted. He had somehow contrived to travel through the channels on his back, feet-first like the rest of us, but he had clutched Dillon to his chest. The guard had clamped one massive hand over the Princeps's mouth to keep him from swallowing the worst of the water.

"Hurry with the blankets," he said. "We can't be sure our escape was undetected. We have to dry off and reach the seaside cavern before the Guard finds us here."

"But Janna—" Taggart started to say as I finally found the strength to stand. I staggered toward Goran and the blankets.

"Janna is not coming." Nessan's jaw was tight. "She stayed behind, to do her best deflecting the Guard. When they come to the library, she'll try to convince them we never passed that way."

When they came to the library. Not *if.*

I pictured the woman's smooth face, her inky fingers. How could she have the courage to stand against the Primate's Guard? How could she face a dozen men as efficient as Nessan had been when he trussed up Dillon and carried him down the waterway?

"If she is taken, then you must make her sacrifice count," Caw said. *"Hers and Sleek's."*

He was right, of course. If the library clerk was captured, her darkbeast would not last past the next full moon. I shuddered at the thought of Janna taking my place in the dungeons beneath Bestius's godhouse. I had to assume the Inquisitors would be harsher with new prisoners now that we Travelers had escaped, making them all look foolish.

I swallowed hard and said to no one in particular, "What is this place?"

Before he answered, Nessan took a dagger from his belt, the one he had used to strike Dillon. Now he used the blade to cut through the net that still bound the Princeps, swearing as the knife caught on some of the tighter knots. Dropping the ruined net to the floor, he finally said, "An ancient refuge."

"When was it built?" I peered into the gloom, as if I could read a date on the rough walls. A detached part of my mind realized that I must finally be thawing, must finally be recovered from my passage through the waterways, if I could push for such information.

"During the Dark Age," Nessan grunted.

I'd heard of the Dark Age, of course. It was a time when monsters stalked the land, before First Primate Kerwen gained the favor of the Twelve, before the Family Rule had been crafted to keep order. Every once in a while a shepherd found evidence of the Dark Age in the hills above Silver Hollow—pitted iron blades or crusted coins.

"How far do the tunnels go?" I asked.

Nessan barely spared me a glance as he briskly rubbed Dillon's arms and legs. "They can be reached from all the ancient unums in Lutecia."

"Unums?" I asked.

Nessan glared at Taggart, but he did not stop ministering to the Princeps. "Does she ever stop asking questions?"

"Not often," the old Traveler said with the barest hint of a smile. "Enough, Keara," he said to me. "The unums were ancient places of worship. Each is underground, in the heart of today's godhouses. In the Primate's palace."

A unum. Like the room where Paton had stored his saltbite. Like the room where Janna had seen us off, beneath the Primate's library.

So the unums were connected by Lutecia's underground rivers. And the rivers led to this chamber. And this chamber—

"Squeak says the Princeps is awake." Caw's voice cut through my speculation.

I glanced at Dillon. Nessan was still tending to him. The Guard had rolled one blanket, setting it carefully beneath the Princeps's head. He had another tucked tight around Dillon's body while he used a third to scrub at Dillon's calves.

Goran seemed unaware of the change as he asked, "But what good are the waterways, if they only trap us here?"

The Guard's voice was grim as he looked up from his labor. "We aren't trapped. Those stairs over there lead to the open sea."

"The open sea!" Goran's voice ratcheted up in disbelief. "We nearly froze in the tunnels. We'll die in the sea!"

Nessan snorted. "Trust the Darkers, boy." He shifted to get better access to Dillon's arms. "There's a cove cut back in the cliffs. The Darkers have wood there, and more blankets, and a skiff. It'll be night, and you can build a fire before you skirt the coast."

"'You?'" I asked before Goran could express his outrage at Nessan's dismissive tone. The pronoun made me suspicious. If he wasn't planning on coming with us, what was to keep him from turning in us traitors, all for the glory of the Primate?

"Chirp would not take kindly to our being harmed," Caw remonstrated.

"I'm not even certain that Chirp—"

Exists. I was going to say *exists*. I was going to say that perhaps I had imagined the cricket, hallucinated the insect darkbeast in the panic of our rush to be free from Vala and Paton and the Primate's court.

But I never got the chance to finish the thought.

All at once Dillon exploded in a flurry of blankets and shouted rage. He grappled for Nessan's dagger, gripping the weighted blade even as he fumbled for the torn net. Shouting, furious, he flung the seine around the Guard's arms, doing his best to tangle his enemy.

Nessan reacted as a trained warrior. His hands flashed into a hidden pouch at his waist, emerging with a pair of shining iron stars that sliced through the netting without an instant's hesitation. At the same time, he allowed himself to fall backward, kicking out with one booted foot toward Dillon's hand.

But he stopped himself in the middle of the movement. With an audible *oomph*, he landed short, managing not to break his charge's wrist. In fact he lay on the stone floor as Dillon scrambled behind him, as the Princeps leveled the Guard's own blade against his neck.

"Easy, boy," Taggart said, the first of us to recover.

As if in reply, Nessan's darkbeast cricket crept from beneath his cuirass. The insect twitched his antennae forward and back, as if he were trying to ease Dillon's hand.

"There," Caw said. *"Perhaps you will not doubt me again."*

I did not spare any thought for answering my darkbeast. Instead I watched as the Princeps tightened his grip on Nessan's knife. The Guard's eyes were bright as he spread his hands, as he tilted his chin up just a little to give Dillon better access to his throat.

"Come, boy," Taggart said. "Give us the knife."

"Never!" Dillon's voice was raspy. I knew how disoriented I had been when Nessan choked me into submission. How much worse must the Princeps feel, after having been knocked unconscious and dragged through the waterways?

"You don't want to hurt the Guard," Taggart said, in the same voice that he might have used with a wild dog.

"He struck me!" Dillon looked wildly about the chamber. "He brought me here against my will."

"He brought—" Taggart started to explain, but Nessan cut him off.

"I acted to save your life, Your Highness." The Guard's voice rang out as if he were reporting for duty. He stared at Dillon without blinking, almost as if he were not aware of the knife quaking against his flesh. "It would have been a danger to leave you in the library, Your Highness. The Travelers had stirred up too much anger, too much rage."

Dillon shook his head, although the movement turned him a frightening shade of green. His hand shook harder as he adjusted his grip on the blade. "You struck me. You struck the Princeps of Duodecia."

"And I will make an offering to Marius in contrition."

"You laid your hands on me! You bound me in a net!"

"And now I throw myself upon your mercy, Your Highness."

I gaped as the Guard leaned his head back even farther. He

was inviting Dillon to slay him. He was offering up his life, here in this rocky grotto, where none of us would be alive if he had not led our flight from the Primate, from the rest of the Guard.

Dillon's hand shook as if he'd contracted palsy from our journey through the waterway.

"Say something," Caw prompted.

"He'll not listen to me. He'll not do as I say."

"Then quote someone else."

And so I listened to the wisdom of my darkbeast. I thought about the instant I had met Dillon, in his brother's study, in front of the maquettes of Howell. I thought of how the Princeps had lectured me about the sculptor, about how he had crafted his ill-fated argument before the Primate, about all the things he had studied in the library, under Janna's guidance.

Forcing my voice to be firm, I said, "I suppose there's *some* philosopher who has written at length about your right to slay your faithful guard."

Dillon barely glanced at me as he asked, "What do you mean?"

"I know you've read a thousand texts, likely more. Janna could probably find a dozen scrolls back there, directly on point. What would they say?" Purposely, I threw off my blanket and shifted my weight, spreading my feet wide the way Dillon did when he quoted. I clasped my hands behind my back. "A Primate's Guard who acts to save the life of his charge should be punished to the full extent of the law, if any harm should come to that charge despite the Guard's best intentions."

"You're mocking me," Dillon said.

"Oh," I said. "Was that the wrong text? Perhaps another would apply?" I shifted my feet to make it clear that I was quoting from another imagined text. "If your servant shall attempt to rescue you, accuse him of assault and take full vengeance upon his body. And if he offers up his neck to you with no resistance, then recognize true guilt before you have your satisfaction."

"You're twisting what he's done here!" Dillon's voice was shaking now, nearly as much as his hand.

I dared not yield now, when I nearly had the advantage. I shifted one more time and cleared my throat before I quoted from the Family Rule. "Your brother shall be the oak in your forest, offering you the shelter of his leaves to protect you from the summer sun. Yea, even when he is threatened by the foulest of winter storms, know that his strength and his mercy shall protect you, long after he is fallen. Blessed be thy brother."

A sob ripped through Dillon's chest. "Nessan is not my brother!"

No. Dillon had two brothers. One was dead, and the other had challenged him for power in front of their father, in front of the entire court of Duodecia. Perhaps my quotation from the Rule had been misguided. Nevertheless, I had learned much as a Traveler, including the principle rule of public performance: If someone missed a line, continue as if nothing had happened.

I insisted, "Nessan is more than your brother. He swore an oath to protect you. He risked discovery of his deepest secret to guide you here to safety."

"He's a Darker!"

"As am I!" I shouted. Suddenly I was tired of trying to cajole Dillon, of trying to coax him to see the truth. "I don't understand you," I said. "You argued for mercy for me and my fellows in the throne room, before your father. You spoke out in favor of us, even though you knew we had spared our darkbeasts. You thought that we deserved another chance, that we should be free from the grim demands of the Twelve. But what are you now? Primate and Inquisitor all wrapped into one? Have you passed judgment on this loyal soldier? Do you demand his death?"

Dillon gasped as he flung the blade across the chamber. "No!" he cried. "I would spare him!"

Goran scrambled for the knife before it could reach the channel of swift-flowing water. Dillon fell to his knees, filling his lungs with great, noisy breaths. I started to step toward him, to offer him comfort, but Taggart's hand fell on my shoulder.

Nessan climbed to his feet. The soldier laid one heavy hand on the crown of Dillon's head, as if he were a priest offering approval for a sacrifice made upon a godhouse altar. As he stood there, calm and commanding, the Guard nodded once at me, offering up his silent gratitude.

"Very well," Taggart said quietly, breaking the charged silence. "We must move on without any more delay."

With varying degrees of dread, we all turned toward the shadowed staircase.

PART FOUR

Impatience

I celebrated my ninth nameday in the middle of a drought. We'd had no rain since before the Flower Moon, not a drop. Thunder Moon brought my nameday, and we feasted on redfruit bread to celebrate the fact that I was another year older. But the Silver River ran low, exposing rocks that even the oldest villagers had never seen. The Red Moon came, and still no rain.

And then the fires began.

Daric saw the lightning strike when he was tending sheep. He'd led the animals far up the slopes of the hills, hoping to find a few mouthfuls of grass that had not yet baked. He saw the jagged white tree of lightning flash from the rainless clouds, heard the crash of thunder, and then the dance of red and yellow and orange fire crawling across the plain.

The flames ate their way toward the Silver, and there was nothing anyone could do. Mother wrapped her most precious herbs into knapsacks, ready to seize them at a moment's notice. The cooper lashed wood together, making half a dozen rafts to ferry us to the other side of the river. We took turns walking to the high point on the Great Road, looking toward the foothills, watching the smoke grow closer, closer, ever horribly closer.

We had no godhouse for Tempestia, not in tiny Silver Hollow. Nevertheless, people began to make offerings to the goddess of weather. They built up piles of mud on the riverbank, channeling water to flow between them like the chutes of water in Tempestia's distant Lutecia godhouse. They braided stalks of wheat into chains, reminders of the Holy Play that some had seen performed years ago, when the Travelers had last stopped in Silver Hollow. They carved tiny swoop-winged swallows out of wood, baked them out of bread, anything to imitate the sigil of the goddess.

And the offerings worked.

Tempestia showed mercy on us. She sheltered us with her cloak of rain. She washed out the fire just as ash started to fall on the village.

Everyone in Silver Hollow rejoiced. Men broke into casks of cider that had been aging since the previous fall. Women baked honeycakes, well before the Autumn Equinox. Children roamed the streets day and night, playing their slide whistles and trying to imitate the swallows that soared among all the Twelve in the nighttime sky.

Everyone celebrated. Except for Mother.

Instead Mother collected every sack she could find. She dragged Robina and Morva and me out to the charred fields. She told us to look for firecaps, for the rare fungus that only appeared after fire had scorched the earth. The spongy balls could be boiled and preserved in salt, stored for future use as a cure for ague and catarrh. But they blew their spores on the second day after a fire, became as worthless as the ash where they appeared.

It was filthy work, looking for the dirt-black globes. Burnt grass crumbled underfoot. Brambles had hardened into sooty tangles, anxious fingers that snagged hair and clothes alike. Bushes were seared away until only knife-sharp sticks remained, dangerous to anyone who took a tumble.

For an entire day we walked, collecting firecaps, storing them in our sacks.

At last our bags were full. We stumbled home, us girls nearly asleep on our feet. Mother let us nap on the floor of the cottage while she collected firewood, while she toted water from the well. Only when the cauldron was full and boiling did she awaken us.

"Keara-ti," she said. "You're the youngest. You can stay by the fire and boil the firecaps while the three of us retrieve the rest. Remember— one layer at a time, spread across the top of the pot. Count to one hundred, then store them in the salt. You'll be finished by dawn, or an hour after."

I nodded, grateful that I was being spared more time in the fields. Robina and Morva looked exhausted as they collected torches and followed Mother back out to the scorched earth.

Caw waited until they were gone before he rattled the bars of his cage. "I suppose those things could make passable treats if you rolled them in honey instead of in salt."

"They taste disgusting," I said, remembering the one time Mother had dosed me with the stuff. "They work well though."

Caw watched as I dropped a dozen firecaps into the pot. I counted slowly before I scooped them out, using Mother's favorite wooden spoon. "I don't suppose all this labor is making you hungry?" *he suggested.*

I tossed a few dried apple rings into his cage and went back to my work. Measure out the fungus. Count to one hundred. Scoop up the stinking results. Cover them with salt.

I completed three batches, four, five. By then my arms were aching. The back of my throat itched with the stench of the firecaps. I was bored with counting, even when I changed things and went by twos, by fives, by tens.

I eyed the firewood stacked beside the hearth. If I added a few extra sticks to the fire, the flames would burn hotter. I could count to seventy-five instead of one hundred. Save myself one quarter of the time.

"I wouldn't try it," *Caw admonished.* "You were given very clear instructions."

"I'll be careful." I tried to sound as if I were certain of the results.

In any case, I would only test one batch. If it didn't work, I would let the flames die back to their lower level. I would complete the full count.

"Seventy-three, seventy-four, seventy-five." I scooped out the dozen firecaps. They looked exactly the same as the others. They stank in precisely the same way. I added them to the salt.

Another ten batches, and I was only halfway done. My hair was curling in the steam of the pot, and the air in the cottage seemed solid with stench. Surely I could add a few more firecaps to each batch. I could make them two deep, and they would be none the worse for wear.

Caw shifted in his cage, swallowing his words but pinning me with one gimlet eye. "What?" I asked. "I know what I am doing!"

"I am certain that you do."

His tone annoyed me. I decided I would prove myself to him, show him I was every bit the herb woman my mother was. All my proof required was careful calculation, attention to detail. I could build the flames up even higher and drop the boiling time more. I would be finished well before Mother returned with my sisters—and with more firecaps.

"Keara—"

"Caw!" I drowned out his warning with one sharp cry of exasperation. He turned his back on me, staring at the wall, until I was fairly certain he had fallen asleep.

I finished up the firecaps in half the time that Mother had predicted. Pleased with myself, I opened the cottage door to release the stench. I sprinkled the final layer of salt over the fungus. I let the fire die down until it was safe to bank the coals. And then I crawled over to the lavender-scented mattress I shared with Mother, collapsing on top of our thin summer blanket.

I was sound asleep when Mother screamed my name. Confused, I struggled to sit up. "What?" I asked. "What happened?"

Mother grabbed me by the arm and dragged me over to the hearth. She shoved me to my knees beside the clay pot where I had stored the firecaps. "Look!" she cried. "Look what you have done!"

My belly turned at the mess before me. All of the fungus and salt had melted into a sludge—a thick porridge that was black and slimy and smelled a thousand times worse than the original firecaps had done.

"I—I don't know what happened," I stammered.

"I'll tell you," Mother said. "You cooked too many firecaps at once. Over too high a flame. For too short a time."

"She figured it all out in one try," *Caw said, awake now, and watching closely from his cage.* "Admirable woman, your mother."

I shot him a withering glance. "I'm sorry," *I said to Mother.* "I didn't realize—"

"Did I not tell you precisely how to prepare them?"

"But I thought it would be faster—"

"Do you think I make up rules just to entertain myself?"

"Of course not. I only thought—"

"You didn't think at all. You believed you could do whatever you wanted to do. You were impatient, and you've ruined the entire batch of firecaps."

In the silence that followed Mother's condemnation, I could hear the villagers outside singing the Morning Song in final thanks to Tempestia. The cider would be long gone now, and all the honeycakes eaten. The celebration was over, and we had missed it completely—my mother, my sisters, and me.

And we had no firecaps to show for our sacrifice.

Mother sighed and gestured toward the leash that hung from Caw's cage. "Go ahead. Take your impatience to your darkbeast."

"Mother—"

"I don't want to hear more excuses." She nearly tripped over her sack as she headed toward the door. Soon I heard her splashing water at the neighbor's trough.

I stomped across the cottage and slipped the frayed leash over my wrist. "I only thought to cook the firecaps faster," I muttered to Caw. "I wanted to be ready when Mother came back with more."

"Oh, really? It seemed to me that you were tired of counting."

"I thought I would finish and get you fresh honeycakes!"

"Don't add lying to your wrongs. You only wanted to get your task done as quickly as possible."

"It was boring!"

"It was necessary."

I glanced at the slop I'd made, then at the sooty sack that was half-filled with the last of the firecaps, the ones my family had gathered while I cooked and slept. I knelt beside the hearth, fiddling with the banked embers until I had a fire going. It took a long time for the water to boil, long enough for me to find another pottery jar, another canister of salt.

I realized Mother had gone somewhere after washing up at the trough. Most likely she was in the Women's Hall, telling everyone how I had disappointed her. Again.

I sighed and started counting out the first batch of firecaps. "I'm sorry," *I said to Caw.* "No honeycake, and now you have to smell this stink again."

"Ah," *he said.* "The tragic life of a darkbeast."

I dropped the firecaps into the boiling water and counted out loud, slowly, number by painstaking number. "Ninety-eight," *I said as I lifted the wooden spoon.* "Ninety-nine. One hundred."

I scooped out the firecaps and spread them on a fresh bed of salt. Without hesitating, I placed a new layer in the cauldron, beginning another slow count to one hundred.

Caw waited until I had completed a half dozen batches. Then he said, "I take your impatience. Forget it. It is mine."

The darkbeast magic jumped from my fingertips up my arm, all the way through my body. The sensation was as rich as cider, as sweet as honeycakes. All at once, I felt as if I had slept through the entire night, as if I were capable of doing anything, anywhere, anytime.

Caw counted out the next one hundred with me, and the next, and the next, and the next, until all the firecaps were done.

Chapter Eighteen

Nessan collected his knife from Goran. He crossed to the pile of blankets against the far wall and gathered half a dozen in the torn halves of his net, before moving to Taggart and launching an animated whispered conversation.

"Go ahead," Caw said. *"Take another blanket for yourself."*

"I don't need one."

"Fine. Then bring it to Goran."

I turned around to find the Traveler standing alone, at the spot where he had pulled me from the rushing waterway. "He has one," I whispered.

"Then bring him another." Caw's voice was insistent.

"He doesn't need me," I said. Goran had stopped shivering, and

his clothes no longer dripped. He obviously did not need another blanket.

Caw clicked his beak three times in rapid succession. *"Keara-ti, when do I ever make unnecessary demands of you?"*

"When don't you?" I muttered. But I picked up a couple of blankets and brought one to Goran. As he draped one over his shoulders, I wrapped myself in the spare. I refused to acknowledge to my darkbeast how much warmer I felt.

Uncomfortable with Goran's silence, I kicked a stray pebble into the waterway.

"Go on, then," he said. "I can see how impatient you are. Go back to your Princeps."

I was shocked at the bitterness in his tone. "What do you mean? *My* Princeps?"

"He's the one you're worried about. There! You're reaching for that stupid pouch of herbs even now."

I pulled my hand from my tunic as if the saltbite burned me. I had not even realized I was checking for the sealed leather container.

Goran eyed my actions with his lips set in a bitter line. "You carried his precious darkbeast for him, so that he can kill Squeak at the Hunger Moon. You made your arguments to him. Go keep him company now."

"Dillon couldn't carry Squeak on his own. And just now he

was frightened and confused—anyone would be, after that blow to the head. He needed my help to understand that Nessan did not mean him harm. You know I would have helped you if you had needed me. If Wart had."

"Would you?"

"What do you mean?" I was confused by the anger in Goran's voice. Anger, mixed with sorrow and something else it took me a moment to name. Jealousy.

He demanded, "Would you have helped me the way you just helped Dillon?"

"How can you even ask that? Of course I would! We were Travelers together. You stood by me at the cath. You forsook everything you knew to join Caw and me. To save Wart."

He merely stared at the flowing water, as if it contained all the answers to all the questions ever asked in the history of Duodecia.

"Goran-tu," I said. "You and I were chained together in the godhouse. You're the one who pulled me out of the waterway here. I will never forget all that we've survived together. All that you have done for me."

He nodded, swallowing hard.

I fingered the darkbeast bracelet that still circled my wrist, tighter for its recent dowsing. Perhaps I needed to pull it off. Maybe I needed to return it to its rightful owner. My fingers roamed over three of the knots, reluctant. Afraid.

I was spared the need to respond further, though, because Taggart called us over to the stairs. "We must get moving. We have to reach the cove before moonset."

Of course. The moon was just past full. As soon as it went down, we had to be ready for the open water. My skin itched at the delay. Knowing that we were going to leave Lutecia, I wanted to make our escape immediately.

I transferred some of my nervous energy into the long walk down the stairs. At first I thought they would be like the passages inside the godhouse, the steps inside the palace that had led us to the unum. I assumed there would be a single flight, twenty stairs maybe, and then we would reach our destination. Perhaps there would be a carving—the strange twelve-rayed sun around the empty circle. Lines moving away from the square.

But there was none of that.

Instead there were switchbacks, landings where we changed direction, flight after flight after flight. At first I counted them, impatiently ticking my fingers against my thighs. After the twentieth one, though, I lost track.

I could hear everyone breathing around me—Taggart in the front, then Goran. Dillon behind me. Nessan at the very back. We took the steps in unison, as if we were a marching army. My knees started to ache, and then my thighs burned. I tried to remind myself to be grateful that we were climbing down; I was not certain I could have made the trek up all the stairs.

At last there was a lighter patch of black in the darkness before us. When I stopped moving, my legs shook, as if they could no longer hold me. Taggart breathed, "Nessan?"

The Guard grunted as he reached the flat floor around us. There was a scrape of fabric against leather, and then another scratching sound. A light flared up, blue as sapphires, strong enough to show the cave that Nessan had described—deep and narrow, with uneven floor and walls.

Captivated by the eerie glow, I saw that Nessan held a wand in his right hand. The tip of the wood burned an eldritch blue, and the very heart of the flame was orange. I caught a whiff of rotten eggs, nearly overwhelmed by the clean scent of pine. I wondered what other magic the Guards had at their disposal, although at the moment I could not imagine anything I would like more than this steady, instant light that Nessan had kindled without a flint.

Just as I completed that thought, my stomach growled, loud enough to echo in the cavern. All right. I could imagine something better than light. Food. And lots of it.

Caw said, *"My thoughts exactly."*

Nessan nodded, as if he'd heard my darkbeast. Or maybe he'd only heard my empty belly. "There should be supplies in those barrels." He nodded toward the closest walls, and I could make out the stacked containers next to an overturned skiff. Goran and I made short work out of prying them open. The seals on each container burst with a loud crack, proving that the contents had indeed remained safe and dry. Soon we were gnawing on dried beef and hardtack, with handfuls of walnuts and rounds of dried apples to finish the feast. One of the barrels was filled with cider, and another yielded fresh, cold water.

Each of us humans ate as if we'd never had a meal before. I had to consciously remember to set aside bits for Caw, to make sure he had enough of the apples he loved, to offer him thirds and fourths on the hardtack. All of the darkbeasts gorged—even Flick and Wart, who would ordinarily have preferred some form of living food.

After our meal, we had nothing to do but wait. Nessan strode to the front of the cave, looking out over the sheltered cove and the silvered ocean. He took a stance that made it clear he was watching, protecting, guarding us from any challenge that might come by way of the sea.

Taggart took advantage of the break to sit against the wall. The old Traveler worked the muscles of his calves methodically, poking and prodding with gnarled fingers. Flick seemed concerned; he skittered from one of Taggart's shoulders to the other, occasionally darting out his tongue, as if he could read anxiety in the air.

Before long, Goran sat beside his grandfather, taking over the task of massaging those tired limbs. As I watched them, emotion swelled in my throat. I could remember sitting beside Mother when she had spent long days sorting seeds. I had rubbed at her shoulders, trying to ease her weariness.

I wondered what Mother was doing that night. Was she looking at the Snow Moon? Was she wondering about me, about whether I was alive, about whether I would ever return to Silver Hollow?

The pang of loss made me think of Janna, left behind in the Primate's library. Did Dillon miss her, even now? Was he still dwelling on what she thought of him after his failed argument in the throne room?

I dragged myself to my feet and crossed to where the Princeps sat on the steps that led back to the waterway. He was staring at Squeak, letting the jet-black mouse scrabble from one hand to the other, over and over again.

"I'm glad he made it through without harm," I said.

"I thank you for saving him." Dillon answered immediately, but his words sounded stiff, distant.

"Caw helped. I was able to think warnings to him, and he passed them on to Squeak."

Dillon nodded gravely. I realized he might not have known that darkbeasts could speak among themselves. I had not learned that until after I spared Caw. The Princeps said, "If Squeak had died in the passage, I'm not sure what I would have done. With the full moon last night, there would not have been time to bond to a substitute creature. I would have needed to postpone my nameday ceremony."

His nameday ceremony.

Of course, Dillon still intended to execute Squeak. The Princeps had not learned anything from watching us Lost, from living with us, from arguing for us to fall under his authority. My belly tightened, and I wished I had not eaten my third helping of walnuts.

"You could not have expected otherwise, Keara-ti," Caw said.

"I could. I did. After he has seen what you mean to me, what all our darkbeasts mean to us . . ."

"He has been raised to duty. He is a boy who chose to yield to his father's command rather than completing the studies he loves. You could not expect a Princeps to walk away from all he believes to be right."

"Believes to be right," I repeated, emphasizing the first word with bitterness. I started to reach out to pet Squeak's head, but I stayed my hand. People weren't supposed to touch others' darkbeasts. We weren't supposed to care.

"It's time," Nessan called, striding back from his post at the entrance to the cave. "Gather near."

For a moment I thought Dillon would not join us. The

Princeps moved, though, slowly and stiffly. I wondered how much his head ached from where Nessan had struck him with the knife.

The Guard nodded when we had all drawn close. "All right. The moon is nearly set. When she goes beneath the horizon altogether, we'll carry the boat down to the beach. Keara, you bring the oars. There are two, along with a pole."

"Why a pole?" Goran asked, before I could.

"You're going to travel up the Limus River. It was silted in long ago. The water still flows, but it's shallow in places, and you'll need the pole instead of oars."

"Where are we going?" I asked.

Nessan glanced quickly at Taggart. The old Traveler nodded. There was no reason to keep secrets from one another. The Guard lowered his voice almost to a whisper and said, "Portus."

"Portus?" I repeated. I glanced at Goran, to see if the name meant anything to him, but he only looked as confused as I felt. I turned my attention to Dillon.

The Princeps stiffened under my gaze, but he obliged me by reciting. "Portus. The abandoned port of Lutecia. It stands twenty leagues from the current city. Following an earthquake during the ninth year of the reign of Primate Nevan, the Limus changed its flow and Portus was abandoned entirely. Primate Egan oversaw the stripping of marble from all the public buildings and the deconsecration of the godhouses. No one has lived in Portus for more than two hundred years."

I looked back at Nessan and Taggart. "No one? Then why are we heading there?"

Taggart's eyes narrowed. "The Princeps has memorized well. But that does not make his words true."

"Janna had me memorize all of Sinclair's *History of Shipping in Duodecia!*"

Taggart merely raised one eyebrow, in that infuriating way he had mastered.

"Janna misled me?" Dillon asked, his voice tinged with disbelief. He still had not adjusted to the fact that Janna was a Darker, that she had interests beyond her library shelves.

Nessan cleared his throat, obviously trying to distract us from the Princeps's discomfort. The strategy worked, but only after the Guard added, "Come. It is time for you to divide my weapons."

"What?" We were so shocked that only Goran could speak.

Rather than respond with words, Nessan began to move. In the shadows of fading moonlight, his face lit by the strange blue fire he had kindled, he set his tools upon the cavern floor.

The knife that we had already seen used. The two portions of tangled net. The pair of sharpened disks. One arm-length torch, twin to the one he had left with Janna. A handful of the sticks that burned blue. A needle-thin stiletto that he slipped from a boot. A half dozen blades intended to be thrown, produced from somewhere near the small of his back. A garrote, woven into his hair. A chain of iron links, wrapped three times around his waist. A handful of caltrops, their iron teeth glinting on the stone, waiting to stab an unsuspecting foot. Four sticks as long as his forearm and sharpened on either end.

"Go ahead," he said. "I'm keeping my sword."

I gulped. I'd nearly forgotten that weapon. It seemed superfluous in light of all the others lying on the floor.

Taggart's voice was grim. "There's nothing that will change your mind? I won't be much good defending these children, if we're hunted by the Guard."

Nessan only shook his head. "You won't be followed. I'll set a false trail, heading east."

My insides trembled. I'd known the man for less than a day, and already I had come to depend on him to protect me. I whirled on Dillon. "Say something to him!"

The Princeps responded immediately. "Take me with you."

Nessan looked pained. "I cannot do that, Your Highness."

"You must. You are sworn to obey me."

The Guard's throat worked, and for a moment I did not think he would speak aloud. "I am sworn to you, my lord," he said at last. "And to your father. But before that I was sworn to my darkbeast. And through him, to the Darkers."

"Free me!" Dillon shouted. "I swear I will not betray you!"

Nessan merely shook his head, sorrow glinting deep within his eyes. "I made my choice when I stole you from the library, my lord. You became a danger to the Darkers the instant you learned of the waterway. And now that I've told you of Portus . . . Forgive me, Your Highness. There is no other way. You must travel with the Darkers."

"So they can use me as a hostage?" Dillon's accusation was hot.

"So they can remain safe. And free. The humans, and their darkbeasts, too."

For once the Princeps had no argument, no memorized words that sprang to his aid. He shifted his weight, and I thought he might force Nessan to manhandle him, to deliver another blow or wrap him in the nets once more. He must have realized, though, how such a struggle would inevitably proceed. At last he swallowed hard and crossed his arms over his chest. The gesture looked like surrender.

Nessan took it as such. "Thank you, Your Highness. Now please hand me Squeak's cage."

"What?" Dillon became outraged all over again.

"Your darkbeast's cage, my lord. Everyone saw it in your father's throne room. I will take it with me, leave it on the trail I build. No one will look toward Portus after they find solid evidence of your heading west." The soldier extended his hand, waiting patiently.

Dillon fought another silent battle. He had to know that Nessan could take the cage by force if necessary. With slow gestures the Princeps held out the cage and said, "You have broken your vows to the Guard, Nessan."

The soldier looked grim. "My oath was to keep you safe, my lord. And while you do not believe me now, your safety remains most important to me. I work today to bring you a long and healthy life."

Dillon snorted. Nessan merely stared straight ahead, a tiny muscle working in his jaw. Goran and Taggart watched, apparently at a loss for words.

Caw broke the spell, saying to me, *"You should take a couple of the throwing knives. A bit of netting might be useful, and maybe the chain. And take two of the fire sticks. They're a lovely shade of blue."*

I thought a wordless objection. I was not ready to leave Nessan, not yet. I was even less prepared to force Dillon against his will.

"This decision is not about you," Caw chided. *"Help Nessan by respecting his choice. Let him lead our pursuers astray. All will be well with the Princeps."*

Caw had no way of knowing that. He could not foretell the future. Nevertheless, I sighed and collected my booty from the cavern floor.

By that time, the moon had set. At the Guard's instruction, we hurriedly carried the boat and oars and pole to the water. I went back for the blankets, and then we all worked to bring the barrels of food and water.

All of us but Dillon. He stood in the mouth of the cave, no longer objecting, but refusing to help.

That changed once we were in the actual boat. Despite Goran's grumbling, Dillon was appointed to row first. I understood that Taggart intended to keep an eye on the Princeps, to exhaust him through hard labor. To that end, the Traveler sat in the aft, steadying the pole that we could not yet use. He tasked me to sit in the very front, keeping an eye out for rocks and other dangers.

Nessan pushed us out from the shore, ignoring the freezing water that quickly soaked his breeches. I bit back a cry as we broke free into the waves, as salty spray hit my face.

Nessan stood in the shallows, his shoulders thrown back as if he were a statue. It was too dark to see if Chirp crept free from his armor, but I knew the cricket was there. Nessan's hand closed into a fist, and then he extended his arm, straight and proud, toward the horizon.

Dillon bent low over the oars. He could not have responded to the salute if he had wanted to.

"Oh, grand," Caw said ironically, as a choppy wave broke over the bow. *"More water. Precisely what I was hoping for tonight."*

Never had my darkbeast echoed my thoughts more exactly. I turned my back to the shore and leaned out over the bow, searching for rocks that could end our journey before it had begun. I could not be certain if the water on my face was salt spray or tears.

Chapter Nineteen

By mid-morning we found the muddy mouth of the Limus River. At first I was pleased to escape the waves, the crash of salt water against my face, the unchanging up and down of the boat on the water. Then I realized that we had our hardest work ahead of us.

The river had not been destroyed by the earthquake so many centuries before. But it had been silted in, layer upon layer of muck accumulating until the flow of water was almost choked off. In places our boat scraped against the riverbed. In others the water resembled the mud that plastered over the shepherds' huts, back home in Silver Hollow.

Taggart was the first to use the pole. He pushed off against the mucky river bottom as Dillon tried to work the oars. The earth-choked river fought us, resisting our every effort to move up the sluggish stream.

In short order we changed our tactics. Goran and Dillon coordinated pulling on the oars while Taggart poled. We took breaks often, changing position. First I took over one of the oars, then the pole, then back to the other oar before I rested.

We could have used Nessan's strength. More than once I wondered how our passage would have been different if the soldier had traveled with us. He would have doubled our speed up the river, at the very least.

Nevertheless, his absence likely meant that we were spared pursuit from the Primate's Guard. I tried not to think what it would mean if he fell into conflict with his fellow soldiers. Not when Nessan was armed solely with his sword. Not when he had Chirp hidden beneath his armor. I tried not to worry, but a part of me suspected that I should be charring mardock roots, that I should be lining my eyes with the dark circles that symbolized mourning.

During my breaks from laboring on the boat, I fingered the throwing blades I had taken from Nessan's stash of weapons. I longed to practice with them, but I did not have the chance.

Two days, three days, four. The scenery on the riverbank remained the same—dry winter grass, crumbling muddy embankments. It was hard to believe that we were making any progress at all.

Each night we tied up to a dead tree. We ate from the Darkers' barrels, chasing the dry food with cider and water. We slept fitfully on the soggy ground.

I thought that Dillon might try to run, especially when we were still close to Lutecia. But Taggart apparently believed otherwise. He did not try to restrain the Princeps in any way. Instead he gave Dillon space, letting the boy maintain his sullen silence.

More than once I caught the Princeps looking eastward, as if he could make out the path Nessan had taken. Often Dillon bent his head low over Squeak, whispering secrets to his darkbeast.

As the sun rose on our fifth day, I took advantage of my turn to rest, distributing the last of our hardtack and dried beef. "Wasn't Portus the chief harbor of Lutecia?" I grumbled. "How can it be so far upstream?"

"*Patience, Keara-ti. It's not far, as the raven flies.*" Caw sounded inordinately pleased with himself as he settled on my shoulder. "*Are you going to eat that apple?*"

I handed him half my portion of dried fruit. "How much farther then?"

"*Another three loops of the river. Large ones though.*"

"We might as well get out and carry the boat on our backs." I squinted at the coppery water, eager to be done with this part of our journey.

"*Or take advantage of the time to figure out a strategy for what lies ahead.*"

"Strategy? Why do we need a strategy?"

"Just because you're arriving at a hidden enclave, with darkbeasts and a reluctant Princeps and half of Lutecia in pursuit?"

"They're not really in pursuit, are they?"

"Not that I've seen," he conceded. *"Not up the river, at any rate. But who's to say they're not traveling across land? One poor darkbeast can only explore so far. I get tired, you know. And hungry."*

He bobbed his head, and I gave him my last bite of hardtack. My belly had tightened at his warning, in any case. I was too nervous to eat.

The sun climbed higher in the sky, and we negotiated one great loop in the river with me working the oars with Goran. I took over the poling position as we completed the second loop. Then I moved to the other oar, doing my best to match my stroke to Taggart's.

His reach was longer than mine, although his motion was slower. I needed to lean into the labor, using all the muscles in my back. I lowered my head so that I could extend my arms a trifle more.

Therefore I was taken completely by surprise when a voice called out from the shore, "Hail and well met!"

I jerked upright, fighting the panic that threatened to close my throat. Caw settled on my shoulder, a little too close to my ear for comfort. I offered him my wrist as an alternative perch, but he merely rustled his feathers. He clearly wanted the higher vantage point.

A man stood on the riverbank, shielding his eyes from the sun so that he could better see us. He looked perfectly ordinary—medium height, medium weight, medium complexion. He had brown hair, and I was willing to bet that his eyes were brown as well. If I had passed him in the streets of Lutecia, I would not have looked twice—not at him, and not at the boy and girl who flanked him.

The children were younger than any of us in the boat, probably around eight or nine. Out of habit, I looked for their darkbeasts, but I found none. That wasn't surprising—most children left their companions in cages unless they were actually in the process of offering up failings.

"Are these the Darkers?" I asked Caw.

"I can't tell. If they are, their darkbeasts aren't close by."

I fingered my bracelet of ferret fur, as if it might help me to divine whether the people on shore were friends or enemies.

Taggart leaned heavily on the pole as he spoke to the man. "Well met indeed. How much farther to Portus?"

The man laughed. "You're here," he said. "Such as it is." He waved us closer, and a rotting wooden dock became apparent, just beyond a stand of sere grass. "Not many come to see us these days."

There was a question embedded in the statement, but no aggression. Taggart merely shrugged and said, "A friend suggested I travel this way. Said there were interesting things to be found in the ruins of the city."

The man shrugged. "Don't know that I'd say there's anything interesting. Unless you have a liking for broken roof tiles and cracked mosaics."

Taggart nodded. "That's what my friend said. A chance to study the old ways. From before the river changed."

The statement was cast off, a few meaningless words, drivel that might have been expected from some sort of traveling scholar. If the man on shore was what he seemed—a common peasant working a patch of earth out of sight of the Inquisitors and Lutecia and the great roads that crisscrossed the primacy— then he could hardly be expected to react to Taggart's explanation.

But I thought I saw something as the man listened. I sensed a glint of understanding, a tensing of his tanned hands. It was gone before I could put a label to it, but he had definitely reacted to the phrase "old ways."

The man's voice was easy as he said, "We haven't much, but you're welcome to share in what we have. Cast your rope here, and we'll secure your boat."

"Blessings of Pondera," Taggart said, invoking the goddess of hospitality as he threw a line ashore. The man caught it easily, clearly familiar with his task as he wrapped the rope around a faded wooden post.

Taggart climbed up first, as befit a man of his age. Standing on the dock, he stretched his back, taking the time to roll his neck slowly, to work out the kinks that came with spending nearly a week in a too-small boat.

I caught a flash of annoyance on the Princeps's face—he clearly expected to have been given priority, as befitting his station. After scrambling to the dock, he held himself stiffly, his arms straight at his sides.

Squeak darted up Dillon's arm, as if the mouse wanted a clearer view of our new surroundings. Dillon frowned, and moved to shove the darkbeast in his pocket, but the mouse chittered and climbed to the top of the Princeps's head. Dillon must have thought some sharp rebuke, though, for Squeak descended quickly. Still, the animal stayed in full view on Dillon's shoulder.

"Young sir," the man said in greeting. Dillon merely inclined his head. He might have been welcoming a visiting ambassador to the palace.

Before Dillon could say or do anything to betray us, Goran clambered out of the boat. I noticed that he had hidden Wart. In fact Taggart's Flick was tucked away as well. There was no reason to disclose our darkbeasts until we knew if we were among friends.

Of course Caw was nowhere near as easy to conceal.

Apparently sensing my unease, Caw took flight with a throaty cry as I scrambled up to the wooden dock. At least the man on shore seemed to notice nothing amiss. Instead he bobbed his head toward me and said, "Greetings, young one."

No title for me. Not that I expected one. And I should be grateful that I could still pass for eleven, that no one suspected I had already celebrated my twelfth nameday. No one could be certain Caw was supposed to be dead.

The man raised his fingers to his lips, stretching his mouth in some odd way before he made a piercing whistle. One short blast, two long, one short. When he was through, he nodded to the children who hid behind his legs. "Go ahead, then. The others will meet us at the green." The boy and girl took flight, too shy to respond with words.

I was surprised that my legs were so unsteady on the wooden dock. My knees did not want to work, and it took conscious thought to move forward without stumbling. "Ah," the man said. "You've been on the river for some time."

"This is our fifth day," Taggart said.

"You came from Lutecia?"

"Close enough." The Traveler made it sound as if we'd set out on a pleasure excursion, a casual journey up a choked river, for no reason other than to admire the wildlife.

The Portus man was no fool, though. His eyes darted to our

boat, to the breached and empty barrels. We had no clothes other than our salt-stained black garments, no supplies for a legitimate expedition aside from our piles of blankets. Without consciously deciding to do so, I ran my fingers over my darkbeast bracelet and checked to see that my saltbite pouch was still hidden away. They were my only two possessions in all the world, and it suddenly seemed important that both be kept safe.

If the man noticed, he did not comment. Instead he shrugged and said, "No reason to make you repeat your story. We'll be on the green soon enough, and you can tell us all then."

The "green" wasn't. No grass was planted in the ragged square. Rather, cracked flagstones gave way to dusty weeds. The mortar between the stones had worn away, and my feet slipped as I walked, forcing me to pay attention so that I did not twist an ankle.

The square was surrounded by a low arcade of buildings. In several places their roofs had fallen in, but it was easy to see that the space had once been a thriving market. The remains of a god-house filled the center of the green—the open-walled circle of Nuntia. Alas, the square travertine columns typical of the goddess of messengers were broken off near their bases. Portus was a skeleton of a town.

A wind skirled across the green, and I set my teeth to keep from shivering.

The people of Portus were responding swiftly to our host's

whistle. A man and a woman ducked out from one of the nearby storefronts. Two women came from another. A passel of children ran into the square, chattering, kicking a hide ball between them until they spotted us and the oldest boy scooped up the toy.

So it went, with men, women, and children emerging from the ruins around us. While an occasional child had a jet-black creature on a shoulder or forearm, no other darkbeasts were in evidence. From everything I could see, the folk of Portus were ordinary people. There was nothing that marked them as different. Nothing that indicated they were heretics. Traitors. Lost.

Nessan had told us to journey up the river, and Taggart had agreed, but both men had been wrong. We had failed in our search for the Darkers and found only a colony of ordinary people.

"*Caw?*" I asked, too disappointed to put my real question into words.

"*I don't see more than you do. The children are bound to their darkbeasts in common ways, with mudroyal and ladysilk. I cannot find anyone with the strange tie of Saeran's people.*"

Perhaps that should have brought me comfort. At least we weren't likely to be betrayed the way we had been in Barleytown.

Before I could wonder more about the terrible mistake we appeared to have made by coming to these distant ruins, a woman stepped forward from the small crowd. As with the man from the dock, there was nothing striking about her—she seemed like an absolutely ordinary goodwife, summoned from her cottage on a perfectly ordinary day. Her clothes were made of homespun. Her apron was newer than her dress.

"Greetings," she said, and there was an edge to her voice, a shrillness as if she were accustomed to yelling at small, disobedient children. "Welcome to Portus. My name is Minna, and I have been elected Speaker of the People."

Speaker. I did not know the title, but the intent was plain. Before Minna could say anything further, Dillon stepped forward.

"Greetings Minna Speaker. I am Dillon, son of Hendor, Princeps of Duodecia. These people have kidnapped me from my father's court and forced me here against my will." He swung an accusatory arm in our direction. "They are Darkers, sworn to honor their darkbeasts more than their ruler. To arms, good people! To arms, to free your rightful lord!"

My breath froze in my lungs as every one of the Portus people turned to stare at Taggart, Goran, and me.

Chapter Twenty

As Dillon made his accusation, my heart stopped beating. My lungs stopped breathing. My mind stopped working.

Caw's talons tightened on my shoulder, and Taggart muttered a curse beneath his breath. Goran knelt down and when he came upright again, he held Nessan's long stiletto in his hand.

But the real change around me was in the people of Portus. They moved like ants on a hill, like bees in a hive. They had a purpose, a goal. They knew where they must go, what they must do.

And the thing they needed to do was restrain Dillon.

The Princeps put up a fight. He twisted like a fish on a line, bellowing out protests as if he expected an army to rally to his cause. He fumbled for one of Nessan's throwing knives but never got it clear from the sheath at the small of his back.

The fight was not fair. In moments the people of Portus had cast ropes about the Princeps. They bound his arms to his sides, lashing the bonds a half dozen times around his chest. They tossed him to the ground and tied knots around his ankles. They cast a hood over his head, a rough hempen sack that must have been dusty, given the number of times Dillon sneezed.

I was breathing hard enough that my fingertips began to tingle. Even in my dazed state, I recognized a familiar sensation. As Caw shifted his balance, I realized that it felt like the glowing moment when my darkbeast took my failings, when he made me be a better person.

I gaped at the people of Portus, and I saw that every person—man, woman, and child—now displayed a darkbeast. Birds and reptiles, mammals, amphibians, and insects, each animal gathered close to its partner. Eyes glinted. Scales gleamed. Teeth sparkled, blinding white against black.

The darkbeasts stood out even more because they were displayed against the dusty clothes of common folk. These Darkers were ordinary people. Ordinary people who looked distinctly unwelcoming. Distinctly displeased to have us—or at least Dillon—in their midst.

Minna waited until two of the burliest men had hauled the

Princeps to his feet. Then she proclaimed, "Dillon, son of Hendor, Princeps of Duodecia. Hold your tongue, and we will do nothing more to harm you. Do I have your word?"

Silence.

Minna nodded to Dillon's two captors, and they tightened their massive hands upon his arms. Dillon flinched, but he did not cry out.

"Your word, Princeps?"

"Aye." The word was muffled through his hood, but Minna gave a tight nod. One of the men stripped off the hemp sack.

"Very well," Minna said, and then she turned to Taggart. "What names do the rest of you claim?"

"I am Taggart Traveler," the old man said. He twisted his wrist, displaying Flick in all the lizard's glory. Rather than introduce the animal, though, he inclined his head toward Goran and me. "This is my grandson, Goran. And a child of my heart, Keara."

I flashed a quick look to Taggart. He'd never given me a hint of the esteem he now proclaimed to these strangers.

The Speaker nodded tightly. "Taggart," she said, as if she were memorizing his name. She nodded toward Flick, then to Wart, who suddenly crouched on Goran's open palm. "Goran. Keara." I shivered as the Speaker's gaze met mine. Those eyes were nothing, though, compared to the appraisal of her darkbeast, a stoat that draped around her neck like a stole. That creature jerked to attention, obsidian gaze hard and unblinking.

"She is jealous," Caw said.

"Of what?" I could not think of a single thing I had that anyone else might want.

"Of Minna's safety. Of the Speaker's well-being."

"We represent no threat to that! Tell her! Explain."

"I don't think the stoat will listen to a common raven like me."

"Now is not the time for humility!"

"I always find it wise to be humble when I might become someone's dinner."

I swallowed hard. It was unlikely a stoat would capture a raven. But I understood the warning behind Caw's words. I should be humble, at least until the Portus settlers decided on what to do with me. I barely resisted the urge to run my fingers over my darkbeast bracelet. I ached for that release of tension, for the sensation that all would be right in my world.

But there was no release to be found, not there in the central square of Portus with dozens of people staring at me. Minna spoke: "Very well. Taggart. Goran. Keara. And Dillon, son of Hendor, Princeps of Duodecia." Dillon stiffened at the sly mockery of his title, but he held his tongue. "We Darkers must speak. We must decide how to handle so many newcomers in our midst. Trevan? Kendrick? Will you escort our guests to the safehold?"

Safehold. Not darkhold, as Saeran had called her underground warren of caves. I tried to take comfort in the difference of names.

The two broad-shouldered men made short work of guiding us across the square. For Dillon, they each took an arm, holding him steady as he hobbled with rope-shortened steps. We were marched past a half dozen doorways, abandoned shop entrances. The first two had gaping doors at the back, obvious routes of escape for anyone intent on fleeing. The next few rooms had solid enough walls, but the ceilings had caved in, leaving the spaces open to the elements.

When we reached a satisfactory chamber, the men pushed us all inside. Quickly enough, we were searched, and all of Nessan's weapons were taken from us. The Darkers missed my pouch of saltbite, though. The leather must have been too soft; they could not feel it through my clothes. I took silent pleasure in their failure.

After the search, the guards stripped off Dillon's ropes, apparently trusting their ability to keep the Princeps from running. Our captors took up positions outside the door—one looking out toward the square, and the other facing inward, toward the four of us.

I stared at the ground, waiting to hear what Taggart would say. The floor was built out of tiny black and white tiles that glinted in the light streaming through the doorway. I could make out a ship and a dozen clay jars, like those used to store oil. This shop must have sold stowage on the boats that once used Portus as a harbor.

"What do we do now?" Goran whispered.

Taggart shrugged. "We wait."

And so we did.

We waited for the entire afternoon, as the sun coursed across the sky. We waited while two women brought us supper—bowls of good fish stew, thick with doughy dumplings. We waited while two men relieved Trevan and Kendrick, taking up their own efficient, dispassionate guard posts. We waited as our captors parceled out a stack of blankets, making it clear that we would have no fire against the night's winter chill.

A dozen times I started to say something to Dillon. But I held my tongue, confused. I could not understand him, not truly. I could not understand how he could give me his brother's saltbite with one hand, and try to betray us with the other. I did not know if he was my friend or my bitter enemy.

Every time I opened my mouth to speak, the Princeps leveled grim eyes on me. My words froze in my throat like pebbles. I blinked back tears and turned away. Sometime during the night, I slept.

As our second day in Portus bloomed full, Trevan and Kendrick returned. Wordlessly they once again took up their stations.

I grew impatient with the delay, pacing our prison cell,

measuring it foot by balanced foot. I tested the back wall, eager to find loose bricks. I rehearsed the steps I would take to the door, to Trevan, to Kendrick, if I decided to fight for my freedom.

"Nothing to be gained by dancing that dance," Caw advised.

"Nothing to be gained by sitting here," I retorted.

"Ah, now that you do not know."

"What? What possible advantage could there be in sitting another day, another night? However long they make us wait?"

"Such an impatient girl," Caw said. *"I clearly failed as your dark-beast if you cannot tolerate a little harmless waiting."*

I bristled at the reprimand, but I did not get a chance to respond. Instead I saw a shadow drift across the door. I took three full steps forward before one of the guards held up an impassive hand.

Minna stepped into the shop. "Taggart Traveler. You may come with me."

The old man had been sitting against the wall in a patch of sunlight, soaking up what passed for heat. He climbed to his feet slowly, taking his time to straighten his salt-stiffened clothes. As he walked to the door, he drifted a hand over Goran's head, over mine. He turned his gaze on Dillon, and then he said to all of us, "Be strong, children."

I could hardly swallow as he followed Minna out the door. He did not look back.

I stared out the doorway, not quite able to believe that [...] had been taken from us. Taggart, who had guided every ste[p of the] way. Taggart, who had made the mistake of taking us to [the] false darkhold, but who had stood fast when we were captur[ed.] [Tag-]gart, who had been weakened in Bestius's godhouse, but ha[d done] all he could to ease my plight and Goran's, too. Taggart, w[ho had] been forced to watch as Vala and the Travelers made a mo[ckery of] everything the performer had ever valued, but who had bee[n able] to escape in the end. Taggart, who had led us to this new g[roup of] Darkers, who had poled the skiff with grim determinatio[n even] when we were all tired and hungry and cold beyond measur[e.]

Dillon continued to stare straight ahead as if nothi[ng had] changed.

But Goran now crouched against the wall, in the sun [light] his grandfather had left behind. Goran's head was bent [over his] fists, and I realized he was whispering to Wart. I could [not tell] if he was promising or begging, if he was struggling for [hope or] yielding to despair.

I knelt beside him.

"All will be well," I whispered.

"You have no way of knowing that." His skin was pulle[d tight] over the bones of his skull, as if he were starving. His ey[es were] wide, and in the dark interior of the abandoned shop, they [seemed] to be nothing but black.

"You must have faith, Goran-tu." I set my hand on his shoulder. "As long as we remain together, you can have faith."

And those words comforted both of us as night fell. We ate more food, which I could not remember a moment after I had swallowed. We lay down beneath our blankets. But I barely slept for the entire night.

Minna appeared the following morning, as Trevan and Kendrick returned to guard us. "Where is Taggart?" Goran shouted.

The Speaker only said, "Goran Traveler. You may come with me."

My friend swallowed hard. "I'll go nowhere without Keara," he said, curling his fingers into fists.

"You'll come, or I'll have Kendrick carry you."

"Go," I whispered.

I tried to take comfort in the way Goran kept his eyes on me the entire time he crossed the shop. He turned back as he ducked through the doorway. He craned his neck to look over his shoulder as he stepped out of view.

It was my turn to lean against the wall where Taggart once had rested. I placed Caw in my lap and smoothed his feathers, over and over, until he grew unhappy with the attention and flew to sit on the window ledge.

"Leave it be," Dillon said, as the afternoon sun slanted through the doorway. His voice was gravel after so many hours of silence.

"What?"

He nodded at my wrist. "The bracelet. Counting the knots won't bring Goran back."

I had not realized I'd been fiddling with the darkbeast bracelet. Just to prove that Dillon did not control me, I touched each knot three more times. But then I forced my fingers to be still. Dillon was right. I wasn't helping Goran. And now that I was aware of my action, I wasn't even soothing myself.

In the middle of the night, Dillon whispered, "Keara." When I did not respond, he repeated my name more urgently, and then he said, "Keara-ti!"

It was the first time he had ever used the endearment with my name. I was so shocked that I sat upright. Even in the faint moonlight, I could see that he was staring directly at me. "What?" I asked, embarrassed by the intensity of his gaze.

"I did not mean for this to happen," he said. The words were barely louder than a whisper, but they were charged with intensity. "You must believe me."

"No," I said. "I don't. I don't have to believe anything you say."

Hurt cut across his features, as if I'd still possessed Nessan's sharpest blade and used it to exact revenge on the Princeps. His voice was very small when he said, "When have I lied to you, Keara-ti?"

Lied to me? Perhaps never, not precisely. But his role as Princeps was directly opposed to mine as a Darker.

Unbidden, my thoughts went to the leather pouch Dillon had given me back in the godhouse. He *had* risked a great deal for me, for all of us. He had reached out when we were prisoners. He had challenged the entire order he had ever known—stood against his father, his brother.

And in repayment, I had been party to his kidnapping. I had stood by as Nessan bashed him over the head, as Dillon was man-handled through the waterways, forced into a boat and up the river to this dilapidated settlement.

"It wasn't supposed to be this way," I whispered. "I wish you had come with us willingly. By now you should understand what we did, and why."

As if to underscore my words, Squeak peeked his head out from Dillon's sleeve. The mouse's nose twitched so violently that he seemed to be speaking to me, trying to convey an entire conversation through pantomime.

Dillon sighed. "I've been raised for one duty my entire life."

"That's not true! You were raised to be a scholar! You only became the Princeps last year!"

He shook his head. "It's simpler than that. And far more complicated. I've been raised to do my father's bidding. I've been raised to fill whatever role the Primate designates for me. Scholar. Princeps. If he ordered me to become the Inquisitor Ducis, I would do that as well."

"And if he's wrong? If the thing he orders you to do is wrong?"

"He is the Primate. He makes the laws. By definition, if he orders me to do it, it cannot be wrong."

"He makes the laws, I'll grant you that. But there are things older than the Primate's laws, Dillon. The truths of the Twelve. Ways of believing. Ways of living." I grasped for words, trying to express my argument, impatient with the shortcomings of language. "In the Dark Age, there was no Primate. There was no law. And yet there were things that were right and things that were wrong."

"It's not that simple," Dillon said.

But it was. It had to be. I took the pouch of saltbite from my tunic. Dillon swallowed hard when he saw the herb. "Here," I said. "Take it."

"I gave it to you. It's yours!"

"But you think you were wrong for stealing from the god-house. It must pain you to see the laws of your father broken."

He stared at the pouch, unblinking. I wondered if he was remembering Vala Traveler's revel. If he saw the Villain-Keara stumbling about the stage, if he heard the mocking narration.

He reached out, and my heart clenched at the thought that the saltbite would be lost to me forever. It was more valuable than any of the herbs I had ever gathered with my mother. There was a part of me that had always assumed I would bring it home to her, that I would share my treasure with her.

But Dillon would take it now. He would take it away, because he wanted no part of my life, my darkbeast, my rebellion.

His fingers closed around mine, and he gently folded my hand around the pouch. "It is yours, Keara-ti. Yours to do with as you will, now and forever."

I swallowed hard. Dillon's words were a confession. By admitting he could break at least one of the Primate's laws, he admitted others could be broken. Perhaps he finally understood why I had spared Caw, why I had assumed the status of the Lost. Maybe he knew, and he accepted.

The Princeps met my eyes. "Go to sleep, Keara-ti," he said. "We do not know what tomorrow will bring."

I nodded and waited until he released my hand. I held his gaze as I stowed away the leather bag, and then I said, "You too, Dillon-tu. We must be prepared for anything."

We slept then, bundled in our blankets. Even in my dreams I longed for the comfort of Goran and Taggart, for the familiar company I had kept for so long.

And in the morning, I was not surprised by the sunrise. I was not surprised by the light meal of bread and redfruit jam. I was not surprised by the changing of our guard. And I was not surprised when Minna appeared in the doorway.

But I thought I would never be able to voice a response when the Speaker said, "Keara of Silver Hollow. You may come with me."

Chapter Twenty-One

Caw fluttered on my shoulder as I followed Minna across the square. I heard a scuffle behind me. Dillon shouted my name, and I barely resisted the urge to turn around. Trevan and Kendrick would not let him follow. I was certain of that.

Minna might have been deaf, for all the attention she paid to the commotion behind us. Instead she picked her way across the courtyard with the determination of a woman who knew her destiny. Somehow *her* feet did not slip on the eroded flagstones. *She* was not at risk of turning her ankle at every step. I scrambled to keep up with her, fighting to maintain my dignity.

And dignity was what I needed when we ducked beneath the shattered threshold of a building that had been a godhouse for

Patrius in ages past. I recognized the signs of the father of all the gods—marble columns, a stripped altar that must once have been decorated with silver.

Minna wasted no time crossing the formerly holy space. We found steep stairs at the back, along with an already-burning torch. One level, two levels, three—we descended into the earth below Patrius's godhouse. At last we reached a chamber with a rough floor. Rough, I remembered, like the rooms of the waterway beneath Lutecia.

But this room was different as well. There: a wooden table, with a large jar centered on its surface, a smaller cup beside it. There: Three dozen people, standing, staring, as if I had interrupted the titheman's visit back in Silver Hollow. There: A mosaic design on the wall—a sun with twelve rays set out in black and white tiles.

There: Goran and Taggart standing at the back of the room, their faces drawn.

I managed to take a full breath for the first time since Minna had claimed me. My companions lived. They had not been spirited away by the Darkers, executed for bringing the danger of Dillon into the community. Given their grave expressions, though, I feared that I might not be extended the same mercy.

Minna stepped forward before I could fully absorb that thought. "Greetings, Darkers," she proclaimed.

"Greetings, Speaker." They answered as one, even Goran and Taggart.

"We are met this morning to determine the fate of one who wishes to join our community. Keara of Silver Hollow has passed her twelfth nameday. She stands before you with her darkbeast, Caw. She asks for refuge in our community, for safety against the Inquisitors, the Primate, and all who would do her harm."

The words had the rhythm of a revel. Minna had clearly said them before, many times. The rough edges were worn smooth, the jagged meanings washed clean.

Nevertheless, they were new to me, and every declaration jangled. I felt exposed to the Darkers, vulnerable.

I braced myself to plead my case. I was ready to speak with fine words, to spin out glorious tales of all that I had done, all that I had suffered in my efforts to keep Caw safe from Bestius's priests. I was ready to perform like a Traveler.

"What words would you say to us all, Keara of Silver Hollow, before we cast our votes?"

Votes?

Why would the Darkers *vote*? Certainly Minna had authority over them as their Speaker! Surely I only needed to satisfy one of the Darkers, the one who held my fate in the balance like the Primate's titheman had done so many years in the past.

"Wouldn't that be lovely?" Caw said.

"You knew about this? You knew they each would vote?"

"I had heard . . . rumors." His wry tone made me look toward Goran and Taggart. They, too, must have been subjected to the decision of the crowd. Their darkbeasts must have relayed the information to Caw. Alas, I had no time to chide him for keeping secrets from me.

Caw shifted on my shoulder. *"This isn't like being home in Silver Hollow. You have to do more than please your Mother. More, even, than satisfying your Primate. Each of these people has a say in your future."*

I cleared my throat and tried to remember every Traveler's trick I had ever learned. Stand straight. Rest one hand on the edge of the table to make my presence seem more authoritative. Lower my voice to seem less like a child. Project my words so I could be heard at the back of the room.

And speak with passion.

"People of Portus," I said. The words came out weak, though, scrawny. I cleared my throat and started again. "People of Portus, on my nameday at the Thunder Moon, I did what I knew was right. I saved my darkbeast from slaughter on Bestius's altar. I spared Caw, and I fled the only home I had ever known. Since then, I have joined the Travelers, fled the Inquisitors, and stood before my Primate. Now I hope you will show me the mercy I hoped for in all those places. I hope you will welcome Caw and me into your society."

Taggart stared at me from the back of the chamber. He seemed disappointed in my performance, unswayed by my words. Even Goran appeared to question whether I'd made my case; he refused to meet my eyes.

Minna, though, nodded before she stepped up to the table. "Keara of Silver Hollow has spoken. But she has not told the entire story. She mentioned her bond to her darkbeast, but she overlooked her ties to the Princeps, to the child who stood upon our green and denounced us all."

Angry words flashed onto my tongue before I could measure their importance. "I'm not tied to D—!"

Minna silenced me with a slow, imperious stare.

"I mean..." I faltered before starting again. "I am loyal to Taggart and to Goran, whom you have already welcomed into your midst. I am loyal to my darkbeast, to Caw."

Minna's response rang to the back of the stone chamber. "Did you not speak with Princeps Dillon just last night? Did he not call you Keara-ti, and you call him Dillon-tu? Did you not say that together the two of you must be prepared for anything?"

I wanted to accuse Minna of spying on me—she or her guards had obviously listened in on every word Dillon and I exchanged. I wanted to lie, to tell her that I had never said anything to the Princeps; we had spoken no words at all. I wanted to walk out of the unum, to return to sunlight and fresh air and freedom.

I swallowed hard, though, and lifted my shoulders, making sure that Caw was visible to every Darker in the room. "Aye," I said at last. "I spoke to the Princeps. But that is because he is my friend. Because he was brought here against his will. Because I believe he can love his darkbeast as much as I love Caw."

I glanced at Taggart, at Goran, to see if they were persuaded by my words. If I could not convince my *friends*, what hope could I have of winning over the Darkers? But the chamber was too dim; the Travelers stood too deep in shadow. I did not know if I was actually making my argument or merely sealing my fate.

Minna waited, as if to see whether I had more to say, but I did not trust myself to make any further argument. My words would have to stand for themselves. When I gave the Speaker the most minute of nods, she stepped closer to the table, to its jar and cup.

"What say you, Darkers?" Her voice echoed off the stone. "Will you include Keara of Silver Hollow in our community?"

As the crowd murmured, the Speaker lifted the large jar from the center of the table, turning it upside down to prove that it was empty. After she returned the container to its proper place, she indicated the smaller cup. "Black means this one joins us. White means she is cast out."

Cast out? What did that mean? Was I to be abandoned outside Portus's crumbling walls? Or would the Darkers drive me away, set me on the Primate's road without food or companions? I firmly forbade myself from imagining worse fates, even more dire actions that the Darkers could take to protect themselves, to save their darkbeasts.

Taggart was the first to vote, shouldering his way through the crowd.

Staring directly at me, he plunged his hand into the cup. I heard him rattle the contents for just a moment, and then he selected a square tile. He held it above his head as if he were presenting a treasure for all the world to see.

The stone was the size of his thumbnail, and it was jet black on all sides. Only when Taggart seemed satisfied that everyone had seen his vote did he cast it into the jar at the center of the table.

Goran followed suit, swaggering as he made his way through the crowd. He did not make as much of a show choosing his tile, but he looked directly at me as he cast it. His smile was quick and sweet, and I remembered the boy I had first met on the edge of the Travelers' camp, the one who had once called me a sneak and a thief. Goran had become my friend. He cast his vote to keep me in his life.

After the Travelers had voted, the other Darkers took their turns. All of the men and women approached the table; each chose a tile. The children stayed on the edge of the crowd, staring at me with interest. They were not yet adults in their society; they clearly were not allowed to decide the future of their lives or anyone else's.

"I cannot stand the waiting," I thought to Caw. *"Not having control over what they all decide."*

"I can only imagine how difficult that must be."

Caw's reply made me think back to the Thunder Moon. We had stood in another shadowed room then, one lit only by the glow of a brazier. Caw had resigned himself to a fate he could not control. He had been bound to live—or die—by a vote of one, by *my* decision about whether I would break with all tradition and save my darkbeast.

I had never thought about how long those morning hours must have seemed to him as he waited and wondered, as he heard the snatches of joyous Morning Song tossed about the village.

Now Minna cast the last vote herself. I tried to divine which color she chose, whether she selected a tile that matched the stoat wound about her neck, a tile that would welcome me among her people. She stared at me as she dropped her choice into the jar, her eyes unblinking. I had no way of guessing. No way of telling what she wished for me, for my future.

When she was done, she turned back to the crowd. "Is there any Darker who has not cast a vote?" The question had the ring of tradition, and no one seemed surprised when she was greeted by silence. "Very well, then. We shall tally the results."

With a matter-of-fact gesture, Minna tipped over the jar, spilling its contents upon the table. I had hoped the tiles would all be black. I had feared they would all be white, except for the two that Goran and Taggart had deposited. Instead I saw a jumble that looked like someone had taken the unum's sun mosaic and shattered it into a meaningless mess.

Minna sorted the tiles rapidly, flicking black to one side and white to the other. The piles were roughly the same size; there was no guessing the result merely by looking.

As the Darkers craned their necks for a better view, Minna counted. She worked her way through each pile twice, then nodded before she faced me with the results. "There are nineteen black votes for you to join our ranks. And there are nineteen white votes against."

A tie.

I stared at the Speaker, wondering what would happen now. Her lips were tight, so thin that they nearly disappeared against her face. She narrowed her eyes as well, looking at each of the Darkers in turn. Her gaze lingered long on Taggart and Goran, on those two black votes.

Without the Travelers, I would have been cleanly defeated. Sent forth from Portus. Or worse, kept from ever leaving, so that its secrets were kept safe. Or worst of all, dispatched, laid to rest, *killed* so that I could never threaten the community of Darkers.

"*Careful,*" Caw cautioned. "*Don't step too far down that road.*"

As Minna's gaze lingered on my face, my fingers started to tremble. This felt like the opposite of Caw taking one of my failings. Rather than soaring toward freedom, toward release, I grew more burdened with every beat of my heart. My lungs fought to expand, battled to take even half a breath. My shoulders curved like I was the most ancient and world-weary of grandmothers.

"Very well," Minna said, and her voice was heavier than all the stone that made the unum. "The people have cast their vote. And yet the people cannot decide. Keara of Silver Hollow, you are spared in this round of voting. But you must prove yourself to us Darkers. Show that you are worthy of our community. Worthy of being counted among our number."

"How am I to do that?" In my mind I shouted the question in defiance. In reality, though, my words emerged as the faintest of whispers.

"Watch. And wait. And perhaps you will see a path." Minna's words sounded more like a threat than a promise: "We will vote again in twelve days."

Chapter Twenty-Two

I cornered Taggart that evening, as soon as I was certain we could speak without being overheard. "What is to become of Dillon?" I asked.

"Worry about yourself, Keara," he said gruffly.

"Taggart," I complained, drawing out the second syllable of his name. He had called me a child of his heart. I could not believe he would refuse to answer if I remained standing right before him.

The old man rubbed his hand over his face, stretching the flesh toward his chin as he sighed explosively. "The boy left them with no good options. By denouncing us on the green, he made his position as clear as the crystal goblets he used at his father's court."

"He didn't know what he was saying!" I protested.

"Is that so?" Taggart's eyes pierced through my lies.

"He understood," I conceded. "And he meant to denounce us. But we can convince him that he's wrong. We can make him understand that he should spare Squeak, just as we have spared our own darkbeasts."

Taggart sighed. "He's the Princeps, Keara. The Primate's son. His entire life has been spent serving his father's every command. That won't change now. Now, or ever."

I wanted to protest. I wanted to say that Dillon would set aside his training if they gave him half a chance. He resented being plucked from his studies when Paton was called to serve as Inquisitor Ducis. He despised the way his brother had manipulated him in Bestius's godhouse. But every argument I fashioned came back to the words Dillon had spoken on the green. He had denounced us to the Darkers, and there was no real reason to think he would ever change his mind.

My voice was very small as I asked, "So what will Minna do?"

"Not Minna alone. All the Darkers, acting together. That's the way they do things here." Taggart paused, obviously unwilling to answer my real question. Finally, though, he conceded. "Dillon is a child now, and he is safe from harm. The Darkers will merely keep him prisoner until his nameday. Until the Hunger Moon."

"And then?"

"The nameday rites are sacred, Keara. They'll let him kill that darkbeast mouse."

"They can't! Not when they've sworn to protect their own darkbeasts!"

"Their own, Keara! Not another's." Taggart sighed in obvious frustration. "The Darkers still worship the Twelve. They dare not risk the wrath of all the gods by forbidding a child to enter into the rites. Dillon will have a choice, as we all did. The Darkers will not keep him from sacrificing Squeak."

I swallowed hard. "And after that?"

"After that, Princeps Dillon will be a man."

I heard the words that Taggart didn't say. I heard the threat to Dillon's safety—the Darkers could never be safe as long as the Primate's adult son was as a captive in their midst.

Dillon's life would be forfeit, once he came of age.

And there was nothing I could say, no argument I could make that would change anything. Besides, I had only twelve days to prove that *I* was worthy to join the Darkers on my own. Twelve days to show that the community could trust me. Twelve days to make each individual Darker *want* to be my friend. I had twelve days to prove that I valued the Darkers' society more than I had the companionship of the Princeps, even when we were both imprisoned, when we had both been frightened and afraid for our lives.

If I'd been Goran, my task would have been easy. He had a

way about him, a light, casual friendship that worked equally well with men and women, boys and girls. It didn't matter whether Goran was playing the fool or working hard for the good of the community—everyone watched him and appreciated him, grateful for all he offered.

I set my jaw, determined to catch whatever reflection I could from his good nature.

The next morning, we started working in the root cellars. The Darkers had planted fields outside the stony limits of the abandoned port city. Of course, they had harvested their crops long before we arrived, taking care to get the root vegetables out of the ground before the deep frost came.

Turnips were piled high in one stony chamber, along with onions and leeks. There were smaller mounds of carrots and parsnips, and a single, massive heap of rutabagas. Goran set to work, spreading dirt in an even layer against the wall. He lay down carrots side by side, careful to keep the vegetables from touching. Caw flapped to a perch atop the rutabagas when I knelt beside Goran and started to help.

"Shouldn't they have done this by now? We're halfway to the Hunger Moon." I'd meant my question just for Goran, but a boy who was working nearby overheard me.

"We were too busy setting out provisions for the Route," he said. His tone made it clear that any idiot would have known as much.

"What's the Route?" I asked, sifting another layer of earth on top of the orange and burgundy roots. Mother always preferred the maroon carrots—she said they dated from the days of Recolta herself and had the goddess's blessing of sweetness upon them.

"What's the Route?" a girl repeated, calling my words across the cellar like a taunt. I curled my fingers into fists in the loamy earth, even as Caw shifted on his mountain. I knew that he was moving to draw my attention, to keep me from saying the first angry words that came to mind.

Goran shrugged, reaching for some parsnips to add to the next layer. "Actually, I was wondering the same myself."

The boy sat back on his heels, apparently eager to take a break from our labor. "You know. The Route. The passage Darkers take when they travel to the west."

"*Like* that *means anything*," I thought to Caw. I wasn't an idiot, though. I didn't say the words out loud. Instead I waited for Goran to follow up, knowing he would get the Darkers' full cooperation.

"Where do they go in the west?" Goran obliged.

"You really don't know anything, do you?" The words were harsh, but the boy laughed as he spoke, turning his sneer into a boyish offering of camaraderie, of friendship. "We can't keep too many Darkers here in Portus. We're only a way station, a place for loyal friends to rest and recuperate. If every Darker settled here, the Primate would know before long. Every once in a while, darkbeast kestrels fly over. We can't chance them reporting to their young masters about a large settlement in the ruins."

"And there was that hunting party that rode through last spring," a little girl said. Her eyes were as wide as the rutabaga I buried in dirt. "We all needed to hide then, in the deepest tunnels beneath the ruins."

Goran nodded gravely. "And so, you help new Darkers move on?"

The child straightened her back and nodded solemnly. "Most of them. They go west. To the next way station."

"And where is that?" Goran asked.

"Enough!" said the older girl, the one who had baited me in the first place. "We can trust *him*—he's been voted in as a Darker. But you know not to tell any outsider about the Route. It could cost the life of every Darker we've ever sent that way if *she* learns more."

I wanted to protest. I wanted to say that I could keep any secret Goran could, and more besides. But I knew I needed to make friends with these people. I needed to prove I was trustworthy. And so I swallowed my pride and reached for the next vegetables, laying a long row of parsnips into the earth.

"*Excellent, Keara-ti,*" Caw crooned inside my head. "*Perhaps our years of conversation have finally all paid off.*"

I was cheered by my darkbeast's words of praise, even as I resented the way the older girl moved closer to Goran. She didn't need to lean over him that much, just to settle the next row of turnips. And she *definitely* had no reason to reach in front of him for earth to spread; there was plenty beside her. But I held my tongue and hoped that my silence was breeding allies.

That night at dinner, I was so tired from our hard labor that I nearly fell asleep in my food. That would have been unfortunate— the meal was fish roasted on a bed of turnips and onion and fennel. Each bite seemed to have more flavor because of my work that afternoon. I wondered if I was eating the vegetables I had actually touched earlier in the day.

We ate at several long tables in a vast room. The refectory had likely been a warehouse when Portus had served the Primate's ships. After supper, when people pushed their benches back from the tables, Minna called upon Taggart to tell a story. I sat on the floor with a number of the Darker children, eager to hear whatever tale he would spin. I pulled my knees up to my chin and closed my eyes, the better to be transported by the Traveler's story.

My mind, though, quickly wandered. I thought about Dillon, alone with his guards in the tumbling-down storeroom on the green. Had someone brought him fish for dinner? Had anyone spoken to him—all that day or the day before?

"Don't do it," Caw cautioned.

"What?" I tried to sound surprised.

"*Your friendship with the Princeps is the reason you lost the vote. Do not risk upsetting the Darkers now.*"

"*But he's alone out there.*"

"*Not alone. He has Squeak.*"

A lot of good that would do him. Dillon thought of his dark-beast as a mindless creature, a stupid animal ripe for the slaughter as soon as the moon grew full.

"*Exactly,*" Caw said, even though I had not directed my words at him. "*Perhaps a little solitude will encourage him to seek out his dark-beast's companionship. That can only be for the best, for all involved.*"

I shifted on the floor uneasily. I could not imagine stubborn Dillon changing his attitude just because he got a little lonely.

"*It does not matter what you can imagine. You have no business talking to a prisoner. Not when you must convince the Darkers that you are true and loyal to their cause.*"

I sighed and settled back against the bench. I knew Caw was right, even if I wanted to argue.

"*Reward me for my words of wisdom,*" my darkbeast promptly said. "*A bite of currant bread would be welcome, you know.*"

I rolled my eyes, but I clambered to my feet and crossed to the serving boards. There was a handful of other people around, offering tidbits to their darkbeasts. Caw chortled as I gave him a particularly fruit-laden bite of bread. By the time I returned to my bench, Taggart had finished telling his tale.

I continued to worry about Dillon that night as I slept in the Women's Hall. The dormitory was still novel to me, even though I'd slept there the night before. It wasn't like the wooden structure at home, the massive cottage that housed all the unmarried women in Silver Hollow. In Portus the Women's Hall was just another stone building, another warehouse converted to a new purpose. Mattresses were spread across the stone floor, crackling with dried husks, fragrant with lavender. I wasn't surprised to find that I was assigned the bed farthest from the fire. The old woman to my right snored loudly all night long. I used the sleepless hours to think and to plan, to figure out ways that I could win the confidence of the Darkers. Maybe I could help Dillon after I had helped myself.

For several days I made good progress. I tried to emulate Goran's easy grace with everything I did. I encouraged Caw to reach out to other darkbeasts, to talk to them, to join in their silent conversations.

I showed the Darkers how to weave their onions and garlic together, demonstrating a complicated braid that Mother used to keep the bulbs from spoiling. I heated rosemary by the fire using a single flat stone—another one of Mother's tricks to bring out the fragrant oil in the herb. One of the girls was going to throw out some fronds of butterroot, but I explained how the greens could be boiled into a salve and applied as a defense against cracked skin as long as the winter wind blew cold.

A few days into our labor, we restocked the boat that had carried us from Lutecia. A group of women oversaw the provisioning. We filled two barrels with sweet water from the farthest well in the settlement. We added a keg of venison strips that had been baked beneath the winter sun, desiccated by the constant wind. They were tough, but full of nourishment. Rings of apples filled a massive basket, and bell-shaped slices of pears were laid into a keg, the fruit dried so that it would never rot in the cave beneath the Primate's city. A final cask was filled with walnuts.

Every bite of food was checked once, twice, three times. If there was any touch of mold, even the faintest whiff of rot, the provisions were set aside. They'd be good enough for the colony, but not for storage. Not to rest beneath the Lutecia waterways, ready to nourish the next Darkers who tried to find their way west.

Five days after my failed vote, I stood on the rotting dock that jutted into the Limus River. I watched as Minna herself checked and rechecked the placement of the barrels and baskets and kegs in the boat. I saw her stoat test the knots with his own sharp teeth.

"Very well," the Speaker said at last. Her words were directed to the two brawny men who sat in the skiff, but she spoke them loudly enough for all to hear. "Travel safely to Lutecia. And may all the Twelve watch over you, granting you and your darkbeasts a safe return."

The animals in question—a jet-black pigeon and a rather

large spider—bobbed their heads, clearly understanding the danger they presented to their adult humans on the journey. We all watched as the men cast off the ropes that had bound the boat to the dock. The foursome headed down the silty waterway, making slow progress in the morning light. I stared long after they rounded the first bend in the river.

"How will they get home?" I asked Caw in a quiet voice as we headed back to another day of hard work in Portus.

"*They'll travel by land,*" he answered. "*Their path will be easy enough close to Lutecia. It will only grow hard once they leave behind the Primate's roads.*"

I squelched a pang of guilt. Our little group was responsible for depleting the Darkers' supplies. We were the reason that those two men needed to take such risks.

"*That's the way of the Route,*" Caw said. "*That's the cost of saving Darkers.*"

I renewed my vow to aid the Darkers, to help the colony in any way I could. I was so firm in my resolve that I took the long path back to the kitchens, rather than cutting across the green. I didn't want anyone to see me passing by the storeroom where Dillon was still imprisoned. I didn't want anyone to misunderstand my intentions.

My good behavior lasted nearly another week. Until the day before the Darkers were scheduled to vote again upon my fate.

Chapter Twenty-Three

My problems started in the afternoon.

The morning was filled with an expedition to the copse at the extreme northern end of Portus's ruins. We worked hard to collect all the deadfall wood, loading it onto drays so that we'd have enough fuel to last through the winter.

After a quick lunch in the refectory, we settled down to an afternoon of repairing tools. I was charged with working over a vast net, checking the individual knots to make sure that fish could not tug them loose and escape downstream. The work was mind-numbing. Finger-numbing as well—the hemp fibers cut deep as I pulled them taut.

I was working with two other Darkers, and we needed to

move in unison so that we did not tangle the net. I tied my knots quickly, drawing on my years of helping Mother with fibrous herbs. The other girls, though, worked much more slowly. Three times I needed to wait for them to catch up.

Each pause heated my temper. Matters weren't helped any when Gavina, the older of my companions, sniffed at the line of knots I'd just finished. "I suppose those will do," she said.

"What's wrong with them?"

"Nothing. If you don't care whether the hemp is tied overhand or underhand."

I bristled at her dismissive tone. "What difference does it make?" I asked.

"None. If you don't take pride in the appearance of your work."

I started to tell her that the fish would not care which directions the knots faced. I bit my tongue, though, just before I spat the acid words. My retort would not earn me any friends. And tying the knots underhand would take me only a little longer. In fact it might keep me from working so far ahead of the other two.

I flexed my fingers and dove back into the work, taking care to twist my knots precisely as Gavina and Bryna did. That kept us working in companionable silence for a long while, until the rush lamp was burning low, and my belly was crying out for supper.

I planted my fists in the small of my back, rubbing hard to ease cramped muscles. Bryna scarcely looked up, although the sound of her clicking tongue echoed off the rafters. "You've gone too far there," she said, pointing to the ragged bottom of the net, to the last knots I'd tied. "We need to add stone weights to the last row."

"Someone should have mentioned that before I got there."

"*Someone*," Gavina said pointedly, "should have been a little more patient. We're all working on this together."

I started to tell her that *one* of us was working, and the other two were just sitting in judgment. *"Keara!"* Caw thought, his voice harsh as he roused himself from his perch on a nearby table.

I swallowed my words and squared my shoulders, ripping out the last row of knots that I had so carefully tied underhand. A whistle pierced the air just as I finished—one long tone followed by two short blasts. Dinner was ready, at last.

My companions took their time folding the net. They had to know our food was getting cold. Nevertheless, Bryna turned her head to a critical angle, evaluating our handiwork. Gavina suggested that we stretch it out and fold it up again. I almost groaned at Bryna's enthusiastic agreement, but I helped. And I helped again when Gavina wasn't quite satisfied that the corners lined up perfectly.

By the time we got to the refectory, a tic was jumping in my cheek. Caw sat on my shoulder, his talons gently opening and closing on the fabric of my tunic. I glared at him, but he merely cocked his head toward the serving tables. "*Are those apple scones?*" he asked. "*Make sure to get two.*"

Two for him, he meant. I'd be lucky if I got a bite in edgewise.

We three were the last of all the Darkers to arrive for the meal, and we needed to wait at the end of the long line. I craned my neck, trying to make out the food. There were the usual loaves of bread, the baskets of apples and pears. A round of cheese squatted at the far end of the table.

But one platter sat in the midst of everything—a leg of mutton, glistening with melted fat. My mouth watered—there had been precious little meat in our winter meals, and most of that had been stewed until it carried little flavor.

I could imagine the rich meat in my mouth. My teeth ached to tear into it. My stomach growled again, loudly enough that several of the nearby Darkers laughed.

And still I waited. The line crept forward like bindfloss moving down a riverbank. One person needed to sort through all the apples to find one that was perfectly round. Another rejected half a dozen pears before she found the one that suited her.

While we waited, Gavina and Bryna engaged in an animated discussion about needlework, about the best way to make flowers look lifelike on cloth. I had a few opinions myself—I'd watched Mother create wonders with a needle and thread.

But instead of joining the conversation, I turned to the side. I edged one step closer to the table. Another. I passed Gavina and Bryna, and when they did not seem to notice, I studied the food that remained.

The choicest bits of mutton were long gone. In fact there were only a couple of slices left, rough chunks that had been hacked from the thinnest part of the leg. Fat congealed on the surface. Still, it was meat. It was meat, and I was starving.

I was just reaching toward the mutton when a calloused hand clamped down on my wrist. "Hold, there!" It was Gavina, and her fingers were as cold as the Silver River beneath the Snow Moon. "How did you get up there? You were behind me in line, no?"

Her voice rose with every word, so that she was nearly shouting at the end. All the Darkers looked up from their trenchers, freezing with their own food halfway to their mouths. I felt my cheeks flush as red as the wrinkled apple close at hand.

"Sorry," I choked out. "My mistake."

"Impatient whelp," Gavina said. Somehow she spoke the phrase like a Traveler, managing to make herself heard at the far end of the hall, even though her words seemed to be just a casual muttered curse.

I watched as she speared the last few bites of mutton, sharing them out between her trencher and Bryna's. I collected some bread and fruit and slumped over to the tables.

Of course there was no space to sit where I wanted to, near Goran. And I certainly wasn't going to join Gavina and Bryna.

I pushed my way toward Taggart, toward the bench where he sat with several of the oldest Darkers. He was facing away from me, all of his attention pinned to the story he was telling about some ancient Primate, about the way things used to be in ages past. I put my sorry apple on the table and offered a bite of dry bread to Caw.

"The scones would have been better," he chided.

"Take what you're offered, you miserable beast."

Silence.

I would have thought it impossible for the entire refectory to become so still, and with such speed. Nevertheless, all the hearty chatter died away in a heartbeat, all the lighthearted banter, all the discussion of mutton and cheese and good winter food.

Every eye in the room was pinned on me. On me and on Caw. On the darkbeast I had just maligned in public.

"She spoke in jest!" Caw's voice was loud inside my skull. I knew he was not directing his words to me—he was reaching out to every other darkbeast in the room. He was shouting to every other animal, in hope that they would share the news with their human companions. In hope that someone would laugh, that another person would shrug, that the entire incident would blow away like a tuft of thistledown on a spring day.

Desperate to redeem myself, I made a show of plucking out the soft heart of the bread on my platter. I offered it to Caw on my open palm, inclining my head in invitation. In shame.

He took the treat and bobbed his head gratefully, flapping his wings and thrusting out his chest as if I'd offered him one of the Primate's finest cakes. "*Again,*" he whispered inside my head. "*Flick says to take Taggart's scone and give it to me.*"

Under any other circumstance I might have suspected Caw of telling tales for his own benefit. Of *course* he would say that Flick thought I should take the scone. Of *course* he would bargain for the sweetest treat I could reach.

But one glance at Taggart told me my darkbeast spoke the truth. The old Traveler didn't reveal anything by the curve of his lips or the set of his shoulders. But I was close enough to see his eyes. I was close enough to see his honest fear for me, for my future, if I could not convince the Darkers that I truly honored Caw.

My hand trembled as I reached toward Taggart's scone. I ripped the sweet in two and found the section veined with the most apple. I proffered the treasure to Caw with a flourish, as if I were casting pearls before the Primate's slippered feet.

He downed the rich chunk in one gulp, shivering from the tip of his beak to the point of his tail. When he was finished, he stretched toward the rafters and let loose a gurgling croak that sounded for all the world like laughter.

In fact, Taggart joined in the merriment, adding his own hearty guffaw to Caw's. The Traveler's act was so convincing that half a dozen Darkers joined in. Even the people who did not laugh relaxed enough to go back to their own meals, to their private conversations.

"*Eat, Keara-ti,*" Caw urged. "*They must forget that anything was ever amiss.*"

"*I didn't mean it,*" I said.

"*I know that.*" Caw's understanding washed over me like a soft blanket. "*You were tired and hungry.*"

"*And impatient,*" I said, hating the admission, knowing that I'd made that confession so many times before.

"*That too,*" Caw agreed. "*But mostly disappointed that you didn't get to taste the mutton. At least, this way, one of us is happy. I got my scone.*"

Any other night I would have chided my darkbeast. I would have told him that he had manipulated things for his own advantage. I would have argued that he had no business stealing Taggart's treat.

But that night, in that company, knowing that the vote on my acceptance was scheduled for the following morning, I sat as quietly as I could and hoped that no one else took notice of me, ever again.

I did not sleep that night. Instead I lay on my pallet and thought of all the things I'd done in the past twelve days, all the ways I'd tried to make the Darkers accept me. And the more I thought, the more I feared I had failed.

"*Sleep, Keara-ti,*" Caw said, sometime after Mortana had stridden across the sky.

"I can't," I whispered. "I'm so afraid of what will happen."

"*Whatever happens will happen. Your being gritty eyed and yawning will make no difference.*"

I knew he was right. But I also knew I could not obey my darkbeast. Not this time.

I left my pallet when the first touch of dawn kissed the horizon. It was cold outside; my breath fogged, and I clutched a woolen shawl close around my shoulders. Fleetingly I wondered if Dillon's guards had given him extra blankets for the night. He was a prisoner, of course, so they might not have done so. But he was still the Princeps. His title might count for something.

I walked to the western edge of Portus, to the fragments of crumbling wall that marked the end of the settlement. Stones were strewn across the plain, as if some mighty wind had blown parts of the old city into the grass. There were no paths there; the Primate's roads had long since crumbled in disrepair.

How did the Darkers make their way west? How long was the journey? What awaited them when they arrived at the next stop on the Route?

I longed to know. I longed to be free of these Darkers, from the society I feared I would never be permitted to join.

And yet the very thought of traveling anywhere in the primacy raised gooseflesh on my arms. Sparing Caw had placed a price on my head, a value that had soared the instant that Saeran handed me over to Bestius's priests. In fact, it must have increased a thousand-fold when I fled Lutecia, taking Dillon with me against his will.

I thought that I had feared the Inquisitors before, back in Silver Hollow and on the long road I had traveled with Taggart and his people. I had fretted about their punishment, about their trying to bring me back from the Lost.

Now, though, I feared that the Inquisitors would kill me.

The Inquisitors, the Primate's Guard, and anyone else who sought to keep proper order throughout the primacy. Only the Darkers stood between me and nearly certain death. I needed Minna's people to welcome me into their society, permanently and without reservation.

"*We should be heading back,*" Caw thought from his familiar perch on my shoulder. "*Didn't you hear the whistle? The others are breaking their fast.*"

"I can't eat, Caw." I only spoke the truth. The thought of food turned my stomach.

For once my darkbeast let a meal pass without comment.

Soon enough we heard more whistles—three short blasts, and then a long, drawn-out call, ending on a high note. We were all being summoned to the unum. Caw and I made our way in silence.

This time Goran and Taggart did not lurk at the back of the crowd. Each was surrounded by friends, by colleagues. I sensed the moment when both Travelers noticed my presence; they gave away their awareness by little things—standing a bit straighter, angling their gaze away from where I stood. Both Goran and Taggart were talking to the people around them, telling breezy stories, but I was not deceived.

However indirectly, they were talking about me. They were making one last bid for the vote to go in my favor, for me to be free.

Minna stepped to the front of the crowd. She echoed her stoat's sharp gaze as she surveyed her people. Speaking the same formulas she had used twelve days before, she greeted the Darkers, and they responded in kind. She introduced the matter at hand—me—and she gave me a chance to say a few words before the vote.

I cleared my throat. The last time I had tried to use Travelers' tricks; I had tried to appear stronger and taller and braver than I was. This time I retreated into my true self, into Keara of Silver Hollow.

"I've spent the past twelve days learning your ways. I see the safety you create here, the Route you set. I understand how you protect other Darkers, ones still trapped in Lutecia, others who might come from anywhere."

I looked at the crowd as I spoke, trying to gauge what they thought of me. There, next to Taggart—that woman had a kind face. She and the tall man beside her, they both looked at me with smiles. They would vote for me to join their society.

Goran had found me allies as well. Two boys whom I had last seen burying turnips in the root cellar. A girl who had offered Caw a bite of seedcake just two days past.

But there were other gazes as well, harder ones. Gavina and Bryna, glaring at the edge of the crowd. Minna herself.

All night long I had considered the words that I would speak at this moment. I had considered invoking Taggart and Goran, reminding the Darkers how much they had already come to like my Traveler companions. I had thought about whether I should mention Dillon at all, if I should try once and for all to clarify my relationship to the Princeps.

In the end, though, I knew that I stood alone before the Darkers. They would make their decision about *me*, not about my companions.

I lifted my hand high, raising Caw so that he could be seen by all the Darkers, even the ones in the very last row. "I love my darkbeast," I said. "The finest thing I've done in my life was to rescue him. I want him always to be safe. I want to live here, with you, with all of you who also saved your darkbeasts."

And that was all. Nothing about Dillon. Nothing about the Travelers.

Minna nodded sharply before she turned to the table. She made short work of displaying the empty jar. Taggart took the lead, as he had during my first vote. This time, though, he did not display his black tile. He did not give his action the illusion of any extra power. Rather he acted as if he were making the only choice a reasonable man could make, casting the only vote that was simple and fair. Goran followed, setting his own tile into the jug with grim efficiency.

And then I watched as each of the Darkers came forward, selected their own tiles, cast their own votes. The process seemed to take forever. Minna came last, and then she called for anyone who had been forgotten.

I caught my breath as she emptied the jar. The tiles were mixed, black and white. I closed my eyes as she separated them, but I could hear each marker scrape across the stone of the altar. There was a long silence, and I assumed she was counting up the totals.

"*Caw?*" I thought, when I could not stand the suspense any longer.

My darkbeast did not have a chance to respond, though. Not

before Minna's voice rang out, echoing off the walls of the unum. "The tie remains," she proclaimed. "Nineteen white tiles. Nineteen black."

I opened my eyes to see what that meant, what the Darkers were going to do. Everyone was talking. Taggart was demanding that Minna count again, that she make sure she had not missed any tiles. Goran was checking with his friends, visibly questioning whether they had cast their votes as he intended.

Minna's stoat twitched his whiskers as the Speaker completed her recount. "The tie remains," she said again. "Go forth, Keara of Silver Hollow. Leave this sanctuary and wait aboveground while we Darkers determine your fate."

Chapter Twenty-four

Later I learned the terms of the Darkers' debate. Some people favored letting me enter their ranks; a tie should be resolved in my favor, and in favor of my darkbeast. Others called for another twelve days, another chance for me to prove myself. And some said that I should be cast out of Portus, taken by boat down the clogged river, left close enough to Lutecia that I would meet whatever fate the Twelve chose for me. Six people voted for me to be put to death that day, to protect the Darkers. To preserve the Route.

In the end, the Darkers decided not to decide. They would let me stay in Portus until the Hunger Moon, until Dillon celebrated his nameday and sacrificed Squeak. After that, the Princeps would present an even greater challenge—would the Darkers kill him? Banish him? Send him along the Route, far enough from Lutecia that he could never be a threat?

Whatever the Darkers chose, I suspected my fate would be tied with Dillon's.

The wait until the Hunger Moon spun out. Each individual day was achingly long, filled with the work of any community in winter—repairing tools, mending fences, spinning and weaving and stitching damaged clothes.

The nights stretched even more. I lay on my pallet and stared at the dormitory ceiling, listening to the women snoring around me. Caw kept watch nearby, and I sometimes thought a question in his general direction, just to confirm that I was still alive.

And yet, as long as those days and nights seemed, they tumbled after each other like brambles down a cliff. I blinked, and my twelve-day respite was over. Dillon's nameday had arrived.

The whistles rang out at dawn—one short blast, two long, one short. We were summoned to the green. Minna led the way to the ramshackle storefront where the Princeps had been held prisoner for weeks. As his two guards stepped away, the other Darkers pressed close—they wanted to witness whatever would happen, however the Princeps would react.

Minna's voice was as sharp as swordleaf in the cold morning air. "Nameday greetings, Dillon of Lutecia."

The Princeps had clearly prepared for this event. He had brushed his clothing as best he could. He had wetted down his hair, combed his blond tangles with his fingers. His darkbeast had been ministered to as well—Squeak's fur stood up in spikes along his back.

Dillon bowed stiffly and said, "Thank you, Speaker."

There was none of the celebratory air that had accompanied my own nameday. No one sang the Family Rule. No one clothed Dillon in fine, embroidered robes and laughed and danced beside him. We were all silent as we made our way through Portus's dusty streets.

Minna stopped in front of a building that had once been a tavern. "We have long searched for Bestius's godhouse in the ruins, but no trace of it remains in Portus. We have created the best we could, under the circumstances."

Dillon nodded gravely toward the tavern door. "This will serve the purpose, I am certain."

There should have been a priest present. There should have been a formal greeting and chanted prayers.

But the Princeps acted as if all those traditions were being properly observed. He held himself straight and tall. He settled Squeak on his palm, displaying the mouse for all to see.

The Darkers fell still. There was anger in their silence, focused rage against all that Dillon stood for, all the Princeps represented.

A space had cleared around me; I was separate and apart from the others. The Darkers seemed to believe that Dillon's dedication to the old ways was somehow mine to control.

As everyone stared, the Princeps reached into his pocket. He did not hesitate as he pulled out something. No, *three* somethings, I realized. Three gold coins. The weak morning sun glinted off them, as if Aurelius himself had stepped into the square. I wondered how Dillon had hidden them when we'd been searched, if they had been sewn into the lining of his clothes or merely buried deep within a pocket.

"I would make this nameday gift to Bestius's priest, if any were here," Dillon proclaimed.

A nameday gift, one fit for a Princeps—more money than I had ever seen in one place. Dillon's offering made me ashamed of the humble gift I had made to the god of darkbeasts on my own nameday. I had spent hours dyeing wool with mardock root; I had used all my meager skill to weave a blanket in the god's honor.

How much more would Bestius have appreciated three glinting golden coins?

Minna, for once, seemed uncertain of how she should proceed. Dillon was the one who turned to her, who bowed again with the careful precision of a man trained at court. "My thanks, Speaker." He pressed the coins into her reluctant palm.

He paused then and looked out at the assembled Darkers. He

took the time to meet the gaze of every man, every woman, every child. He lingered over Taggart, and I thought he almost spoke to the old Traveler. He hurried when he got to Goran.

And then he stared at me, writing an entire volume with those green eyes. I wanted to tell him that I understood. He was destined to be Primate when his father died. He was bound to follow all the ways of the Twelve and sacrifice his darkbeast.

Nevertheless I wanted to plead with him, to beg him to spare Squeak and join with the Darkers.

I said nothing, though. My only motion was to dig deep within my pocket, to pull out the leather pouch of saltbite I had carried for so long. My fingers curled around the herb, and I held it aloft in my own private salute.

Dillon saw me. He nodded. And then he passed inside the tavern-godhouse.

If we were anywhere else in Duodecia, all the village children would have danced around the building. They would have chanted, *Kill the darkbeast! Kill the darkbeast!* We would have smelled festival meats roasting on nearby fires. We would have poured out tankards of cider and ale. We would have been prepared to welcome a new adult into our midst, to cheer him for his courage in ridding himself of the foul creature of his childhood.

I tucked away the saltbite, a little embarrassed now that my moment of silent communication with Dillon was over. Caw let me take him from my shoulder and brush my fingers down his back. I gathered him close against my chest as if I could protect him, as if I could keep him safe from the cruelty of others.

I had not seen Dillon select a weapon to execute Squeak. It would not take much, of course. The sole of a boot would suffice. Poor Squeak was much smaller than Caw. Much more vulnerable.

I closed my eyes, thinking back to my own nameday. I had been so nervous, standing in Bestius's godhouse, the incense brazier my only light. Caw had been willing to die. He had *expected* to die. He had encouraged me to do all that I must do, reminded me of my obligation to Mother, to Silver Hollow, to all of Duodecia.

I had heard the priest returning to the inner chamber. I had understood that it was then, or never. I had known that the decision I made would change my life, would make me different for all the rest of my days.

I had opened the door of Caw's cage, and I had told him, "Be free."

"I take my freedom," Caw had said, where he had nestled against my heart. *"Forget it. It is mine."*

I could still remember how he had burst out of the doors of Bestius's godhouse. He had beat his strong wings, battering Bestius's priest before he soared high above our village. I had thought that he was gone forever, but he'd come back to me that night. He had settled on my shoulder as we left behind the only life we had ever known.

"I would not change it," I said to him now. "Not one thing."

He croaked a quiet disagreement. *"Vala. You would change her."*

"Only to make her understand. Only to make her see what I see."

"She certainly would not understand this."

For a moment I did not understand what my darkbeast meant. I thought he referred to our whispered conversation, to the dusty streets of Portus, to the clutch of grim Darkers around us.

But then I realized Caw referred to more than that. He had glimpsed something in the dark recesses of the tavern. He had understood a truth I had not yet learned.

For Caw had seen Dillon emerging into the sunlight, with Squeak displayed on the flat of his palm.

The mouse groomed his whiskers as if he had not a care in the world. His tail twitched to keep his balance, and he cocked his head at a questioning angle as Dillon raised his arm high.

"Behold!" the Princeps called in a voice that echoed all the way to the ruined harbor. "Behold my darkbeast! Behold the living symbol of my choice to stay among you."

He lowered his arm, and he turned toward Minna. "If, Speaker, you will allow me to stay within your midst." He made the slightest of bows toward the assembled Darkers, toward the crowd that was now whispering and pointing and exclaiming over the oblivious darkbeast mouse. "Of course, I understand you all must vote."

Squeak must have told him about the procedure, passing on knowledge from the community of darkbeasts.

"Of course," Minna said without emotion. The crowd moved as one to the unum, and the speaker led us down the dim steps.

"I never thought he'd do it," Goran whispered to me.

I wondered at that phrasing. Had Goran always believed that Dillon would slay his darkbeast? Or had he been completely certain that Squeak was safe?

Before I could ask for clarification, Minna began the formulaic call to order. "Greetings, Darkers," she intoned. If anything, she was more still than I had ever seen her, more suspicious.

"Greetings, Speaker." I raised my voice with the others, even though my belly was flopping like a new-caught fish.

"We are met this morning to determine the fate of one who wishes to join our community."

I knew these words. I had heard them before, when the Darkers voted on me. They were custom. Tradition. Part of the ways that had kept this community safe for so many generations.

Minna continued. "Dillon of Lutecia has passed his twelfth nameday. He stands before you with his darkbeast, Squeak. He asks for refuge in our community, for safety against the Inquisitors, the Primate, and all who would do him harm."

I watched Dillon's face as Minna spoke, as she named the threats arrayed against us. Dillon had lived in the midst of the very Inquisitors who desired our demise. The Primate was his own father. How could we ever be certain that his conversion was true? How could we be assured that he was actually one of us?

Minna obviously had the same concerns. She looked like she was choking down a triple dose of bitterroot tea as she turned toward the Princeps. "What words would you say to us all, Dillon of Lutecia, before we cast our votes?"

Dillon might not have known the precise parameters of the ceremony here in the unum. But he was accustomed to pomp, to regal protocol. He cleared his throat and came to stand before the Darkers.

"Good people of Portus," he announced. "I thank you for this opportunity to speak to all of you, on this, my twelfth nameday. In the name of Bestius and all his sacred darkbeasts, I greet you." He bowed slightly, managing to take in all of the crowd with his gesture.

This was not the nervous scholar who had argued ineffectively before his father's court. This was a young man who knew precisely what he wanted to say, who was comfortable with every word of his speech, and with his audience as well.

He held out his hands, displaying his empty palms as if to prove that he bore no ill will. "I know that many of you mistrust me because of my lineage. You fear my brother, the Inquisitor Ducis. Every day of your lives is spent finding ways to avoid my father, Primate Hendor. And yet, I say to you good people that you need never fear me!"

Dillon's words echoed off the ceiling of the unum. His voice grew even stronger, even more rich as he said, "I know that I could speak with you all day. I could tell you how I spent my long time in captivity, thinking about darkbeasts, about Bestius, about all the matters of our faith. I could tell you how I observed my guards, how I saw that they were good men, even when they were firm, even when they enforced the laws of your community. I could tell you how I looked through the window of my chamber, how I caught glimpses of men and women, of boys and girls, all dedicated to the hard work of carving out a life in Portus. I could tell you how I saw the error of my past ways, and how I decided to change, to join you forever."

Many of the Darkers stood straighter at his words. They were proud of all that they had accomplished. Others, though, narrowed their eyes, realizing just how much they valued the life that Dillon's presence threatened.

"I could tell you all of that, good people," the Princeps continued. "But I will not ask you to believe *my* words. I will not ask you to accept that my heart has changed."

There was a flurry of whispers. What could Dillon mean?

How could he remain silent when such an important vote was on the line?

The Princeps raised his hand high above his head. Squeak scrambled up his arm to take a seat and look at all of us. The mouse's whiskers twitched, as if he did not quite share his master's ease before the crowd. The shy beast darted glances left and right, but he did not attempt to flee.

Dillon spoke, even though every eye was now on his darkbeast. "My dearest wish is that I will be allowed to prove myself to you with deeds in the days and months and years to come. Until then, I hope that you will listen to the one who knows me best. To the one creature to whom I cannot tell a lie. Squeak?"

For a heartbeat, I thought that Squeak would tell me words I already knew, truths I already believed. I waited for the darkbeast mouse to reach inside my mind and tell me that he had faith in Dillon, that he knew the Princeps was now truly dedicated to the Darkers.

Of course, he didn't. He couldn't.

But Caw spoke to me. *"I've always known that boy was clever."*

"What? What do you mean?"

"Squeak is talking to all of us darkbeasts. He is telling us that he knows his companion is true. . . ." Caw paused, clearly listening to more of Squeak's explanation. *"He can see inside the Princeps's heart now, as he has every day since Dillon's birth. Dillon has been changed*

by his time with you, Keara. With you and the Travelers. With Janna, his teacher. With Nessan, who was sworn to be his Guard. Dillon, son of Hendor, Princeps of Duodecia has truly decided to join the Darkers."

I thought back to Dillon's arrival in Portus, to his denouncing us, to his vicious fight in the face of impossible odds. He had not believe in the Darkers then. He had not accepted our rebellious ways. But he'd had weeks to think about things. Days and days to reflect on all that had gone wrong in Lutecia, on all that we Darkers stood for. And through all of that time, Squeak must have been speaking with the other darkbeasts, relaying lessons learned by all the adults who had spared their companion animals, all the children who expected to do so.

Dillon had used his time in custody to examine all the facts before him. And like the scholar he had always longed to be, he changed his mind when everything he once believed no longer added up. He accepted new information, developed new beliefs. He set aside the errors of his childhood, and he stepped forward as a man.

I looked around the unum. People were nodding. They were clutching their own darkbeasts close. The room was unnaturally quiet, as dozens of silent conversations proceeded at once.

And, one by one, I saw the Darkers understand. I saw them accept the words from their own bonded animals, absorb the message that Squeak conveyed. The mouse would never lie to his fellow darkbeasts, and the Princeps could not lie to the mouse. Dillon's conversion must be true.

Minna stepped forward and gestured toward the tiles on the altar. Her voice trembled slightly as she reminded us, "Black means Dillon and Squeak stay with us as full members of our group. White means they are gone."

It seemed to take forever, as each person stepped to the table. Taggart displayed a black tile, making his support clear. Minna voted carefully, precisely, taking her time to plant a hidden tile deep inside the pottery urn. Goran was furtive, cupping his marker inside his hand, masking it so carefully that his fingers might have been empty when he placed his treasure inside the jar.

Minna took her time emptying the urn. She used her body to block everyone's view of the tiles as she sorted them. I could see something in the set of her shoulders—surprise, maybe. Or determination. I drummed my finger against my hip in impatience, willing her to move faster, to count more quickly.

Finally, though, she stepped back from the altar, and the vote was displayed for all to see. Thirty-seven black tiles. And one white one, glimmering like a shattered bone upon the altar.

"Welcome, Dillon Darker," the Speaker said. "Welcome to your new family."

Everyone closed around the Princeps, extending a personal

greeting, exclaiming over Squeak. Taggart shook Dillon's hand heartily, as if they had played a great revel before a most important crowd. Minna offered a tight nod, and then she reached up to stroke her own stoat darkbeast.

My eyes, though, kept returning to the one white tile.

Goran stood beside me, watching the joy among the Darkers. His lips were set, and his hand was in his pocket, a sure sign that he was seeking strength from Wart.

I wanted to ask him if he had cast the white stone. I wanted to know if he had voted to cast Dillon out from Portus. I wanted to know if Goran hated Dillon.

"He is like you now," I said. "A Darker and a rebel."

"So it seems," Goran said. Once again I could not parse the meaning of his words. I could not say if he meant that Dillon was truly an ally, or if he thought the Princeps only acted like one. I wondered if Goran knew himself.

Before I could decide whether or not to ask him for a clarification, Taggart pushed his way to the front of the crowd. "Minna Speaker!" he said.

I knew that voice. I had first heard it on the green in Silver Hollow, back in my home village, when I had been captivated by the Travelers' magic. Then, I had thought that Taggart's words would reach all the way to Pondera's godhouse at the southern edge of my village. Farther, even.

Now, though, Taggart only needed to reach the Speaker. The Speaker, that was, and all the other Darkers.

"Minna Speaker," Taggart repeated. "I ask that you conduct one more vote. Ask the Darkers to decide whether Keara of Silver Hollow should be permitted to stay within our boundaries."

"And why would I do that again? Two votes have been taken." Minna actually sounded curious.

"The first, though, was shaded by Keara's association with the Princeps, by her speaking to him while they both were held in custody. Surely matters have changed, now that Dillon is welcome among our people. Any shadow that fell upon Keara because of her friendship with our former prisoner should now be dispersed."

Taggart made it sound so simple. If Minna argued with him, she would certainly sound petty and biased.

Every Darker in the room turned to the Speaker. I could sense many different emotions—outrage, curiosity, even amusement. Minna took her time measuring the responses, gauging the reactions of the community she managed so ably.

And then she looked at me. She studied my face as if she were memorizing the specific curve of my brow, the precise quirk of my lips. She shifted her gaze to Caw, to his ebony feathers, frozen on my shoulder as if he were the very maquette of a raven in Bestius's Lutecian godhouse.

At last she nodded. "Very well, then. One last vote. Black

means Keara of Silver Hollow stays with us. White means she is gone."

Gone. I still did not know if that meant banished or worse.

This time I did not close my eyes. This time I watched as every Darker voted, Taggart first, then Goran, then Dillon and everyone else. Minna ended the voting and spilled the tiles, spreading them across the altar.

They weren't all black. That would truly be a gift from the Twelve, a miracle from the gods. But all of us could see that there were more black tiles than white. In a glance, it was clear that I was finally to be welcomed among the Darkers.

Minna did not bother with a precise tally. Instead she said, "Welcome, Keara Darker. Welcome to your new family."

I inclined my head gravely. "Many thanks, Minna Speaker. I am grateful to be here."

And then it was over—all the mystery and the waiting and the uncertainty. Many people gathered close, offering their greetings, calling me by my new name. Others left the unum in unhappy silence, but I could not bring myself to care. Not then. Not when I had just been granted a reprieve.

"Good day," said one of the oldest Darkers, a woman who often sat near Taggart during meals.

"Good day," I responded, sparing a smile for her long-whiskered rat of a darkbeast.

"It is *a good day when a darkbeast is spared,"* Caw said as the pair strode away. *"Whatever else may follow, today is a good day."*

"Aye," I whispered, and I realized that my cheeks ached a little from grinning so hard. "Today is a very good day."

Caw had spoken the truth. We had found the true Darkers at last. Now we could help others flee Lutecia. We could place others on the Route toward freedom, toward a place where all darkbeasts could live out the natural span of their lives.

When all the other Darkers had left for the refectory, Goran waited for me at the base of the stairs. "Welcome, Keara Darker," he said.

"My thanks, Goran-tu."

He laughed out loud at my use of the endearment. As we climbed the steps out of the unum, he laced his fingers between mine. We picked our way across the stones to the refectory, listening to the sounds of feasting from the rest of our community.

By the time we arrived in the dining hall, there was only one currant scone left on the serving table. I checked quickly with Caw, and he agreed with my decision. I squeezed Goran's hand and told him I would return. And then I crossed the room and offered the currant treat to Squeak, welcoming the darkbeast mouse into the community of Portus.

Epilogue

S ap Moon has come and gone.

With Goran's help I am getting to know our fellow Darkers. It's a slow process—these people are accustomed to keeping their secrets, to hiding from the Primate, from anyone who would harm their darkbeasts.

Every day I think about Saeran's colony in the woods. I think about how I longed for those false Darkers to be true. I think about how I wanted to belong, the way it seemed that Goran did.

And I think about Bestius's godhouse. Despite everything that happened there, I honestly believe the Inquisitors want to help the Lost. They think they can guide people back to the Twelve, to faith, to safety, all by making them memorize endless lists of facts.

All by making them conform, no matter who they are, no matter what they think.

But things are not so simple here in Portus.

In Portus each of us is responsible for our own decisions. We can speak before the group, making an argument for whatever we think is right. We can cast a black tile or a white one, depending on what we believe.

Sometimes at night I wake up and reach for the darkbeast bracelet that still hangs around my wrist. I don't know when I became so accustomed to counting its knots, to easing my anxiety with its familiar feel.

Other nights my fingers reach for the pouch of saltbite. I still want to share it with Mother, to bring her an herb so rare and so valuable that she'll never see it on her own.

I've only spoken to Dillon once about the choice he made in the tavern godhouse. I was surprised to catch him short on words, uneasy setting forth his copious knowledge. He explained that he had grown lonely in his storeroom prison cell after Minna summoned me away. He had tried to talk to the guards, but they had ignored him, refused to engage in even a single spoken word.

In his solitude Dillon had turned to Squeak. He had communicated with his darkbeast more in those few weeks than he had in a lifetime before. He had offered up all his thoughts, all his beliefs, all his questions about the way the world worked.

And he had come to realize that Squeak was more than a simple mouse, more than a common darkbeast to be used and discarded like outgrown clothes. Dillon came to understand what I had known all along—I and Taggart and Goran, Janna and Nessan. He realized that he was not willing to complete his nameday ritual. He could not kill a friend.

Sometimes I see Dillon standing on the eastern wall of Portus, looking down the silted river toward far-off Lutecia. I suspect he misses his home. Misses the books in Janna's library, anyway. But it will be a long time before he sees them again, if he ever does. He's committed to the Darkers now.

Alas, it's not safe for any of us to travel. Not with the Primate's Guard and Inquisitors seeking out the kidnapped Princeps, seeking out the Travelers who were brought before the Primate's throne in the contest for power between the Primate's sons.

For now we four will stay inside Portus's crumbled walls. We'll plant seeds in the spring. We'll pull weeds in the summer. We'll harvest crops in the fall. And after that we'll see what is happening in the wide world. We'll learn if we can strike out on the roads, return to the life of a Traveler, or turn to something new. Something more.

Caw thinks it's just as well we're staying put. He enjoys the company of all the other darkbeasts. And the variety of treats. He has somehow convinced the Darkers' cooks to bake more scones for every meal, to provide more sweetmeats for hungry animals and humans alike.

I watch the sun rise, and I watch the sun set, and I know that things are bound to change. But for now I'm content to stay in Portus with my friends, old and new. With my friends, and with my darkbeast. I truly cannot ask for anything more.

I think that Dillon will become more comfortable with all of us over time. Squeak regularly communicates with Caw and the other darkbeasts.

Taggart seems happy here. The people of Portus respect him like the Travelers did of old. They look to him for wisdom, maybe because of his age or because of the long years he spent traveling through Duodecia.

Of course Goran has made friends too. He always does.

He makes time for me, though. A few days ago, he proposed that we make masks, that we sew together some costumes. Together, we're going to teach the Darkers some of the Common Plays. After all, that's what we Travelers always do—perform for the crowd.

I'm a Traveler, and a Darker too. Who knows what revels tomorrow will bring?